Rita's Ring

Gregory T. Glading

ISBN

Hardcover:978-1-966565-44-4

Paperback:978-1-966565-43-7

Acknowledgments

As a former working, professional wrestler, I wrote this novel to give back to the business and the people who made it a thrilling epoch of my life.

About the Author

Rita's Ring is Gregory T. Glading's seventh published novel. He has lived on four different continents and visited over 40 countries. A graduate of Temple University, he is a retired professional wrestler and a US Army Special Operations combat veteran of Operation Iraqi Freedom.

Contents

Chapter 1

Florida, July 1958

Ceiling fans blended cigar smoke, humidity, and heat. The audience fanned themselves with folded programs, bunched newspapers, or empty popcorn boxes. Chains rumbled. The crowd grumbled and craned their heads at a portal, gasping as he entered. A feline-spotted mask cloaked his face. Long, straggly black facial and head hair splayed from his mask. He wore matching spotted tights. His pectorals were striated, meshing with defined abdominals. His shoulders and back tapered from wide to narrow, his limbs strong and balanced. A chain circumscribed his waist and torso. A stocky Asian wearing a 1940s suit and derby hat held one end of the chain; a slender European dressed in a safari suit and pith helmet held the other. They pulled him toward the ring. The crowd booed and jeered. Some threw popcorn and trash. His handlers briefly loosened the chains. The masked wrestler lunged at the crowd and growled. They screamed and backed away.

The ring announcer's voice bounced off the brick walls and concrete barrel ceiling of the Wauchehuchi Armory. "Now the moment that you've all been waiting for. Our main event of the evening. A fight to the finish for the vacant American Federation of Wrestling World Title. He's being led to the ring by his manager, Professor Sakamoto, and his handler, Nigel Earl. Trapped in the wilds of the Amazon, raised by jungle cats. He has no name. Weighing in at 240 pounds. The Jaguar."

A beefy middle-aged man wearing oil-stained pants and a grubby T-shirt cupped his hands. "Remember Pearl Harbor! Go home, you Jap bastard, and take your savage with you!"

"I hate you!" An elderly woman shook her closed umbrella. "I hate you. I hope you die! I hope Abede kills you!"

A young woman licked her lips while fixating on the wrestler's physique. She abruptly stopped and jerked her head to her male companion. "I bet he looks like a monkey under that mask."

Her skinny, pimple-faced companion replied, "You got that right: he's nothing but a musclehead."

Sakamoto, Earl, and the Jaguar stood in the ring. The wrestler's resistance rattled the chains. He waved his arms, slashing at the ring announcer.

"Now about to enter the ring. He stands six foot eight inches tall. He weighs four hundred and twenty-five pounds. He hails from Kenya, Africa. Ladies and gentlemen. Abede. The African Lion!"

The crowd roared as Abede entered the ring. Many reached out to touch him. He wore faux lion skin with maned, teeth-bearing headgear. Abede flashed the crowd a wide smile and shook his fist. The crowd stood and cheered. The AFW's owner, chief promoter, and booker, Al Cohen, made it clear to Wauchehuchi County that Abebe would never wrestle in a segregated venue. The county complied by a council vote of 7-1, as a World title bout would be the county's most important event since President Grover Cleveland's campaign speech. Many Mexican residents and migrant workers mingled with the black and white crowd, most united to see Abede defeat the Jaguar and his Japanese manager.

Sakamoto and Earl removed The Jaguar's chains; Abede doffed his gear and handed it to an attendant.

'*Ding!*'

At the sound of the bell, the Jaguar leaped from his corner. He twisted in mid-flight, making his leap appear higher. He landed on Abede's shoulders. He caught the Jaguar and staggered backward. After regaining his footing, he slammed The Jaguar to the canvas. The ring quaked and rumbled. The crowd shook their fists and voiced approval.

"Kill him! Kill him!" A gray-haired woman in a pastel dress swung her handbag. "Finish him!"

Abede pulled his opponent to his feet and flung him into the corner turnbuckle. Abede charged, turned, and slammed his back into him. The corner post gave like a reed in a gale. The Jaguar collapsed onto his rear: arms draped on the ropes and head dropped. Abede stalked back to the center of the ring. He nodded to the crowd.

"Yeah! Yeah! Crush him, man!" A young Black wrestling fan wearing a soiled white tank top shirt shouted. "Crush him!"

Abede charged like a bull elephant. At the last second, the Jaguar stood and jumped onto the top turnbuckle. He pounced skyward, somersaulted, and kicked Abede's chest with two feet. Adebe staggard into the ropes. The Jaguar jumped and wrapped his knees around his neck. The Jaguar extended his body and arms; he twisted, rolling him to the canvas. He kept his legs locked around Abede's neck and squeezed. Abede pounded the canvas. With each strike, the crowd encouraged him by clapping and cheering. The Jaguar continued to strangle him with his legs. Abede rhythmically kicked the canvas. The crowd clapped and cheered in unison. He shimmied to the ring apron. The referee ruled his foot outside the ring and made The Jaguar release his hold. The Jaguar paced back and forth like a caged animal. He then attacked Abede with his fists, knocking him into the corner. The Jaguar grabbed his wrists, leaped, and used his feet to flip Abede over. The Jaguar lurched over and savagely stomped him. Abede climbed to one foot and shook his head. His opponent kept stomping. With each head shake, the crowd clapped and cheered. Abede stood and shoved The Jaguar into the corner. The African Lion brandished his right fist and rubbed it in his left hand while smiling at the crowd.

"Si! Si! Daselo a el! Daselo a el!" One of Abede's fans shouted.

"Hit 'im! Kill 'im!" An adolescent boy wearing black glasses jumped up and down.

The Jaguar staggered forward. Abede cocked his arm back. He

waited for the audience's approval. He then struck The Jaguar. The Jaguar flopped on his back. He remained motionless. Abede leaped upward and landed with a leg across his throat. He bounced with a thud. Abede then stood and fell, leading with an elbow strike to his opponent's chest. The Jaguar lay still. Abede raised his arms overhead in a victory pose. The audience roared. Abede threw himself into the ropes, dove arms extended and splashed his 425 pounds on top of the Jaguar. Abede remained on top, pinning his shoulders to the mat. The referee tried to place his hand between his shoulder blades and the mat. He then slapped the mat. "One!" He slapped it a second time. "Two!"

Professor Sakamoto then lassoed a chain around The Jaguar's ankle. Sakamoto and Earl pulled him to the ring apron. "Look! Look!" Sakamoto pointed to the Jaguar's foot outside of the ring. The referee tapped Abede and made him release the hold. Abede scowled at the referee before pulling the Jaguar to his feet. He put him in a bearhug, ran, and slammed him into the ring corner. Some in the audience groaned; others cheered.

"Again!" A young fan with a well-greased ducktail haircut and a box of cigarettes rolled under his t-shirt sleeve yelled. "Smash his candy ass again!"

Abede ran him into the corner a second time. The ring post bent backward. He then lifted the Jaguar overhead and slammed him to the canvas. Abede then ran to the ropes for a slingshot boost. Earl tripped him with a chain, ran into the ring, and wrapped it around his legs. Sakamoto ran in and battered Abede with the chain's other end. With Earl holding him back by the legs, Adebe could only flail his arms at Sakamoto. The Jaguar recovered and stomped Abede. The referee grabbed the Jaguar and tried to restrain him. The Jaguar lifted the referee and threw him out of the ring.

The crowd erupted. Debris rained into the ring. In came a folding chair, two glass bottles, and several oranges. The security guards and a police officer less effective than rubber cones. The other wrestlers ran into the ring and circled The Jaguar, Sakamoto, Earl, and Abede. An orange hit a wrestler in the head, and a bottle hit another wrestler's chest. A din of English and Spanish invectives and anti-Japanese slurs ensued.

'Ding! Ding! Ding! Ding! Ding!'

"Ladies and Gentlemen! Ladies and Gentlemen!"

The ring announcer had distracted the crowd. The Jaguar, Sakamoto, and Earl escaped the ring and sprinted down the aisle toward an exit portal. They slammed and locked the dressing room door behind them.

"Your winner by disqualification."

The referee raised Abede's arm.

"From Kenya, Africa! Abede the African Lion!"

The audience halted their hostilities and cheered.

"However, the by-laws of the American Federation of Wrestling stipulate that a wrestler cannot win a World title by disqualification. Therefore, the title remains vacant."

"Boo…" The crowd voiced their disapproval.

Abede grabbed the ring microphone and spoke in a faux accent. "He's not even a man. He's an animal. A wild beast. He wants to be an animal? I will fight him where an animal belongs. I want him where no one can interfere. I challenge the Jaguar to a cage match for the vacant World championship!"

***

"Mama! Mama!" Eight-year-old Rebecca Mendez pointed at their Philco tabletop TV. "He cheated! I hate Professor Sakamoto! He always cheats for his wrestlers."

Rita Mendez checked the oven before going to her daughter. "Now you know it's all show." She chuckled. "Wrestling's like Tom and Jerry. They're not fighting for real. Same as the Three Stooges. You know that Moe, Larry, and Curly only pretend to hurt each other."

"Shemp's also funny."

Rita chuckled. "Like TV and movies, the wrestlers are playing their characters. I doubt Abede is from the African savannah and that The Jaguar was trapped in the Amazon jungle."

"No Mama!" Rebecca held up her hands. "It's real. Look at Abede, the African Lion. He is from Africa, and he's my favorite."

"As you know, Rebecca, some people aren't nice to us just because we're from Mexico. Pearl Harbor was seventeen years ago, and the war ended thirteen years ago. Do you think it's right to make Professor Sakamoto sneaky and have people hate him just because he's from Japan?"

"I don't hate Professor Sakamoto because he's Japanese. I hate him because he cheats. He's sneaky, and The Jaguar is a jungle savage!" Rebecca smiled at her mother. "And how about Hercules Cortez? He's from Mexico, and everybody likes him! He's my next favorite."

"Okay, darling," Rita sat next to her daughter and looked at the TV. "You can watch. Just so you know that's it's just a show."

The TV broadcaster stood on camera with a microphone. The forty-one-year-old broadcaster wore a gray suit with a red tie. "We have breaking news. This is big. Don't touch that dial."

The TV showed a Texaco gasoline commercial, a Schlitz Beer ad, and a spot for Crazy Wally's used car dealerships. Wally raved that he was crazy to sell a '55 Ford Fairlane for under a thousand dollars.

"Gordon Hanson back with breaking news. This is big. Professor Sakamoto has accepted Abede's challenge to meet The Jaguar in a cage match. The place is the Alligator Alley Gymnasium in Gainesville, Florida. The date is Saturday, August the ninth. The time: eight o'clock. This epic battle pits wrestling's big cats for the vacant American Federation of Wrestling world title. Although the arena has plenty of seats, the good ones will go fast. Advanced Tickets will go on sale at all Sears and Roebuck department stores in Florida and Georgia, all Florida Western Auto stores, and select Texaco Gas Stations. If you buy them at any Crazy Wally's used car lot, Wally will pitch in a dollar toward each of your tickets. Why is Crazy Wally helping you buy wrestling tickets? Because he's crazy. You, too, would be crazy if you pass on a two-door, '56 Pontiac Chieftain 860 with one owner and low mileage for under two thousand dollars. Test drive it today. Only at Crazy Wally's used car lot."

"Please, Mama! I wanna go! I love Abede. I hate The Jaguar."

"It's no good to hate, you know that."

"But The Jaguar is so mean, and his manager cheats." Rebecca smiled. "You always told me to be nice and never cheat."

"Yes, we just talked about that, honey, I am proud you learned that it's bad to cheat, and it's good to be nice." Rita chuckled. "Well, you know that I will probably have to work. And Granddaddy's truck might not make it to Gainesville. You'll have to watch on TV."

"But it's not on TV!" Rebecca shook her hands. "We have to go."

"I'm sorry, dear. I know that you want to go. I understand." Rita hugged her daughter.

"I understand, Mama. Christmas time, can we go to wrestling for my present?" Rebecca beamed.

Chapter 2

Bartholomew Johnson drove his green 1951 Chevy Deluxe Sports Coupe along US Rt 1. He chose that model because he wanted a sports car with headroom for his 6-8 height and a back seat for his son and daughter. His petite wife, Stephanie, could fit in any car. He had replaced the 92-horsepower inline six-cylinder engine with a 352 cubic inch FE V8. That engine powered his 425-pound frame as fast as the roads would allow. He switched the stock wheels for stainless-steel American Racing torque thrusters for added performance and appeal. He turned up his radio dial. It played Little Richard's *'Good Golly Miss Molly.'* He tapped the steering wheel with the music and looked to his right, *'Del's Diner. Beer Barrel Bobby told me they serve a great pot roast. And he assured me it was fully integrated.'* Bart chuckled to himself. *'As if anyone has the guts to try throwing me out.'*

Del's diner had picture windows extending from its stainless-steel plinth to just below the black roof façade. A large red neon sign above the segmental arch entrance flashed "Del's Diner." Bart climbed four steps and entered through double glass doors. The booth seats and counter stools were upholstered in peppermint green vinyl. The tile floor had a black and white checkerboard motif. Individual jukeboxes sat at each booth and counter space. Attached to the rear of the ivory counter, clear fountain dispensers sprayed beverages of various colors. Four cake domes holding a coconut cake, a dark chocolate cake, a lemon meringue pie, and a blueberry pie were placed at uniform spacing along the counter. An antique, ornamented cash register sat in the counter's corner. Behind the counter featured three stainless-steel blenders and a five-gallon coffee urn. A neon sign for Miller High Life Beer was on the back wall. Many customers did a double take as the black giant strolled into the diner.

Bart sat at the counter. He put a nickel in the private jukebox and played James Brown's *"Please, Please, Please."* The diner's proprietor, Delbert Anderson, cooked the orders fast as a 'Vegas dealer shuffling cards. His wife, Margie Anderson, took orders and served the countertop patrons. Two waitresses worked the tables and booths. Margie was in her forties and a tad underweight. Her straight nose held horn-rimmed glasses. Brown hair with gray streaks in a bun topped her angular face. She approached Bart with a notepad and a pencil in hand. "What are you having?"

"Well," Bart flashed her a toothy grin. "My buddy Bob, he's hard to forget. He's a huge guy with a big black beard, says you serve the best pot roast in Florida."

"Bob?" Margie lowered her notepad. "Yeah, how can I forget him? He is huge. And how can I forget his long beard and denim overalls? When he walked in, I felt a bit intimidated. But he quickly disarmed me with politeness."

"That's him." Bart pointed his thumb upward. "The one and only."

"Here, I just called him huge." Margie chuckled. "I need a word beyond huge to describe you." Margie blushed. "I'm sorry. You must hear that all the time."

"It's okay." Bart smiled. "I'm used to it." He chuckled. "How about instead of huge, you say enormous?"

"How about ginormous?" Margie chuckled. "I'll tell you what?" Margie beamed. "I'll make it up to you. I'll have my husband give you a 'ginormous' helping of Bob's favorite pot roast."

Bart pointed to the neon sign on the wall behind the counter. "And a High Life sure would hit the spot."

"Coming right up." Margie took a bottle from a glass-doored cooler, popped it open with a bottle opener, and placed it in front of him. Cold mist rose from the bottle.

Bart put another nickel in the jukebox and played Jackie Wilson's *Lonely Teardrops.* He beamed as Margie put a plate loaded with beef, carrots, potatoes, onions, and celery in front of him. While chewing his fourth forkful of pot roast, two young men in blue work clothes with their names embroidered over a white backdrop bumped his arm. "Hey! I know you. You're Abede. The African Lion. Can we have your autograph?"

Bart sighed and dropped his fork on his plate. He took a deep breath and forced a smile. "Sure."

"Gee. Thanks. Yo Margie." The boy with Hank stitched on his shirt pointed. "Can ya lend me ya pen and a piece 'a paper?"

Margie handed Bart two paper scraps. Bart scribbled his signature on both. The boys took the autograph and stuffed it in their pockets. "Thanks, man. Hey, after ya whoop that savage Jaguar guy, how about ya whoop that sneaky Jap, Sakamoto, too."

The boy with Jimmy on his nametag added, "Hey. How about you tear off The Jaguar's mask? I wanna see how ugly he looks underneath it."

"Come to matches. You never know what you might see."

"I hope so." Hank raised his palms. "I don't want a savage and his sneaky Jap manager to have the World champion belt."

Margie walked over to Bart. "I knew you weren't just an ordinary guy off the streets. Is your friend Bob also a wrestler? He never talks about it."

"We're not supposed to, but I guess the cat's out of the bag." Bart laughed. "No pun intended. Yeah. He's Beer Barrel Bobby." Bart grinned. "And speaking of which." He slid his empty beer bottle to the back of the counter.

Margie served Bart another Miller High Life beer. "Do people asking you for autographs bother you?'

Bart chuckled. "Go figure. I played three seasons with the

Washington Redskins, and except at the stadium, I never once got accosted for an autograph. Say what you want about professional wrestling, but I can't finish a restaurant meal without getting asked for an autograph."

A middle-aged Black man wearing a green John Deere cap turned to them. "I sure remember you, and not just from the Redskins, Bubby Johnson. Back at Grambling, with you blocking, I don't think anyone ever sacked the quarterback." He chuckled. "And that's saying a lot, seeing that you never had a mobile quarterback like that Lance Burkett up in Pennsylvania."

"Bubby?" No one ever calls me that anymore." He extended his hand. "Call me Bart. Short for Bartholemew."

"Charly. Short for Charles." The customer shook Bart's hand. He did a double take at their hands' size difference. "Yup. Bartholemew. It's on the back of your Bowman football card. My twelve-year-old son collects 'em. He likes rasslin' too. But he's more about football. He plays halfback on his school team. If he had you blockin' for 'im, he'd score a touchdown every play. Wait 'til I tell 'em I met you." Charles doffed his cap. "Hey, can you sign Bubby Johnson 78 right here?" He pointed to the bottom of the bill.

"Since you remembered my uniform number." Bart chuckled. "And you didn't ask me to speak in my wrestling accent." He snickered. "Sure thing." He signed the cap.

***

Bart's private jukebox now played Elvis Presley's 'Heartbreak Hotel.'

"How was the pot roast?" Margie took his plate and utensils.

"Even better than Bob said."

"Well, I know how to top it off. A slice of blueberry pie. It's on the house. My waitress, Rita, baked it herself."

Mary Jenkins worked the booths on the north side of the diner, while Rita Mandez had the south side. Delbert Anderson gave her that side as it had a backroom entrance. Delbert let Rita bring her eight-year-old daughter Rebecca to work when she didn't have school or if her grandfather was working and couldn't look after her. This allowed Rita to check up on her during slow times.

Rebecca laughed at a Three Stooges short playing on the Andersons' TV. After the show, she peered through the partially closed door opening to look at her mother. Rita winked back at her.

"Ma'am." Bart motioned to her.

Rita lip-synched *'me?'*

"Yes."

Rita nervously walked over to the giant. Rita's height reached the minimum for a ramp model. Her curvy and chesty figure filled her light blue waitress uniform with a white lapel to the brim. Her heart-shaped face, even lips, and celestial nose centered between brown eyes. Florid cheekbones enhanced her smooth light brown skin. Many of Del's customers asked why she wasn't working as a model rather than a waitress. She would reply with a blush and a thank you before taking their orders. Today, she wore part of her dark brown hair in a half-up, half-down bun, her sides curled under the shoulders.

"Margie says you baked this pie yourself." Bart beamed at her. "It's the best I've ever tasted."

"Thank you." Rita lowered her head. "I usually only bake them for the church."

"Well, I, for one, am glad you saved one for us. It was delicious."

Rebecca peered through a small door opening. She beamed and bolted into the diner. "Abede! The Lion! You're my favorite wrestler." She looked up at him with soft hazel eyes.

"So, you watch wrestling?"

"Yes. Every time it's on TV." Rebecca smiled. "But I've never gotten to go for real."

"Now Rebecca," Rita put her hand on her daughter's shoulder. "You know you're not supposed to come into the diner while Mommy's working."

"I'll forgive her if you'll forgive her." Bart grinned. "So, you're Rebecca." He switched to his faux accent. "I'm Abede, the African Lion from Kenya, Africa."

"Wow! I knew you were big." Rebecca beamed. "But not this big. And see!" Rebecca prodded. "I told you that he was from Africa."

"Well, I ate everything my Mama served me. That's why I got so big. Now you're little and pretty. Soon, you'll be tall and beautiful like your mother. Even more important than good looks is a sharp mind. Are you doing well in school?"

"Yes, Adebe," Rebecca chirped. "At first, I had trouble understanding English, and the other kids teased me for it. But now I got caught up. I got four B's and two A's last report card."

"Well, that's wonderful. It's so wonderful," Bart winked at Rita, "that your mother asked me to reward you. I got an autographed photo for you. Wait here. It's out in my car."

Charly looked at them. "You did give me this." He showed them the autograph under his cap's bill. "I'll go out and get it for you."

"Thanks, Charly, it's the green '51 Chevy Coupe. It's unlocked. They're in a brown envelope on the front seat."

Bart sipped his beer while Charly fetched the photos.

"Here they are," Charly returned and handed him a brown envelope.

Bart removed a photo of himself standing before a wrestling ring while wearing his lion garb. Pen in hand, he looked into the little girl's eyes. Her right eye was moist. Both of her eyes had a puppy's gleam. "You know something, Rebecca? I see you're a special little girl. I want to do something special for you. Now only my closest friends," he glanced at Charly, "and Grambling football fans, call me Bubby." Bart scribbled onto the photo and handed it to her.

"Wow!" Rebecca beamed. "Gee Whiz!" She stared at the writing. "Thank you!"

Rita looked over her daughter's shoulder and read, *To my special new friend Rebecca, from Bubby.*

Bart looked at Rita. "Today's the first time I've ever signed a wrestling autograph, Bubby." Bart laughed and pointed at Charlie. "He got Bubby on a football autograph."

"That sure is nice," Rita looked at Bart and paused, "Bubby." Rita put her hand on Rebecca's shoulder. "Thank him again, but I'm afraid you can't stay."

"Thank you again, Adebe, I mean, Bubby."

Bart again looked over the little girl and noticed a large stain on her blouse placket and a tear on the sleeve. She had a matching yellow ribbon in her gossamer light brown hair. Her eyes were soft hazel. "I see that you're wearing a pretty yellow dress. My wife is a designer and dressmaker. She's so good, I will only have to describe you, and she will make you a prettier dress than you ever imagined."

"You can't do that." Rita smiled at Bart. "I thank you anyway. It's a wonderful gesture. But my daughter's been disappointed before. We're doing just fine as we are."

Another tear formed in Rebecca's eye.

"Well, you just wait and see. A week from Saturday, I'll be back." He grinned at Rebecca. "And we'll turn those tears to cheers. And thinking of cheers, I am fighting for the World Championship at the University of Florida's basketball stadium next Saturday in Gainesville. How would you two like to sit at ringside and cheer for me?"

"I truly thank you, and I appreciate your interest in us. I don't have reliable transportation, and I work on Saturday nights." Rita took her daughter's hand, "Come along, Rebecca. Mommy must work."

"Please, Mommy?" Rebecca leaned back. "I've never gone to wrestling before, and this is the biggest match of the Century."

"No. Please." Bart held up his palms. "I insist. I have a daughter almost Rebecca's age. I can tell how happy it will make her. And I will have my wife make her a new dress. No." Bart beamed. "I changed my mind." He held up two fingers. "Two new dresses."

Rita put her hands on her hips. "I appreciate the gesture. It's just not possible for me to take her to your match next Saturday night."

Margie walked over. "How about you get a third pass? For me." She beamed at Rebecca. "I can take you two."

"But the diner?" Rita held up her hands.

"Even though his name is on the marque," Margie laughed. "We all know who's the real boss of this place." Margie laughed while looking at Delbert toiling at the grill. "Jane can work the floor, and I'll have Mary work the counter. Well, Bart, how about you include me on your guest list as a tip for good service?"

Bart smiled and nodded.

"Yippie!" Rebecca jumped up and down.

Rita, at last, smiled. "I thank you both." She nodded at Bart and then Margie.

"And you little girl." Bart winked. "When my wife Stephanie finishes your dresses, you will be the prettiest in the land."

Rebecca and Rita looked at each other and smiled.

Chapter 3

Rita lived with her daughter and father, Pedro, in what was known as a *shotgun house* in a predominantly Mexican neighborhood in Autumn, Florida. Their two-bedroomed, wood-frame house had facing entrance doors at each side of the rectangular structure. The front porch ran the length of the house. The added circulation of the open front and rear doors, the shade of the porch portico, and ceiling fans cooled the unairconditioned home.

Rebecca was too excited to sleep the night before. She spent most of the afternoon looking up and down Grimsby Lane, hoping to see Margie's White 1955 Buick Roadmaster Sedan.

"Come in and eat lunch, darling. Margie won't be here for a couple more hours."

"I'm too excited, Mama. I want her to come right now."

"You barely slept a wink last night. You only ate two bites of your breakfast." Rita affectionately pinched Rebecca's cheek. "If you don't come in and eat, you will run out of energy and sleep through Abede's match." Rita smiled. "He can't win the championship without you cheering for him."

"Oh no. I would never fall asleep on Abede. I'm gonna cheer as loud as I can so that he beats that horrible savage wearing the Jaguar mask."

"Well, then," Rita held Rebecca's hand. "Eating your peanut butter and jelly sandwich and drinking a glass of milk will help you cheer louder."

***

After lunch, Rita read Hans Christian Anderson's "*Thumbelina*" out loud to Rebecca. Before Rita could finish, Rebecca fell asleep. The rumble of a "Nailhead" 322 C/I V8 engine preceded a horn honk.

"She's here!" Rebecca sprung to her feet and ran out the front door.

Before Margie could disembark, Rebecca had sprinted from her front door and climbed into the Buick's rear door.

"You are one excited little girl." Margie kept her left hand on the steering wheel while turning to look at Rebecca.

"I couldn't sleep last night; I was too excited."

Rita wore an ankle-length, ruffled cotton skirt with colorful, floral embroidery topped by a sleeveless white blouse with lace trim. She strolled to the car, looked at Margie, and sat in the front seat.

"Well, will you look at you!" Margie turned and grinned. "Am I taking you to professional wrestling, or are you waiting for Cary Grant to take you to the Academy Awards? You look like a movie star."

Rita blushed and lowered her head.

"I didn't mean to embarrass you, especially in front of Rebecca." Margie drove down Grimsby Lane. "But it's no secret. Customers at the diner always ask me about your relationship status."

Rita half smiled, "If I accepted every marriage proposal I've gotten at the diner, I'd have more marriages than any number of movie stars."

"I understand. I won't make you talk about your late husband, especially in earshot of Rebecca. And I know you're cautious about bringing another man into her life."

"I heard you, Aunt Margie."

Margie chuckled. "Even if you don't want a stepdad, you will always have your Aunt Margie and Uncle Delbert."

***

"Will you look at all of those cars and people!" Margie leaned on the steering wheel. "It looks like we'll have to park at the football stadium."

A parking lot attendant walked over to the driver's window. "You're welcome to park here. But if you don't already have tickets, or you don't wanna pay twenty-five bucks a pop to scalpers, you're wasting your time. The rasslin' is sold out."

Rebecca beamed and chirped, "We're Abede's special guests."

"If you say so, little girl. I'm just the parking lot man."

Rita, Rebecca, and Margie weaved and jostled through the crowd. Many grumbled over being shut out. "Hey, you don't want to disappoint a little girl." A man in his early thirties, gaunt and poorly shaven, approached them. "There ain't no more tickets." He furtively looked around. "Except these. twenty-bucks each." He pulled three tickets from his coat liner. "But since she's such a cute little girl, fifty bucks and all three are yours."

"Abede is letting us in for free as his guest." Rebecca jumped up and down.

"If you say so, little girl." The ticket scalper laughed. "You better hope so because these are my three last tickets, and I'll have no problem selling them to someone else."

"Then I'm sure you'll have no trouble selling them and for more."

"I'm tryin' to do ya a favor." The ticket scalper leered at Rita's eyes before his eyes dropped to her chest. "I hate to see a little girl go home sad."

"And I bet you have a fourth ticket that you'll use to sit next to me." Rita looked away. "Come along, Rebecca." She pointed. "There's the will-call window."

***

Rita held Rebecca's hand and stepped up to the window. "Rita and Rebecca Mendez and Margie Anderson. We're on Bart Johnson's, I mean, Abede's guest list."

An overweight woman with short-cropped, dirty blond hair perused a list, moving her lips as she read. She spoke in a nasal voice, "I don't see you on my list."

"Look again!" Rebecca pleaded. "Abede promised!"

"I'm sorry. You're not on the list. Next!"

"No. I am an eyewitness." Margie intervened. "Abede came into my diner. He told us that he would pass us into the wrestling."

"Sorry. I don't see you on my list." The nasal-voiced woman looked down. "There's nothing I can do. Next."

"Come on, ladies." A large man in denim overalls stepped in front of them. "You ain't on her list? You ain't on her list. Move on." He peered into the window. "Five tickets saved for Skeet Boggs."

"Oh no, you don't." Rita shoved him and glowered. She turned to the will-call lady. "I want to see your supervisor."

The will-call woman nodded to a balding man. Grease kept his thinning follicles in place over the bald spots. "What is the problem?"

"One of the wrestlers, Bart Johnson, Abede, put us on his guest list." Rita pointed to the will-call woman. "She says she has no record of it."

The balding man adjusted his black, plastic-rimmed glasses. "The problem is that you are in the wrong place. Go to the employee entrance on the other side of the building. That's where we admit the wrestler's guests."

***

Rita took their seats four rows from the ring.

"Excuse me. Excuse me." A large man in denim overalls, his plus-sized wife, two young boys, and a little girl Rebecca's age pushed through the row. They sat in the next five seats by Rita, Rebecca, and Margie. "Hey. I remember you three." He smiled at them. "I'm afraid I lost my Southern manners. I let the crowd bother me. We

19

live on eighty acres. We're not used to so many people in one place. It's still no excuse for rudeness. My apologies." He extended his hand. Margie shook his hand. Rita and Rebecca did not. "Skeet Boggs. This is my wife, Tammy May, my boys, David and Bob, and my little Angelica. I named Bob after my big brother. He's a rassler. We had the same problem as you at the will-call window."

"Really!" Rebecca stood up. "Your brother's a wrestler?"

"Yup. He rassles as Beer Barrel Bobby."

"I know your brother." Margie smiled. "He's a regular at my diner. He can't resist our pot roast."

"You mean you're 'Pot Roast Margie'?" Skeet beamed. "My brother talks about your pot roast all the time."

Margie blushed. "He calls me Margie, and my husband, Del, cooks the pot roast."

Rita looked at them and relaxed. "Her husband's name is on the marquee." Rita chuckled. "But Margie's the big boss."

"Abede gave us tickets!" Rebecca chirped.

"I'm sorry, Skeet and Tammy May," Rita extended her hand. "Now I am the rude one. I haven't introduced myself. Now we're even," she chuckled. "I'm Rita, and this is my daughter, Rebecca."

'Uh oh, Rebecca," Skeet chuckled. "Each wrestler only gets four passes. Most promoters only give us two. Anyway…" Skeet paused and smiled at Rebecca. "Even though we're all friends now, I'd still rather wait to tell you who gave us the fifth ticket."

"I wish you could come to our farm and play with us." Angelica smiled at Rebecca. "We have horses. I can show you how to ride 'em."

"Mama! I love horses! Let's visit Angelica!"

Rita blushed. "That's nice of you, Angelica, but…"

"But nothing." Tammy May beamed. "I'll give you our phone

number. Just give us a call, and I'll get Angelica's pony ready for you." She pointed at Rebecca. "In the meanwhile," she reached into her handbag. "One for each of you." She handed Margie and Rita a cup. "This is for when my brother-in-law wrestles." She chuckled, "Sorry Rebecca, I'll give one to you when you turn twenty-one."

The house lights dimmed. A spotlight shone on the aisle from an exit portal.

"Coming down the aisle. He hails from the Cossack Plains of Russia. Weighing in at two hundred and seventy-five pounds. Yuri the Red." Yuri climbed into the ring. He wore knee-high riding boots and a traditional black Cossack chokha coat. The ring lights glowed off his smooth head. His mustache had five curves like scimitar blades, ending three inches below his chin. He stomped about the ring, ensuring each step caused the floor to resound like a bass drum.

A fan jammed his head between Rita and Rebecca. "Go back to Russia, commie pinko prick!"

An elderly woman sitting ringside yelled, "Better dead than red, and I hope soon you'll be dead! Commie!"

Yuri grabbed the microphone from the ring announcer. "Vodka! Vodka! Vodka!"

The crowd stood and yelled at the top of their lungs, "Beer! Beer! Beer!"

Yuri dropped the microphone and covered his ears.

The ring announcer spoke, "Now, coming down the aisle, he's from Tallahassee, Florida, weighing in at three hundred and forty-five pounds, Beer Barrel Bobby!"

"Beer! Beer! Beer!"

Beer Barrel Bobby had straggly hair and a long black beard. He wore denim overalls. He carried a wooden beer keg on his shoulder. He then held it over the ring rope and released the spout. The fans jostled to place their cups under the flow.

"Come on Margie, Rita," Tammy May grabbed Rita's arm. "What's better than free beer straight from the keg?"

Margie smiled, stood, and leaned over with her cup. Rita sat still. Margie lipped, '*Come on,*' and head motioned. Rita reluctantly held out her cup. Bob recognized both from the diner and made a point of filling their cups.

"Beer! Beer! Beer!" The crowd yelled as Bob lifted the keg overhead and shook it up and down. "Beer! Beer! Beer!"

Yuri snuck behind and struck Bobby's back with a forearm. Bobby staggered forward. He turned and slammed the keg into Yuri's chest. The Russian fell into the ropes and rebounded. Bobby dropped the beer barrel, put him in a bear hug, and slammed him to the canvas. Bobby held him in a headlock and squeezed. Yuri managed to place his foot over the lower rope. The referee broke the hold. After they stood in the center of the ring, Yuri kneed Bobby in the stomach. Bobby keeled over. Yuri kneed him in the chest. The Russian wrestler then kneed him rhythmically with each kick in what resembled a Cossack dance. Bob collapsed onto the canvas. Yuri stomped his head.

"Get up Bob! Get Up!" A gray-haired woman shook her handbag. "Don't let that Commie win!"

"Beer! Beer! Beer!" The crowd yelled.

Bobby climbed onto one knee.

"Beer! Beer! Beer!"

Bobby managed to stand. Yuri twice hit him with forearm strikes.

"Beer! Beer! Beer!"

Bobby shook his head in unison with their shouts. He then scowled at Yuri and cocked his fist.

Yuri steepled his hands and begged for mercy.

"Commie coward!" A large fan in blue work clothes punched his left palm with his right fist. "Punch him! American style!"

Bobby slammed Yuri with his right fist. Yuri fell into the ropes. Bobby ran forward, grabbed his arm, and flung him across the ring, into the far ropes. Bobby set himself for a bear hug. Yuri raised his leg and put his foot into Bobby's chest, knocking him to the floor. Yuri did an elbow drop onto Bobby's chest. He lifted Bobby by the hair, grabbed his arm, and flung him into the ropes. Bobby rebounded. Yuri raised his arm to clothesline him. Bobby ducked, slingshot himself off the far ropes, and knocked Yuri to the canvas. He then ran to the other rope, leaped skyward, and splashed on top of the Russian. Bobby pinned him to the mat, tucked his arm under his left knee, and raised his leg.

The referee slapped the mat and counted, "One! Two! Three!"

The bell rang. The ring announcer entered the ring. "Your winner! From the good old U.S.A! Beer Barrel Bobby!" The referee raised Bob's hand.

"Way to go, Uncle Bob!" David stood and clapped his hands.

"That was my Uncle Bob." Angelica faced Rebecca. "He's not married and has no kids of his own. He treats me like his daughter. My dad." Angelica pointed to Skeet, "and him are brothers and best friends. I hope your mommy will bring you to the farm to play with me and my brothers, and you can meet my Uncle Bob."

"Mommy," Rebecca turned to Rita, "When can we go to Angelica's?"

"Maybe Someday." Rita looked away.

"Well," Tammy May clutched Rita's arm, "Here's the phone number I promised." Tammy May handed Rita a paper scrap. "Make that someday as soon as you can."

"Gracias, I mean, thank you." Rita blushed and smiled.

"Mom. She speaks Spanish." Angelica smiled at her mother. "I'm learning Spanish at school. I wanna learn more." Angelica waved at Rebecca. "Hola amiga."

"Hola," Rebecca waved back. "Mommy. Me gusta mi nueva amiga." Rebecca clutched Rita's arm. "Per favor visitemos pronto. And she said I could ride her pony."

The houselights came on. The ring announcer spoke. "Ladies and gentlemen. Our next match will be the main event of the evening. A cage match pitting The Jaguar and Abede the African Lion for the vacant American Federation of Wrestling world title. First. A twenty-minute intermission while we set up the cage."

"Do you all also know Abede from the diner?" Skeet stood.

"Yes. He only came once, but, like your brother, he made quite an impression."

"Did he also love your pot roast?" Skeet smiled.

"Well, as I said, it's my husband's pot roast. And the one who made the big impression on him is sitting here." Margie gazed at Rebecca. "That's why he gave us tickets."

"Well. My brother won largely because your pot roast stuck to his ribs. My wife and I are going to make a beer run. I'll bring you and Rita one too."

"Daddy. May I stay and play with Rebecca."

"Of course, it will be fine." Rita smiled. "I'll be happy to look after Angelica.

***

After twenty minutes, the house lights were still on, and no one had entered the ring. All seats were filled. The crowd stirred and grumbled. They stood and cheered as the ring announcer, referee, and timekeeper at the bell entered the 15-foot-high cage. They erupted as the house lights dimmed and the ring lights illuminated. "Ladies and Gentlemen. Your main event of the evening. One fall to a finish for the American Federation of Wrestling World Title. A

24

cage match has only one rule. The first man to exit the ring, whether over the top or through the door, is the winner."

The spotlight shined onto the aisle. The boos and catcalls echoed throughout. The arena sound system played Martin Denny's "*Quiet Village.*" The serene instrumental created atmosphere. It stirred rather than calmed the crowd.

"Now coming down the aisle, being led by his manager Professor Sakamoto and his handler Nigel Earl, jungle cats raised him. He was trapped in the most remote reach of the Amazon jungle, weighing 243 pounds. The Jaguar."

The Jaguar struggled against his chains. Sakamoto and Earl feigned exertion.

The sound system now played the original 1957 Gallotone label recording of Miriam Makeba's "*Pata Pata.*" The crowd clapped in synch; some danced in place.

"Now. Coming down the aisle. He hails from Kenya, Africa. Weighing in at 428 pounds. Everybody's favorite! Adebe. The African Lion."

The moment Abede exited the portal, the crowd cheered and stomped their feet. The building shook enough to register on the Richter scale.

The referee instructed the wrestlers before following the timekeeper out of the cage.

"Ding!" The bell rang.

The Jaguar ran to the cage wall and started climbing. Halfway up, he performed a backflip and landed on Adebe, knocking him down. The Jaguar got up and climbed higher up the cage wall. He waited until Adebe stood. The Jaguar leaped and thumped Abede's chest with both feet. Abede staggered backward. The Jaguar leaped six feet off the ground and kicked Abede's head with two feet. Abede crashed to the canvas. This time, The Jaguar climbed eight feet up the cage wall; Abede stood and faced him, wobbly and unsteady. The Jaguar leaped like a springboard diver doing a jackknife and clotheslined Abede. He hit the canvas; The Jaguar stood and executed a flying elbow drop, stunning Abede. The masked wrestler headed for the cage door and victory. Abede crawled over, tackled him by the ankles, and pulled him back into the ring. He lifted The Jaguar, and power slammed him. He struck him with an elbow drop, stood, and dropped his leg across the Jaguar's throat. Abede raised his arms in victory and walked three-quarters out of the cage door. Professor Sakamoto suddenly threw salt in his eyes. Abede put his hands over his eyes and stumbled about the ring. The fans screamed at the referee positioned outside of the cage. Pretending he didn't see it, he waved it off. After the referee turned his back, Professor Sakamoto smirked at the crowd and cackled. The fans erupted, many throwing debris at the Japanese manager. The Jaguar raked Abede's eyes. He stammered about in blind pain. The Jaguar struck Abede with a right forearm shiver to the chest and hit him again with his left forearm. Abede fell into the corner. The Jaguar pounced on him and flung him into the other corner.

The crowd started stomping and clapping in a two-beat rhythm. "Abede! Abede! Abede!"

Abede stomped his feet in unison. He recovered and elbowed the Jaguar across the head, put him in a bear hug and whispered to the Jaguar without moving his lips. "Bring it on home." Abede power slammed him to the canvas. Next, he lifted the Jaguar overhead with two arms and hurled him into the cage wall. The cage gave way. The Jaguar fell through the gap at the bottom of the wall and ring apron. He lay motionless on the floor.

Abede raised his arms in victory. The crowd stood, cheering and shaking their fists.

"He won!" Rebecca jumped up and down. "He won! Bubby is now world champion!"

Skeet and Tammy May pursed their lips and looked away.

"Ding! Ding! Ding!"

The referee, the ring announcer, American Federation of Wrestling proprietor Al Cohen, a uniformed police officer, and two security guards entered the cage. Professor Sakamoto helped the Jaguar to his feet and led him into the ring.

"Ding! Ding! Ding!"

"Ladies and Gentlemen. The time of the match: sixteen minutes and 47 seconds. The by-laws of The American Federation of Wrestling stipulate that the first wrestler to leave the cage wins. Your new American Federation of Wrestling World Champion. The Jaguar!"

The referee raised the Jaguar's right arm. Professor Sakamoto guffawed. The Jaguar held the championship belt overhead, swung it like a whip, and stomped around the ring. Abede's jaw dropped. He raised his palms. Al Cohen put his arm around Abede and explained the rules. Abede winced. He closed his eyes and tilted back his head.

The crowd booed. Oranges, tomatoes, and popcorn boxes peppered the cage walls.

"No! No! That's unfair!" Tears streamed from Rebecca's eyes. "My friend Bubby won!" She grabbed her mother's arm and looked into her eyes. "He won!"

"Don't you worry." Tammy May craned her head to Rebecca and Rita. "They'll be a rematch. He'll get him next time. We'll have Beer Barrel Bob get you free passes." She looked at her husband with narrow eyes and furrowed brow, "Won't we?"

Skeet nodded.

***

Rebecca sat between Margie and her mother in the '55 Buick Roadmaster sedan front bench seat. Rebecca sobbed.

Rita put her arm around her daughter. "Don't be sad, honey. We had a fun night. It's all entertainment. It's just for fun."

Margie added, "And they sure did entertain, and you know there'll be a rematch."

"You had a great time tonight. We all did, even if Bubby got robbed of the World Championship." Rita kissed Rebecca's forehead, "The best part is that you found a cool new friend."

Rebecca wiped away her tears. "When can we visit Angelica? I like her."

"I hope someday. They live three hours away. I don't think Grandaddy's truck will make it that far." Rita squeezed Rebecca. "But be happy her uncle won."

"Yes, I'm glad he won. I don't like commies. My teacher sometimes makes us hide under our desks in case the commies drop a bomb on the school."

"Don't worry, my little darling. President Eisenhower knows how to handle the Reds. Remember how well he dealt with the Nazis."

"I second that," Margie steered the '55 Buick around a bend, "I like Ike."

"I bet the commies cheat too. But you said cheaters never win. Not only did Professor Sakamoto cheat for the Jaguar; he also cheated for the Rustler Brothers; they won too."

"Well. The Japanese cheated by sneak attacking Pearl Harbor," Rita chuckled, "And in the end, they lost." Rita squeezed Rebecca's hand. "They'll be a rematch. America and Mexico won the war, and Bubby will soon win the wrestling championship."

Rebecca beamed. "Angelica's mom promised that Beer Barrel Bob would give us tickets to the rematch."

"Yes, she did." Margie passed a '49 Ford. "I heard her. But just to be safe, when Bob comes to the diner again, I'll have your mother bring him an extra big helping of my husband's pot roast." Margie chuckled, "That will seal the deal. You should see how he eats."

"How does he eat, Aunt Margie?"

"A lot."

"What I'm excited about," Rita smiled at her daughter, "is Bubby coming back to the diner the Saturday after next and bringing you the dresses his wife made for you."

"Yes, Mom! I can't wait! And I know that he'll be champion soon."

Ten minutes later, Rebecca fell asleep and snuggled up to her mother.

"It looks like your little angel is sound asleep. I can't help but wonder what The Jaguar looks like under his mask. I've seen hot bodies on men but woo! He wins first prize."

Rita blushed. "You know I wasn't watching it like that. Besides, the last thing I want in my life is a wild man. I have Rebecca to consider."

"Oh, come on Rita, it's all an act. The man playing the role of the Jaguar is no more a savage than Boris Karloff is a Frankenstein monster, or Bella Lugosi is a vampire. Give him credit. He's a great athlete, and who knows? Maybe underneath that mask, he's handsome like Mickey Mantle or Pennsylvania's All-American quarterback, Lance Burkett, and he had the crowd going, even if his Japanese manager helped."

"Why do you look at men that way? You have a husband?"

Margie guffawed. "Take a look in my husband's desk drawer. You'll find a well-worn copy of the first issue of Playboy. Del's fingerprints are all over the Marilyn Monroe centerfold. Anytime we can both get away from the diner and catch a movie, he always takes me to one of her flicks. This is a girl's night out, even if it's taking Rebecca to professional wrestling. She's asleep. What do you say?

You are a beautiful young lady. Gorgeous even. Just about every man who eats at the diner makes googly eyes at you. But you've never had a single date. As you say in Spanish, que pasa?"

"You know I don't like talking about it." Rita took a deep breath. "Okay. You're right. I haven't gone out on a date or otherwise since my husband was killed." She winced. "Can we leave it at that, please?"

"I know, I won't pry. Let me say one last time before I shut up. You are a wonderful mother, and I think you have much to offer a good man as a wife. And I hope that you find the right stepfather for Rebecca."

Rita pursed her lips and looked downward.

"I hope that I didn't step too far over your line." Margie looked down the road. "I'm sorry. I won't ask again."

***

Buzz Arlette sat on a hard bench in the corner of the Alligator Alley Gymnasium's visitors' locker room. An overhead light hung from the ceiling, casting dim shadows on the gray walls. The dank odor of humidity and sweat hung like the soiled wrestling attire and dirty towels hanging on hooks. He grasped the rear edge of his mask with his right hand and pulled it off. He shook his head, sweat sprayed like a lawn sprinkler. After catching his breath, he wiped down his face with a towel.

Bart entered the locker room. "Brother, that was one great match." They shook hands.

Buzz clasped Bart's right arm, "I just hope I don't have to take another bump like hitting the cage and falling between the ring apron gap. The next time, I hope Al has the ring crew loosen the bottom of the wall better. I felt like toothpaste getting squeezed out of the tube."

"Either that," Bart laughed, "Or I throw you into the wall

30

harder.”

“I weigh 240 pounds. You picked me up and threw me like I was a 90-pound cheerleader. With you blocking, how did any team stop Grambling or the Redskins from scoring a touchdown on every play?”

“There was only one of me and eleven of them.” Bart chuckled, “Besides, my playing weight was almost 350 pounds. That's not good for foot speed. Anyway, this is now my bread and butter.”

“Maybe you should cut back a little on bread and butter,” Buzz laughed. “Stephanie is a great gal. And luckily for you, she's a clothes designer. Otherwise, lion skins would be the only thing that fits you.”

“Bubby, I hope no one saw you enter this locker room.” Al Cohen walked in with Professor Sakamoto. “We can’t risk our business by breaking kayfabe.” Al Cohen wore a gray suit with a blue tie. A former wrestler known for his size; he had put on at least fifty more pounds since retiring as a wrestler.

Bart shook his head.

“With that out of the way,” Al smiled. “Fantastic match! The crowd is still in an uproar. It's a good thing I hired a film crew. I'll have it broadcast on television. I will have to book the rematch in the Tangerine Bowl in Orlando or the Orange Bowl in Miami. You just made us the big time. Now we’ll make real money.”

“Did you say *we?*” Bubby smirked.

“I’ll get to that.”

“When Al?” Bart put his hands on his hips.

“What I want to know,” Buzz held up his Jungle cat mask. Strands of long, straggly black hair were attached to the edges. “Is when I can get rid of this.”

“Fifteen minutes ago, you were handed a World Championship belt. That is unheard of for a rookie. I have wrestlers who have worked for me for years and will never wear a championship belt. It's a good thing that you were a college wrestler, have an Asian martial arts background, and you're a fine athlete; otherwise, you'd have to deal with their resentment."

"Oh, they resent him all right." Bart guffawed. "I have to listen to their griping."

"Yeah, they pull plenty of ribs on me behind my back." Buzz shook his head.

"Rookie hazing is part of the business," Al added. "I experienced it myself."

"Don't I know it," Bart shook his head.

"And right now," Al turned to Buzz and placed his hand on his shoulder, "most of the boys know more about the business than you can ever forget."

"I'm not complaining." Buzz held up his mask, "This thing is uncomfortable, but for now, it beats wearing a tie to work every day, and my wild man act has made more money than I could make in years of wearing a suit, fighting traffic, and working in a city. But still Al..."

"Look, you're a handsome man. Anyone can see that. But if I over-expose you and let the public see you as less a wrestler than your potential, it could damage your future in the business." Al put his hands to his side. "Wrestling has more female fans than, say, boxing, but even our female fans need other reasons to pay money to see you. And the men? They need a reason to admire you, to want you to win. Moreover, the kids must see you as a superhero. Creating and pulling that off is not as easy as you think. You are a fine athlete, and you can leap and do somersaults. But our show is not a body-building competition or a gymnastics meet. Besides, I already have two good-looking faces in the Samson Brothers. Growing out their hair challenged the cultural norm, but long hair is par for the course in wrestling."

"At least you didn't make them bleach it."

"You have short hair." Al chuckled. "Can you grow a flowing mane like the Samson Brothers? Look Buzz, I need you as the Jaguar. You're doing a great job, and I am compensating you accordingly. You still have more to learn about wrestling before I can use you as a front-line face. Working a match is both an art and a science. You're natural at this; that's why you got a belt tonight. With time, you will be where I want you and where you want to be." Al pointed, "and no one succeeds without developing positive charisma and rapport with the crowd. Right now, you are learning from the best." Al slapped Bart's back. "Without the Bubby here and his African Lion role, The Jaguar doesn't work. I know my business. Don't think I never hear the rumblings about you being former Grambling and NFL football player Bubby Johnson, and you're really from Macon, Georgia, not Kenya. But you're playing the role so well that the fans who have caught on don't care."

"Well, Al, I admit I am doing this for money." Bart scratched his chin. "Some black community leaders have criticized me for playing a stereotype while others have applauded me for being a unifier. Working for you tips the scales. I appreciate that you won't book a show in a segregated venue or book any of your wrestlers in a segregated hotel."

Professor Sakamoto laughed, "And little does anyone know that I am a real professor."

"Yeah, Japanese theater." Bart laughed and slapped his back.

"There's a lot more to it than that. I teach the history, culture, and traditions of Noh, Kyogen, Kabuki, and Takarazuka. I was last directing a Kabuki production with American student actors and actresses. Unfortunately, the University just had to hire Stephanie to design the costumes." Sakamoto skewed his head at Bart. "I don't know how a black American knew so much about Japanese costumes, but she did a great job. The downside was meeting you."

He tapped Bart's chest and chuckled. "And unlike you unifying people and making white people like a black man, I'm perpetuating the same old wartime stereotypes."

"You're an actor, not an activist," Al added. "You're regularly seen on TV, and wrestling is bringing you more fame than you'd get out of a hundred years of university theater. Besides, Shigeru, it didn't take you long to accept my offer, seeing that I doubled your university salary. And if this gets you a movie role, I will release you from your contract and be happy for you."

"With a last name like Cohen," Bart smiled, "many of the bigots who don't like me don't like you either."

"One of your people invented the bomb," The professor pointed at Al. "And one of your people," he pointed at Buzz, "dropped two on my country." Shigeru chuckled. "But you know we'll get even," he pointed to his temple. "And we'll do it with our brains." Elvis's *'Don't Be Cruel'* played in the background. "You can turn up the volume on that Sony TR-69 transistor radio and thank me later."

"So, when do we get the first Japanese Elvis?" Buzz joked.

Al held up his arms in a halt gesture. "All kidding aside, you guys get it. Heroes and villains. That's what literature and drama are all about, and that's what professional wrestling is all about. Haters will hate. We can't stop a bigot from hating." Al chuckled. "But we can exploit their prejudices and take their money."

"I'm a White Navy brat, but I got 'em convinced I'm a savage from the Amazon jungles. So how about you dispel a certain stereotype the bigots hold against you and do it on behalf of the three of us?" Buzz held out an open palm.

"You know that I must operate this business on a shoestring budget, and I have expenses to account for." Al put his hands on his hips.

"And a full house at the Tangerine Bowl or Orange Bowl will put your ledgers well into the black," Bart added his upward palm.

"You boys did great tonight. We have a lot of promos to do before the big rematch event. In the meantime, I'll have you guys work only with jobbers. No use risking an injury before the big event. And, yes, you all make a good point." Al pulled his wallet from his rear pocket, "You earned a bonus." Al handed Bart, Buzz, and Shigeru fifty-dollar bills."

The wrestlers beamed.

Chapter 4

Rebecca peeked out of the back-room door and into the diner. Rita partially covered her mouth so only her daughter could see her lips move. "He's not here yet." She walked over to two male customers sitting at a booth. One looked in his early twenties and had greased black hair; the other had blond hair and was in his thirties. Both wore shirts with *"Boyd Electrical"* emblems. Jo Stafford's *'You Belong to Me'* played on their booth's private jukebox.

"Good morning, Rita." The older customer rested his elbows on the menu. "We'll have the usual."

"Cowboy breakfasts for both?"

"Yup." He grinned at her. "I learned a new Spanish saying."

"And what might that be, Derek?" Rita smirked at him.

"Casata conmigo?"

Rita chuckled. "And what is Einstein's famous saying"?"

"E equals MC squared?"

"No." Rita jotted down their order in her pad. "Einstein said, 'Insanity is asking the same thing repeatedly while expecting a different answer.'"

"Oh, come on, Rita." Derek smiled at her. "This time I asked in Spanish."

"Do you know what a cognate is?"

Derek shrugged his shoulders.

"It's a word that's the same in two languages. 'No' is the same in both English and Spanish." Rita chuckled. "Hey, I take it you both want your eggs over easy and your bacon crispy."

"Si." Both men laughed.

As Rita walked over to the counter to lodge their orders with Del, she noticed Rebecca again peep from the backroom. Rita winked at her.

***

Buzz Arlette pulled his '56 Chevy Bel Air onto the road shoulder near a four-way intersection. He opened his paper map. The wind forced him to fold it over. *"Damn. According to this,"* he ran his finger along the line marked US Rt 1. *"I should be in Autumn, Florida. All I see is swamps and orange groves. All right, I'll give it five more miles. If I don't run into Autumn and Del's Diner, I better turn back and take a right on State Route 597,"* He looked at the crossroad. *"And head for Jacksonville. I can't be late for my match even if it is with a jobber like Frankie Williamson. He has several years in the business; I respect that, and he takes good bumps. But it's good that Al doesn't let him speak too often."* Buzz chuckled. *"Columbus, Ohio? 'I'm no 'afraid'a nobody. I no run from a nobody.' What Columbus neighborhood did that accent come from? Even his name? Frankie Williamson instead of Hermando Pumarillo? Oh well, Frankie Williamson it is."*

***

A courier leaned his motorcycle against the front steps of Del's dinner. He entered and looked around. "Telegram for Del's Diner."

"I'm Delbert Anderson, the owner. I'll take it." Del tipped the courier and read the telegram. He dropped his head and frowned.

Margie noticed her husband's chagrin. She walked over. "What is it, honey?"

Del handed her the telegram. "Oh, no." She shook her head and pursed her lips. "Rita."

"What's wrong, Margie?"

Margie handed Rita the telegram. It read, "Sorry. Can't make it today. Another time. Bubby."

Rita blanched. "Oh, my goodness, no." Rita crumpled the telegram. "She'll be crushed." Rita saw her daughter's head sticking out from the door opening. Her eyes had brightened, expecting good

37

news. Rita pursed her lips and trudged over to her.

"I'm sorry, Mommy. Don't be angry. It's just that I'm so excited."

"Darling." Rita put her arm around Rebecca. "It's not that. I'm not angry. Rebecca. I know you've had a harder life than most little girls, but Jesus has looked after us. We have food and a roof over our heads, and you have a great future. Having a daughter like you makes me the luckiest woman on Earth. And you're luckier than most, and even if things get worse, we are always to love the Lord and be grateful for every blessing. The most important thing is Heaven after we die. Until then, we must endure trials and disappointments. Honey, I am sorry, but Bubby's not coming."

"No Mommy!" Tears streamed from Rebecca's eyes. "That's not fair! He promised!"

"Life isn't always fair, my angel." Rita placed her hands on Rebecca's shoulders. "Rather than anger, let's be thankful that Bubby gave us wrestling tickets."

"But they cheated him out of the championship, and that no-good Jaguar won! Nothing is fair!"

"Darling, often life is not fair."

"And God took my daddy from me!" Rebecca started bawling.

"We still have Grandpa."

"No! I want my daddy back! And Bubby lied to me!" Rita bolted outside to their rusty '46 Ford 59C pickup truck.

Rita looked at Del and Margie. Margie nodded. "You can have the rest of the day off. Mary and I can cover for you. Rebecca is more important than the diner."

Rebecca sat on the running board of their pickup truck, covered her face in her hands, and bawled. Rita sat next to her and placed her arm around her shoulder. Rebecca buried her face on her mother's shoulder and cried.

***

'All right. This must be it. Autumn, Florida.' Buzz drove through two green stoplights. He took glances at the side of the road. *'That must be it. Del's Diner.'* Buzz pulled into the parking lot.

***

"Mommy, I know how hard you try, and I know Grandpa works hard in the orange grove. But I don't have any nice clothes, and the kids at school tease me and call me names like *'Raggedy Rebecca.'* I never want to go back to school."

"You know that you won't even have food to eat, much less nice things, unless you go to school." Rita hugged her daughter. "I'll try. I'll try harder to buy you better clothes. Everything comes with hard work. Let's go home now. I'll read you Cinderella again."

"Cinderella had a mean stepmother. I have you, Mommy. You're the best Mom in the world. I love you. But I still wish that I had a daddy."

Rita held Rebecca's hand and helped her into the truck. She pushed the starter. After two electric grinds, it turned over.

***

Buzz Arlette entered the diner. He wore brown loafers, navy blue slacks, and a white Lacoste polo shirt with an alligator logo. Short golden blond hair topped his Teutonic, square-jawed face. He stood six-foot-two and had broad shoulders.

Margie greeted him with a menu. "Booth or counter." *'Nice blue eyes, cute nose.'* she thought. *'He looks like a more muscular Lance Burkett.'*

"Neither. My buddy Bubby's wife made a little girl named Rebecca some dresses. He said her mother works here as a waitress. Bubby can't make it, so he had me bring them."

Margie's eyes opened wide as two full moons. She gazed at the

39

unbuttoned placket of his shirt. His striated, muscular chest clicked her mind's tumblers. "Wait right here." Margie ran out of the diner's front door.

Rita's truck belched black smoke as she drove it around the diner, through the front parking lot.

Margie waved at her wildly.

"It's Aunt Margie. She's waving to us."

"Oh my, she's going to ask me to stay. I know you want to go home. Let's pretend we don't see her."

"But that would be cheating, like Professor Sakamoto."

"You're right honey. We better stop and see what she wants."

"Rita! Rebecca!" Margie ran over and braced her hands on the driver's door window frame. "A friend of Bubby's is here! He brought Rebecca the dresses."

"Mommy! Did you hear that!"

"Yes, honey." Rita and Rebecca disembarked.

"He's over there." Margie waved at Buzz. He stood on the entrance vestibule and waved back.

"Stay there," Buzz shouted. "I'll pull my car over."

***

Buzz parked next to Rita's pickup truck and disembarked.

"Buzz." Margie turned her head. "This is Rita and her daughter Rebecca."

"You two need no introduction. Bubby told me so much about you. He sure didn't exaggerate." He gently shook Rebecca's hand. "You are just about the prettiest young lady I've ever met. And you must be her mother, Rita." Buzz and Rita shook hands. They held each other's hands firmly. They made eye contact. Rita blushed, looked away, and retracted her hand.

"Do you wrestle with Bubby?" Rebecca stood on her toes. "You

40

have big muscles."

"No, Rebecca," Buzz chuckled. "I'm his trashman. Everything about Bubby is big, including his trashcans. I get my muscles from lifting them. Well, Rebecca, I bet you can't wait to see what Mrs. Bubby made for you." Buzz opened the trunk of his '56 Chevy Bel Air. He took out a white cardboard box. "I think I know what's in this one. Mrs. Bubby is also from Kenya, Africa. She made this one just for you." Buzz opened the box and showed Rebecca an orange and black dress with floral designs and prints of giraffes and zebras. He handed it to her.

Rebecca held it in front of her. "Mom! Look! It's beautiful!"

Rita looked at her daughter and beamed.

"Rita, you speak perfect English." Buzz looked into Rita's wide brown eyes. "Nevertheless, you have a lovely accent. Where is it from?"

Rita blushed and looked down. "Guadalajara, Mexico."

"Mexico!" Buzz smiled. "Mrs. Bubby must have a crystal ball." Buzz took another box from the trunk of his car. He opened the box and held up a bright red and green Jalisco-style dress with a floral motif. It had a full skirt and a white blouse with a fitted bodice.

"Mommy! It's beautiful! Thank you, Mr. Buzz!" Rebecca took the dress and handed it to her mother.

"You be sure to thank Bubby for me." Rita looked at the dresses draped over her arm and smiled.

"I sure will," Buzz looked into Rita's eyes and smiled. Rita held eye contact for three seconds, blushed, and looked away. "Bubby's wife is a professional dress designer. I don't have a wife, and I surely can't make dresses." Buzz smiled at Rebecca. "Bubby said so many nice things about you that I just had to go to the store. Look at what I got for you." Buzz handed Rebecca a white box with two American-style school dresses. "And you can't wear your new dresses barefoot, so I bought you these..." Buzz reached into his car's trunk and handed Rebecca a pair of Buster Brown *Mary Jane* shoes.

"Wow!" Rebecca held the shoes up to her eyes and grinned. "Thank you! They're beautiful!"

"A beautiful young lady should have beautiful things." Buzz then looked at Rita. "You already have a beautiful mother."

Rita blushed. "You're too kind, Buzz. I can't thank you and Bubby enough." She touched his hands.

"Aww, it's nothing."

"Mommy! I can't wait to go to school and wear my new clothes!"

"It's something." Rita took Buzz's hands and glanced into his wide blue eyes. "It's a bigger something than you can ever imagine." She retracted her hands and put her arm around her daughter.

"You made my day too." Margie smiled at Buzz. "I'm sure Bubby and Bob told you about Del's pot roast. Come on in and stay. I have a big helping waiting for you. It's on the house."

"I thank you very much for your offer, Margie. But today is trash day in Jacksonville. I better get on my way. And Rita and Rebecca, meeting you both was extraordinary for me. I hope to see you both again sometime."

"Likewise." Rita nodded. "Thank you so much for everything."

"Yes! Thank you, Mister Buzz." Rita jumped up and down. They both waved to Buzz as he drove away.

"Rita." Margie smiled. "I felt more than electricity when you two shook hands. I felt lightning bolts."

"Oh, stop it, Margie." Rita blushed. "You're my best friend, and I see you as Rebecca's Aunt Margie." She winced. "But you know that I hate it when you try to play matchmaker."

"Rita, I love you as a daughter and Rebecca as my granddaughter. You know that." Margie put her hands on Rita's shoulders. "So why can't you tell me why you refuse to date anyone? I know I'm on shaky ground to say this, but your husband died four years ago. I'd love to see you move on. Buzz is as handsome and kind a man as has ever come to my diner."

"Margie, I know I'm just a waitress. But still, I'm not going to date a trash man."

Margie guffawed. "Buzz also has a fine sense of humor. Did you see the nice car that he's driving? The stylish clothes? His educated speech? He's no trash man. He's keeping a little secret from you. I think I know what it is. It's nothing bad. Nonetheless, I will leave it for him to tell you. Based on how he looked at you, he'll be back."

Rita blushed and looked away.

Chapter 5

Buzz pulled his car onto US Route One. He imbibed his car's floral air freshener. Rita's visage appeared to him. He smiled. Adjusting the wing windows, he drove back to State Road 597. *'What a wonderful little girl! I'm supposed to be a tough wrestler, fighter, and martial artist. But her smile melted my heart. Buying those dresses and shoes was the best money I ever spent. If only Bubby and Stephanie were there to see how happy their clothes made her.'* Buzz accelerated down the highway. He tuned in to a radio station and cranked up the volume. A doo-wop group called the Jarmels were singing in swing time the Jerome Kern classic, *The Way You Look Tonight.*

The backing vocals sang: La La La La Woah-oh-oh; La La La La Woah-oh-oh.

The lead sang: Some day, when I'm awfully low,

When the world is cold,

I will feel a glow just thinking of you

And the way you look tonight.

La La La La Woah-oh-oh; La La La La Woah-oh-oh

Yes you're lovely, with your smile so warm

And your cheeks so soft,

There is nothing for me but to love you,

And the way you look tonight.

La La La La Woah-oh-oh; La La La La Woah-oh-oh

With each word your tenderness grows,

Tearing my fear apart.

And that laugh that wrinkles your nose,

It touches my foolish heart.

La La La La Woah-oh-oh; La La La La Woah-oh-oh

Lovely, Never, ever change.

Keep that breathless charm.

Won't you please arrange it,

Cause I love you

Just the way you look tonight.

La La La La Woah-oh-oh; La La La La Woah-oh-oh

Mm, mm, mm, mm,

Just the way you look tonight.

La La La La Woah-oh-oh; La La La La Woah-oh-oh

Although the Jarmels sang in up-tempo swing time, Buzz pictured himself and Rita holding each other close as they danced. A boisterous commercial for Crazy Wally's Used Car dealership broke his reverie. After an ad featuring Dinah Shore singing, 'See the USA in a Chevrolet,' the radio played the Flamingo's version of the Warren and Dubin standard, *I Only Have Eyes for You.* Buzz pictured himself looking into Rita's enchanting brown eyes. He moved his face closer to her full and balanced lips. "Dammit!" He banged on the steering wheel upon realizing he had driven past the turn to State Road 597.

***

Rebecca beamed. "Today was the best day ever! Even better than Christmas. I'm sorry that we didn't get to see Bubby. But Mr. Buzz sure was a nice man."

Rita didn't respond. She re-lived touching his hand and her looking into his blue eyes."

"Mom?"

"Yes dear," Rita turned to Rebecca.

"Mr. Buzz was such a nice man."

"Well, yes Rebecca, very nice," She chuckled, "for a trash man."

Chapter 6

Buzz pulled his car into the Jacksonville Coliseum parking lot. He donned a white mask and entered the venue. Bart was the first person he saw. "Bubby! I wish you were there! When Rebecca saw Stephanie's dresses her smile could melt the polar icecaps."

"She's an adorable little girl, that's for sure."

"Yes, she is. I bought her some clothes and shoes from the store. And I'm sure glad that I did. Her mother also appreciated it."

"Buzz, you have no time for that. Al flew in Lou Thesz. You're fighting him tonight to unify the World title. And I mean fighting. Lou is a shooter and a great one. He has more fighting experience than you have experience eating and breathing. You're younger, bigger, and stronger, you have Asian martial arts training, and you wrestled for West Virginia University. If anyone can beat him in a fair fight," Bart pointed at Buzz, "It's you."

"I don't know what to say." Buzz shrugged his shoulders. "What a great opportunity!" He raised his hands. "But I need time to prepare for a match of this style and magnitude. And what about my savage jungle boy act? I wish Al had given me some warning." Buzz tapped his forehead. "Here I thought I had an off-night working with Frankie Williamson."

"You're right. You don't have much time. Hurry up and get changed. I'll get you ready as best I can." Bart led Buzz to the locker room. A radio sat on a bench, playing Dion and the Belmonts' *A Teenage In Love.*' "I will help you stretch and warm up. We can discuss strategy. Remember, Lou Thesz is known for being able to break a man in half."

Buzz and Bart entered the locker room.

"Make way. Make way. Give him room." Wrestler Steve Samson had long, natural blonde hair. "He's fighting Lou Thesz tonight.

Bubby's got to get him ready."

Shaun Samson, his younger brother, was smaller but had even thicker and longer wavy blond hair. Both were regarded as the most attractive faces in the business. "I hope you unify the title and remain handsome. If Lou rearranges your face, you're stuck with that mask, and you'll have to wear it even when not wrestling."

"I know Thesz is tough, skilled, and experienced." Buzz pursed his lips and nodded his head. "I've fought some of the top martial artists in the Philippines, Japan, and Korea. I'm as ready as I'll ever be."

"You better be." Steve chuckled. "Al needs you to win and remain in one piece."

Beer Barrel Bobby added, "Tonight, I'm not wasting my beer on the audience. I'm saving it for after you win the title." He slapped Buzz's back, "And if you lose, we drown it out together." Bob looked at Buzz with a straight face. "And if you wind up in the hospital, or worse, dead, we all drink to your memory."

"This is what I want for tonight." Al Cohen walked into the locker room with Frankie Williamson. "It's easy money for both of you."

"Easy money?" Buzz put his hands on his hips. "I'd be happy to fight Floyd Patterson or even King Kong, I just wish you'd give me some notice. I appreciate the opportunity. But I need more time to prepare for a shoot against Lou Thesz."

Al skewed his head in bewilderment.

Shaun covered his mouth. Steve squeezed his lips shut. Suddenly, Bart broke out in an uproar. Bob guffawed, as did Shaun and Steve.

Al shook his head. "When are you going to learn, Buzz?"

"I knew he'd fall for it." Bob pointed and laughed.

"Not me." Steve laughed. "I never thought he was that gullible."

"You shut up." Buzz smiled and pointed at Steve.

"Until you catch on to their ribs." Bart slapped Buzz's back, "They're gonna keep on comin'."

Al Cohen nodded. "Frankie, you know the routine." Frankie Williamson looked more like the arena's custodian than a wrestler. He had a body as if he ate greasy burgers and fries, with dessert, three meals a day at Del's Diner. His black hair looked cut with garden sheers and his mustache a hostage from a silent movie. "Let Buzz do his thing, lay down about three minutes into the match for an easy payday. Buzz, after Frankie plays dead, do your savage act. Shigeru's not here tonight. It's on you to work up the heat. Bart, you got Spider Nel tonight. Let him have his moments. You know that he's a stand-up guy and a valuable worker. I need him to look halfway decent in losing, but not at the expense of your status. Overall, don't do anything risky. I am negotiating to stage your championship rematch with Buzz at the Tangerine Bowl in Orlando. Steve and Shaun. You're keeping the tag team belt tonight, although I want Spence and Clay to end the match on a disqualification with the rustler wrangle. I trust you four to work out a good match. It's the last time you work together until the big event at the Tangerine Bowl." Al and Frankie left the locker room.

The radio now played Danny and the Juniors' *Sometimes When I'm All Alone.'*

"Hey," Bob walked over to Buzz. "I heard that you met Rita at Del's Diner. I asked her to marry me. She thought I was joking and laughed." He patted his gut. "I guess a hot tamale like her don't go for a 350-pound belly of cold beer."

"I'll take a bottle of cold Corona with a hot tamale every time. What other excuses can you come up with for not getting a date." Bart guffawed almost loud enough to rattle the ceiling. "I weigh over four hundred and Stephanie weighs a hundred after dessert and soaking wet."

"Come on Bob." Steve sniggered. "What's the big idea of asking some chick to marry you? You're having too much fun corralling the arena rats."

"I want what Bart's got." Bob pointed at Bart. "Stephanie's smart and classy. What are arena rats but unpaid whores? But what my brother Skeet's got is what I need. A rugged, all-American farm girl. His wife, Tammy May, met Rita and her daughter at the wrestling show in Gainesville. My niece already considers her daughter her best friend in the world. I understand that Rita is a wonderful mother. Yet in just a few short years, when her daughter's body starts to look like her mother's, she's gonna need a dad and a strong one at that." Bob laughed and pointed at Steve and Shaun. "Someone who can protect her from the likes of you two."

"Well, Buzz." Bart guffawed. "I think Bob here just laid down the gauntlet. You better get your ass back to Del's diner and make your claim on the signorita," He pointed at Steve and Shaun, "Before those two get there and try something first."

"Not only that," Steve pointed at Bob, "We're going to get to Del's Diner before you and eat up all of the pot roast."

"I'll let you two and Buzz fight it out for the girl." Bob grinned at Shaun and Steve. "But I'm not letting anyone eat up Del's pot roast."

"I don't know how you two get all the girls." Buzz chuckled. "With that bundle of hair on your heads, how long does it take for them to figure out if you're a boy or a girl?" Buzz folded his arms across his chest.

"You can laugh at your hair joke the whole time I have the girl on my arm. Meanwhile, I'll laugh all the way to the bank. And speaking of hair on our heads," Shaun picked up his wrestling bag. "I hear Grant 'The Beast' Irons is coming to our territory. He's got more hair on his body than we do on our heads."

"And as much hair on this head as a snowball." Buzz laughed.

"He's got a hell of an act." Steve put his wrestling bag down. "Imagine playing a Neanderthal as effectively as he does. "I mean, you being a football player from Macon, Georgia, and you," he pointed at Buzz, "the son of a career Naval Officer isn't a stretch. But a former defensive end at Ohio State and now an associate history professor at Ohio State in the off-season?" Steve shook his head. "Never in a million years."

***

Rita took down their laundry from the clothesline, folded it into a basket, and took it inside. "I'm finished with the laundry, honey, we can read '*Little Women*' together."

"Gee. Thanks, Mom. Can I watch the end of this first?" Rebecca pointed at the TV. Look! It's Bubby!"

Rita sat down next to her daughter. Bart wore his full African Lion regalia. Gordon Hanson stood next to him with a microphone. "Gordon Hanson here with Abede 'The African Lion.' The big news is that just two weeks from tonight, August 23rd, the battle of the big cats, The African Lion and the Savage Jaguar, will fight in a rematch with the AFW World Title on the line. The place is the Tangerine Bowl in Orlando. Tickets go on sale today at the Tangerine Bowl box office, Sears and Roebuck, and Western Auto stores across the state, and if you test drive any used car at any of Crazy Wally's lots, you can buy your tickets for, now this will sound crazy, twenty percent off face value. Abede, you are not just fighting the Jaguar but you also must contend with his manager, Professor Sakamoto. How do you plan on countering that?"

"Simple Gordon. I hired a manager of my own."

"A manager?"

"Yes. And here he is."

Beer Barrel Bobby stood next to Bart. "If Sakamoto interferes, I'll squash him. Not only that, but I'm on to his dirty tricks. I'll be

50

wearing these." Bob put on goggles and grinned.

"As for the Jaguar," Bart pointed at the camera. "He's not even a man. You see this headdress?" He took off his headdress and held it up to the camera. "It's from a lion that I killed with my bare hands in Africa. The lion is a bigger and stronger cat than the jaguar. After the 23rd, I'm going to have a championship belt around my waist and a jaguar head over my fireplace mantle."

"Mommy!" Rebecca pointed at the TV. I wanna go! And when can we visit Angelica? She's my best friend."

"Later honey. Come on. Let's read together." Rita stopped and looked closely at the TV as Sakamoto and the Jaguar came on. Buzz stared at the camera; his head ticced wildly.

Rita tilted her head as she perused the Jaguar's physique. *'No. He can't be."* She shook her head.

Sakamoto spoke. "A lion? Big and strong, yes. But Abede and that hillbilly, Beer Barrel Bobby? Very stupid." Sakamoto shook his head. "My cat has strength, agility, and ferocity. I have the brains." Shigeru pointed to his temple. "We beat him last time. We beat him again."

"In all due respect, Professor. Your wrestler won on a technicality, and you cheated by throwing salt in Abede's eyes. The rematch will be a fair fight."

"We didn't cheat. I outsmarted him." Sakamoto pointed to his temple. "Nobody asks how you won. They ask, 'Did you win'?"

"If you're going to win this time, it will be fair and square because Abede's got a manager of his own."

"Please Mommy, I wanna go! I want to see Bubby win the championship. And I want to visit my best friend, Angelica. Ask Bubby or Bob for tickets?"

"Rebecca, we haven't been invited to Angelica's farm. They're a very nice family, but it's rude to invite ourselves. Even if they invite us, they're three hours away. I don't know when Bart or Bob are coming to the diner again. It's not good manners to up and ask them for tickets."

"How about Mr. Buzz." Rebecca beamed. "I like Mr. Buzz. He's very nice. I bet he'll get us tickets."

"Buzz is just a trash man. He doesn't have any tickets."

"Look, mom." Rebecca pointed at the TV. "It's the Samson Brothers. They have long hair like girls, but they're cute. They remind me of Tarzan."

"If they're going to grow their hair like that." Rita chuckled. "They better know how to fight."

"We have the skill to beat the Rusler Brothers," Shaun smiled at the camera. "They don't know a wristlock from a wristwatch."

"But if they want a down-and-dirty, knock-down, drag-out fight." Steve brandished his fist for the camera. "We can brawl too."

"Yes. That's one-half of the co-main event: The AFW Tag Team championship. And now the other half - their opponents, the Rustler Brothers, Biff and Cletus." Two burly men wearing black Western hats and black vests came on camera. Biff stepped forward. "See this." He held up sheep sheers. "Out on the range, we read the good book. What Delilah did to Samson was a style and a trim compared to what I got coming to you- Steve and Shaun. The only problem is that we can't tell the difference between you two and Delilah." Biff guffawed. "So, we're gonna sheer you both."

Cletus leaned over to the microphone. "Listen here, partner. We're gonna be punchin' Samson Brothers just like punchin' dogies. Yippi Ti Yi Yo, get along little Samsons." Cletus scowled and pointed at the camera. "Only in this case, we don't need no railroad to get you to the slaughterhouse. We're gonna make sausages and hamburgers out of you right in the ring."

"You heard it here. Two weeks from tonight. The individual

World Championship and the Tag team championship."

"Wrestling is over." Rita turned off the TV. "Before we read together, would you like to sing with me?"

"Yes, Mom." Rebecca beamed. "I love singing with you."

Rita and Rebecca sang together.

"A la nanita nana,

Nanita ella,

Nanita ella,

Mi nina tiene sueno,

Bendito sea,

Bendito sea.

Chapter 7

Buzz turned up his radio's volume. The Safari's *Image of a Girl* made Buzz feel like he was piloting a glider rather than driving a '56 Chevy. Spotting a roadside sign informing him that the town of Autumn, Florida, was only five miles away spurned him to sing along.

"As I lie awake resting from the day

I can hear the clock passing time away;

Oh, I couldn't sleep for on my mind

Was the image of the girl I hope to find

I look straight up at the ceiling above

Thinking of the girl whom I will love

Oh, would it be soon when she exists?

The image of the girl I've always wished."

'Del's Diner at last.' Buzz felt a tingling as he ascended the four-step stairway. He stopped at the entrance, straightened his gray sports shirt collar, and rubbed his hairline, even though his hair was cut too short to comb. He walked in and scanned the premises.

"Can I help you?"

'Please be here.' He looked about a second time.

"Can I help you?"

"I'm sorry. I was distracted."

"And what might be your distraction?" The waitress held her menu below her chest and pushed it upward. She had left her top three blouse buttons unfastened. Her perfume was swathed on her upper chest, drawing both eyes and noses.

"I was hoping to find Rita."

"You and a thousand other guys." She laughed and flicked her below the shoulders, flaming red hair. "I've got a menu for you, but she's not on it. I recommend the pot roast, but if you find chopped liver, that's not me." She squeezed Buzz's right bicep.

"I'm sorry." He glanced at her nametag. "Mary."

"I'm a country gal," Mary laughed. "Some think my Southern drawl means I can't speak proper English. I can help you with Rita though. I know what you're going to ask her. Try asking in Spanish. Repeat after me, Casata Conmigo."

"Casata Conmigo?" Buzz shrugged his shoulders.

"My answer is, yes." Mary squeezed both of Buzz's arms.

"Yes?"

"You just asked me to marry you, and I answered yes." Mary chuckled. "Let's go to the Grand Ole Opry for our honeymoon. We can leave now. No need for me to pack my bags. We'll find a Justice of the Peace on the way."

"You know something, Mary." Buzz looked into her green eyes. Her angular face had him figure her age as early thirties, just a bit older than him. He laughed. "Any other day, I might cradle you, whisk you through that door, and drive you off into the sunset. But today, I have my heart set on Rita."

Margie walked over.

"Margie, it looks like another suiter for Rita." Mary smiled at Margie. "After she tosses this one back in the sea," she placed her hand on his right shoulder, "how about you suggest a good bait for my hook." Mary winked at Buzz.

"Well, Buzz, you can never say I don't know how to hire 'em." Margie put her hand on Mary's shoulder and laughed. "Rita's off today." Margie pursed her lips, closed her eyes, and deeply breathed. "I'm going to do something that I've never done, and God forgive me," She closed her eyes and steepled her hands. "I'll never do it again." Margie jotted on her order pad and tore off the page. She looked around and, looking away, she put the page in Buzz's left hand. "You better go now."

***

Buzz sat in his car and read the paper slip. '1010 Grimsby Lane.' Buzz felt something he hadn't experienced since he was Rebecca's age. Shyness. *'Can I just knock on her door? I know she's not expecting me. What if she has guests? Maybe she has a boyfriend? I don't want to cause a scene, especially if Rebecca is home.'* Buzz fisted the paper, closed his eyes, and inhaled deeply. *"What if she doesn't want me at all? And what do I say to her?'* "Relax, Buzz. You got this. Margie wouldn't give this to me," he glanced at the paper slip, "if she has someone else or doesn't like me". *'I better not come empty-handed.'* He reached into his car's jockey box and grabbed a paper road map. He opened it up over the steering wheel. "There it is." He tapped his finger on the map. "Grimsby Lane." *'Shouldn't prove too hard to find.'*

***

Buzz's heartbeat was louder than his '56 Chevy's 256 cubic inch V8 engine, and his radio was blasting Fats Domino's *'I'm Gonna Be a Wheel Someday.'* He rolled up Grimsby Lane, *'1006, 1008, that's got to be it.'* He checked himself one more time in his rearview mirror, took a deep breath, grabbed the bucket of fried chicken he bought on the way, and walked to the front door. He paused for three seconds, then pushed the doorbell button. He heard rumbling. *'At least someone's home.'*

Rita opened the door and gasped. Her light brown skin turned pale, and her mouth formed a circle. Two seconds later, she looked into his eyes. Her eyes opened and shined like a pair of lanterns. The edges of her lips shot upwards. Her face flushed. Just as abruptly, she lowered her head and looked away.

"She's even prettier.' "Hi Rita, um, I brought lunch." He held up the bucket of fried chicken.

56

Rita raised her head. *'Guapo.'* She tilted her head down a degree. *'Tremendo físico.'* "Thanks anyway," she looked away, "but I've prepared lunch for Rebecca, me, and my father. I don't know how you found out where I live, but I'm afraid you need to…"

"Mr. Buzz!" Rebecca ran up and hugged him.

Buzz placed the bucket of fried chicken on the floor and patted her back.

"You're the grinchiest!" Rebecca beamed at him. "Look at what I'm wearing!" Rebecca curtsied. "Thank you so much for this dress. I can't wait for the kids at school to see me!"

"Mr. Buzz is a nice man. I'm glad that you thanked him again. Please go inside, Rebecca, so I can talk to him."

Rita stepped onto her porch and closed the door behind her. "I'm sorry but how did you get my address?" She slightly narrowed her eyes and furrowed eyebrows.

Buzz looked at her blankly.

"I live alone with my daughter and my father. I work with the public. Many men come to the diner that I don't want to see at all, much less at my door. I think you understand why I don't want a strange man visiting us."

Buzz hinted at smiling. "I'm hardly a stranger."

"You're also physically powerful. Maybe right now your intentions are good. But what if something comes over you?" Rita pursed her lips. "I won't have the physical ability to fight you. Worse, Rebecca is here. It would traumatize her for life."

"I would never…"

Rita held up her hand in a halt gesture. "I don't know that. Don't get me wrong." She nodded. "I like you. I'm working tomorrow. Come see me at the diner." She turned and started to go inside.

"I'll be in Ft. Lauderdale tomorrow. I'm working in Dade, Broward, and Palm Beach Counties all week. This is my last chance to see you." He spread his palms.

She turned back and saw a hint of moisture in his right eye.

"Well, I don't like that you hunted down my address and arrived uninvited." She stood halfway in the doorway.

"I didn't hunt down your address, and I was hesitant to come over."

"Then how did you know I live here?"

"Bubby's business has an expression. 'Kayfabe'. It means to keep insider knowledge from the public."

"Okay," Rita stepped back onto the porch. "You're not a stranger. If you want to be an insider with me, I expect you to tell the truth. How did you find out where I live?"

Buzz inhaled deeply and paused for five seconds. He handed her Margie's handwritten paper slip with her address.

Rita stared at it for three seconds. "Margie!" Rita's eyes widened. "That woman!" She closed her eyes. "I'm sorry. That woman is like a mother to me and a grandmother to Rebecca. You should know that she often encourages me to date. But never have her matchmaking schemes steered me in the direction of any one man, and never has she given someone my address or even my phone number. I have never seen any customer outside the diner socially or otherwise." She looked into his eyes. The corner of her lips twitched upwards. "I trust Margie's instincts." Rita unconsciously pulled out her hairpin, releasing her half-up bun on top of her head. Her dark brown hair cascaded well below her shoulders.

"Margie told me that she never gave anyone your address or phone number." Buzz looked into her eyes and smiled. "She said she never would again. I hope she never has to."

Rita again looked into Buzz's eyes. '*Que me pasa?*' She gently embraced him. Buzz embraced her back. She pulled away two seconds later. "Look, before I invite you in, I need the one hundred percent truth from you. No kayfabe or otherwise. You're not a trashman." She touched his right bicep. "You didn't develop that physique by slinging trash cans into a garbage truck."

"I sent away for Charles Atlas's muscle-building course. You've seen his ads in the comic books. You know, *Dynamic Tension.* It made a man out of Mack. I too used to be a ninety-eight-pound weakling. As you can see," Buzz flexed his biceps, "it works."

Rita chuckled and flicked her hair. "You don't talk like someone who reads comic books. Where did you go to college."

Buzz blushed. "West Virginia University. I was on the wrestling team. Our coach worked our asses off. My father was a career Navy officer. I learned Asian calisthenics while he was stationed overseas, which was most of the time."

"Wrestling. West Virginia University." Rita raised her eyebrows. "That makes sense. However," Rita crossed her arms and tilted her head. "There's something else you're not telling me."

"What do you mean?" Buzz smiled.

"You know exactly what I mean." Rita chuckled. "No more kayfabe. You're a professional wrestler. Tell the truth or…" she pointed at his car.

"I'm afraid you got me, and I sure don't want to leave." He grasped her shoulders, looked into her eyes, and smiled. "Yes. I'm a professional wrestler."

"Who would'a thunk it?" Rita laughed. "I try not to let Rebecca watch too much television." She touched his hand for a second. "Nevertheless, her favorite shows are Tom and Jerry cartoons, The Three Stooges, and professional wrestling. First Bubby, then meeting Beer Barrel Bobby's family, now inviting you into my home." She skewed her expression and shook her head. "Vamos." She started reaching for his hand but then retracted it. "Follow me."

Buzz had also reached for her hand. He instead picked up the bucket of fried chicken.

"Rebecca! Pedro! Look at who's joining us for lunch."

"Yippie!" Rebecca jumped up and down. "Mmm…Kentucky Fried Chicken."

"Now Rebecca." Rita put her hands on her hips. "I worked two hours cooking us chicken enchiladas."

"I'm sorry Rita. I didn't know."

"I appreciate that you didn't come empty-handed." Rita chuckled. "But you'll leave empty-handed." She winked at him. "I accept your gift." She took the bucket of chicken and put it in her refrigerator.

"I'd say that I got the better of the deal." Buzz laughed. "Trading a bucket of takeaway chicken for homemade enchiladas? Every time."

Rita's father, Pedro, was in his late fifties, although he looked ten years older. His skin was weatherworn from years of physical labor in the sun. He looked at Buzz. "Muy fuerte." He flexed his biceps.

"He doesn't speak English." Rita laughed. "But you can see that he's impressed with your physique."

"Mi gusta este gringo." He pointed at Buzz. "El es galen un caballero."

"Papi." Rita turned to her father. "Solo es una amigo." She then looked at Buzz. "My father likes you. He's old-fashioned, take that as a compliment."

The radio played Richie Valens's 'La Bamba.' Pedro snapped his fingers and shook his head in rhythm.

"I'm sure you know that's a traditional Mexican song. We sing it much slower. My father is big on tradition. I'm surprised that he likes this rock and roll version."

"Let's dance." Buzz took Rita's hand.

"No. I need to check on the enchiladas.

"I wanna dance!" Rebeca ran up to Buzz."

"You're on!" Buzz took Rebecca's right hand. He lifted her arm and led her into an underarm twirl.

Rebecca smiled and laughed.

Rita looked at them wide-eyed and beamed.

The next song on the radio was Pat Boone's, '*Speedy Gonzalez*'. Rita and Rebecca laughed, faced each other, held hands, and danced.

***

Rita and Buzz faced each other on the porch. Buzz held both of her hands and looked deep into her eyes. "I had a wonderful time and a memorable afternoon."

"I was a split second away from sending you away." She held eye contact. "I'm sure glad that I didn't." The lub-dub beat of their heats was audible.

"Goodbye, Mr. Buzz." Rebecca ran up and hugged him.

"Well, will you look at who's here?" Buzz lifted her and cradled her.

Rita pecked her cheek.

"I'm sorry that I didn't bring you a present." He put her down. "I want to change that." He put her down. "Wait here. I'll go to my car and bring it to you."

"No." Rita held up her hand. "Please don't."

"I insist." Buzz walked to his car and brought back his wrestling bag. "Just for you." He reached in and handed her a present.

Rebecca's mouth formed a perfect circle; her eyes shined like beacons. She held it before her eyes and then hugged it.

Buzz gave her one of his Jaguar wrestling masks.

Chapter 8

The wrestlers on the night's bill met in the Lakeland, Florida, Civic Center dressing room. Frankie Williamson walked up to Buzz. "You too quiet. Who hypnotized you? Maybe I hypnotize you more so you no mas beat the mierda outta me." He chuckled. "No te preocupes para mi. It's my job. Al pay me mucho dinero." Frankie chuckled. "I no can hypnotize you no mas." Frankie laughed. "I know that look. Only a bonita muchacha can do that to a hombre."

"Throw in an enchanting little girl." Bart walked over and slapped Buzz's back. "And a popsicle will last longer in this damn Florida heat than his foolish heart." Bubby guffawed.

"I am sure you wore your mask." Leslie van Der Westhuisen and his brother, Trevor, lacked the other wrestlers' size. Their skill and amateur wrestling background compensated. "If you took off your mask, she couldn't look at your ugly face long enough to hypnotize you."

"Up your holes with Mellow Rolls," Buzz laughed. "All of you. Nothing happened."

"Yet." Trevor Van Der Westhuisen chortled.

"Who the hell!" Buzz held his Jaguar mask in his right hand and a safety razor in the other. Someone had smeared shaving crème into the beard and hair part of his mask.

The wrestlers guffawed. Buzz noticed that Frankie Williamson looked away and covered his mouth. "Hmm... Maybe tonight won't be a work after all."

"I know you no stay mad at me." Frankie Williamson chuckled. "We're amigos and I can help you romance the bonita muchacha."

"A fat, ugly dude like you," Shaun pointed at Frankie, "help him," he pointed at Buzz, "with the ladies? Are you kidding me?" Shaun Samson guffawed. "I can get him any girl he wants." Shaun rubbed the top of Buzz's head. "First. He's gotta grow more hair."

"Up your hole with a bigger Mellow Roll." Buzz knocked Shaun's hand away.

"You get the girls on your looks alone," Frankie pointed at the Samson brothers. "I must work for it. I had to learn how. That's why I'm better to advise him."

All the wrestlers laughed.

Al Cohen entered the dressing room. A barrel-chested and barrel-bellied man the same height as Al joined him. He wore a custom-fit, gray pinstripe suit and a fedora hat sporting a small feather. "Are we kayfabe?"

The wrestlers stopped laughing.

"Is everyone out of here that shouldn't be here?"

"All clear, boss." Steve Samsom walked over and locked the dressing room door.

"As you know, Hercules Cortez moved to the California territory. You also know why I had to fire Johnny Durham. All of you know that he was a convincing and popular face inside the ring but a pain in the neck outside the ring." Al lowered his clipboard. "None of you are irreplaceable. If any of you prove more trouble than you're worth, I won't hesitate to make the necessary change."

"Good riddance to him, Al." Steve Samson put his hands on his hips. "He caused shit with us too."

"Yeah, he owes me fifty dollars." Frankie Williamson pointed at the other wrestlers. "I no make money like you big boys. I guess mis cincuenta dolares es no mas."

Al continued, "Our newest wrestler needs no introduction. Grant Irons has joined our team." The other wrestlers applauded. Grant tipped his hat. "Our big event in Orlando is only a week away. Tonight is no minor show. We're expecting eight thousand people. I'm hoping that many in tonight's attendance will buy tickets to our

Tangerine Bowl event. Many are excited just to see Buzz and Bubby." Al pointed at them. "I still can't risk you two getting hurt. Buzz, you're working Frankie again and Bubby, I expect another good match with Spider Nel. Grant, I will introduce you by matching you with Barry Howard. The match is secondary to presenting your character. You're already nationally famous. Tonight, I want you to put an exclamation mark on your image. Spence and Clay, tonight is your final appearance before the Tangerine Bowl. Immerse yourselves in your Cletus and Biff mode. More than ever, I need the fans to hate and fear you. Let Leslie and Trevor control the early part of the match with scientific and clean holds. About fifteen minutes in, Trevor, I want you to go to the edge of the ring and raise your arms to the crowd as if you're about to win. Shigeru will sneak up and throw salt in your face. Pretend that it's in your eyes and stagger about the ring. Only then will it become a squash match. Bob and Yuri." Al looked at them. "You're tonight's main event."

"This time," Bubby laughed. "Save some of the beer for us."

Al and Grant walked over to Buzz. "Buzz, you have often asked me to let you travel with the boys. You know I had to have you travel alone to keep your identity kayfabe. Besides, the public expects you to be out of control." Al put his hand on Buzz's arm. "Grant flew in from Oregon. He has no car. I want you two to travel together and room together on the road. Grant always wears business suits with fedora hats, and you keep on wearing conservative slacks and sports shirts. Has anyone mistaken you dressed and groomed as a clean-cut, all-American boy for a jungle savage? Likewise, no one will expect a man in a custom-fit business suit to act like a neanderthal. I think it's safe that no one will make the connection between you two." He looked at Grant. "Buzz has a business degree from West Virginia University. Even though he only has a bachelor's degree and you're working on your PHD, I'm sure Buzz took enough history courses to give you a decent conversation."

Buzz and Grant shook hands.

***

Rita punched her card in the time clock and stood at the entrance between the back room and the diner proper. She made eye contact with Margie and scowled.

Margie walked over to Rita. "What's wrong?" She spread her palms.

"You know what's wrong." Rita put her hands on her hips. "What's the big idea of giving my address to a strange man."

"I'm sorry Rita." Margie lowered her head. "I know you hate it when I play matchmaker." She looked up at Rita with moist eyes. "My woman's intuition told me that he was different."

"How could you give a man that big and strong my address? And knowing I have an eight-year-old girl at home."

"I don't know what to say, Rita." Margie closed her eyes. "Other than that, I'm sorry."

Rita hunched her shoulders. "Well, I know what to say." She then relaxed and smiled. "Thank you." Rita hugged Margie. Margie then kissed Rita on the forehead."

***

The houselights of the Lakeland Civic Center remained on as Barry Howard exited the dressing room and climbed into the ring. The lights dimmed; the spotlight shined on the walkway from the dressing room to the ring. The crowd murmured. Professor Sakamoto walked ahead of him. Hair covered his body as thick as fur. His head was bald and smooth as an eggshell while the skin behind his neck rippled like accordion bellows. The ring announcer spoke, "He's being led into the ring by his manager, Professor Sakamoto. He grew up under the streets of Hiroshima and survived by eating radioactive rats. Weighing in at two-hundred-and-eighty-five pounds, Grant "The Beast" Irons. The venue erupted into an

65

uproar. Grant entered the ring. He ran to the corner and jumped onto the second ring rope. He taunted the crowd by skewing his head and uttering noises while wagging a green-dyed tongue, "Ah-uh! Ah-uh!"

'*Ding! Ding! Ding!*' Grant charged Barry and pummeled him with overhead, windmill-like strikes. Barry fell to the ground. Grant stomped his left foot on the mat and kicked Barry with his right. With each kick, Barry rolled over until he fell from the ring. "Ah-uh! Ah-uh!" Grant stood on the ring rope and tilted his head. He then ran to the corner and bit into the turnbuckle pad. After tearing it open with his teeth, he smeared the stuffing all over his body. "Ah-uh! Ah-uh!" He ran to the other corner and tore open the ring pad. He threw the stuffing about the ring. Next, he exited the ring and started throwing chairs, a table, and the ring steps into the ring.

"Ding! Ding! Ding!"

Professor Sakamoto climbed into the ring and restrained his wrestler. The ring announcer joined him in the ring and spoke into the microphone. "At forty-five seconds into the match, the referee has counted out Barry Howard. Your winner. Grant "The Beast" Irons!" The referee raised Grant's arm. He pulled it away and ran circles around the ring, grunting and vocalizing non-sensical utterances. On the way back to the dressing room, he twice mock-charged the audience, causing them to scream and disperse.

***

Grant, Sakamoto, and Buzz sat on a bench in the heel's dressing room. Al Cohen walked in. "Excellent! Excellent! I could not have possibly asked for more. Grant, you outdid yourself. Your routine had tons of notoriety coming in. You not only solidified your legend, you grew it." Al looked at Buzz. "Buzz, you already know Bubby will take your belt in the Tangerine Bowl." He sat down next to him. "You were unknown outside of the Florida territory until I had you win the AWF World Championship. Grant here already has national

66

fame. Moreover, he has far more experience than you. Don't get me wrong, Buzz, you've done an outstanding job for me, and you have an unlimited future."

"I can smell a *but* coming." Buzz locked his hands behind his head.

Al chuckled. "Yes. I'm afraid with Grant here, your wild Jaguar act is redundant. We don't need two wild men. I thought about tag-teaming you two, but you play an out-of-control jungle captive while Grant is an uncontrollable Neanderthal. The fans won't buy you two cooperating. I want you to continue as the Jaguar. But after Saturday night, I plan on re-working your act and image. We lost Hercules Cortez, one of my most popular faces. We've replaced him with a heel. I need another face." Al placed his hand on Buzz's shoulder, "Moreover, everyone loves a redemption story. In the meantime, you listen and heed everything Grant tells you. He knows more about the business than you can ever forget."

Chapter 9

Bart and Bob sat together in a booth at Del's Diner. Bart played Little Richard's *'Rip It Up'* on their private jukebox. "I gotta play some Little Richard. He's from my hometown. Macon, Georgia."

"Coming up is one from my hometown. Ray Charles and *'What I'd Say'.*" He grew up only about twenty minutes from me in Greenville, Florida,"

Mary approached their booth, flicked a lock of flaming red hair, and handed them menus. "I'm sorry, Mary," Bart read her name tag. "But can we sit at one of Rita's tables?"

"Oh, so you're here for hot tamale?" Mary put her right hand, palm flat on her hip. She arched her back and thrust her chest forward. "But tamales ain't so hot without spicy red sauce." She flicked her hair.

Bart and Bob laughed.

"I knew you two were coming. On Rita's side, you get a regular portion of Del's pot roast. Last night, I shot a buffalo. I spent the night butchering it. I had Del make the whole thing in a pot roast. You only get to eat the whole thing if you sit on my side."

Bart and Bob laughed.

"Here comes the hot tamale now." Mary pointed at Rita.

Rita walked up to their table.

"Be careful of what you say to her." Mary shook her head, splaying her red hair. "Because I also love this hot tamale." Mary stood on her toes and pecked Rita's lips.

"Bubby." Rita beamed. "I can't thank Stephanie enough for making Rebecca those dresses. She was thrilled. Her smile was one for the ages. Now she can't wait to go back to school."

"I'm just sorry I couldn't give them to her myself."

"Oh, don't you be sorry." Mary put her arm over Rita's shoulder. "It worked out just fine for Rita." Mary winked at Bart and Bob. "Better than you can ever imagine."

"Ohh." Bart and Bob grinned at Rita.

"And guess who put you and Rebecca on his guest list?" Bart sniggered.

Rita blushed and looked away. "I better take care of my tables. Thank you again, Bart. And Bob, I met your family. They're lovely people. Angelica and Rebecca are already best friends."

***

"After devouring three plates of pot roast, I hope you two left room for dessert. Ice cream's on me. If either one of you asks for a double scoop of strawberry, you get two bumps on the noggin." Mary thrust her chest.

Bart and Bob laughed.

Mary placed a bowl of vanilla ice cream in front of Bob, and one of chocolate before Bart. "Oh, my bad, it's National Brotherhood Week." She shuffled the bowls like the shell game, putting the vanilla in front of Bart and the chocolate before Bob.

Bart guffawed. Bob laughed so hard that he had to bend over.

"Mary," Bob smiled at her. "I want you to be my guest at the Tangerine Bowl this Saturday night. "There's a great all-night drive-in restaurant nearby. Ya think, maybe after the show, we can go for a late dinner?"

"Are you asking me out for a date?"

Bob blushed and looked away. "Well, um, yes, sort of."

"Sort of? I'll tell you what." Mary squirted strawberry syrup on Bob's ice cream and added a cherry. She thrust her hip to the side and winked at him."

"Uh-oh." Bart pulled his lips into a tight circle. "You da man."

"And save some beer for me." Mary flicked her head, flaming red hair cascading over her shoulders.

Chapter 10

Rebecca jumped up and down, grabbing the hem of Rita's dress. "I can't wait, mom! When's Aunt Margie gonna get here?"

"I can't do magic, honey." Rita chuckled. "If I could fly like Wonder Woman and pick up her car and bring it here, I surely would."

A car horn blared.

"She's here!" Rebecca ran to the door.

An attractive red-haired woman waved to her.

"Mom. It's not Aunt Margie. It's Aunt Mary."

Rita grabbed her handbag, took Rebecca by the hand, and walked to the car.

"You look disappointed, Rita. Were you expecting Prince Charming and a royal carriage? You didn't think your fairy guide could be a redhead and her carriage a 1950 Ford Crestliner? Come on in! This old hulk may not be a new Cadillac, but it's no pumpkin either. But with you, Rebecca, it gets a pair of angel wings."

"I love you, Aunt Mary. You're the utmost."

Rita sighed. "I wasn't expecting…"

"The best things in life are what you least expect." Mary winked. "You better hop in. Orlando is ninety minutes away. They're expecting at least 20,000 people. Good thing Bob got us VIP parking."

"I'm sorry Mary." Rita lowered her head. "You've been nothing but a good friend to me and Rebecca. Thank you for coming and driving us."

"Here's how you can make it up to me." Mary grabbed Rita from behind the head and pulled her face to hers. "Um, mu." Mary vocalized as she planted a closed-mouth kiss on Rita's lips. "And one for you too, my little angel." Mary pecked Rebecca's forehead.

***

Mary turned onto the newly opened Florida Turnpike. "It won't be long now. You two face a tough decision on who to root for."

"I've known all along that it's just a show." Rita chuckled. "Let's say a little prayer that neither gets hurt. Any way you look at it, they perform dangerous stunts."

"I do hope that Bobby beats that commie again."

Mary laughed. "Actually, my darling, Yuri is the polar opposite of a communist. Margie told me that he once ate at the diner. He told her that his parents fled Russia and Stalin. They hate communism."

"I hate Commies too." Rebecca chirped

"You're not to hate anyone," Rita put her arm around her daughter's shoulder.

"Well, Rita, Rebecca, we can make an exception for the commies. They're Godless Atheists who want to drop an atomic bomb on us and blow us to smithereens."

"I read about what's going on in Cuba. Rebecca and I are now American citizens. Nevertheless, I sweat bullets just considering the possibility of Mexico going red."

"Me too Rita. You know, if that happened, those pinko bastards wouldn't hesitate to put missiles on the American border and aim them at us." Mary held Rebecca's hand. "Don't worry. President Eisenhower will never let it happen. We have many blessings in America. But if you so much as believe in God in the Soviet Union, Khrushchev will put you in a box car and haul you off to a prison camp in Siberia and work you to death."

Rebecca chirped, "My teacher tells us that every morning after we say the pledge."

72

"Yuri told Margie those prison camps are called Gulags. Margie also said that he's a devout Russian Orthodox believer." Mary nodded to Rita and Rebecca. "I'm not surprised that he opened up to her like that. Margie becomes a second mother to everyone who meets her."

"She's my Aunt Margie." Rebbeca beamed.

"Well," Mary held the steering wheel with one hand, put a cigarette in her mouth, and lit it with the car's electric lighter, "The Reds may have infiltrated Hollywood, but never wrestling." Mary turned to Rita. "I know that Bobby and Bubby are Southern Baptists." Mary held her cigarette between her forefinger and middle finger and puffed. "Did Buzz talk to you about his religion?"

"No. We're just friends." Rita covered her mouth and looked away.

"Well, Rita, a woman can have a cat as a friend and a woman can have wine as a friend. But if she has a man as a friend, she ends up drunk and kissing her cat."

"Mary, please, not in front of…"

"I heard that!" Rebecca laughed.

"Well, I like your religion." Mary blew a smoke ring and snickered. "Any church that lets you drink real wine is all right with me."

Rita covered Rebecca's ears before laughing with Mary.

***

Mary, Rita, and Rebecca made their way to their ringside seats. All the Tangerine Bowl's 12,000 football seats and the additional 7,000 seats on the field were filled.

"Mom!" Rebecca pointed. "It's Angelica!"

"Rebecca!" Angelica ran over to Rebecca. They clasped arms and danced in a circle. "Mr. Boggs." Rebecca walked over to Skeet. "Is it true that Yuri is not really a Communist?"

"Shh." Skeet Boggs put his finger over his lips. "Shush. The wrestlers have a magic word. 'Kayfabe'. It means you keep wrestling's secrets secret." Skeet smiled at her. "Yuri is from Russia. Let's leave it at that."

"Kayfabe. Secret." Rebecca clamped her lips closed with her fingers. "My lips are sealed."

"Where's Tammy May?" Rita asked.

"She's home taking care of the boys and tending the farm. I wasn't going to come either, but Bob called and told me you were bringing Rebecca." He smiled at his daughter. "So, how can I not bring her?"

***

Skeet sat next to Angelica; Rebecca sat on the other side of her. They played and laughed more than they minded the wrestling. Rita sat next to her daughter with Mary seated on her other side. Rita covered her eyes. "Grant The Beast is horrible. Pobre Frankie Williamson. I hope this is all fake. The Beast is killing him."

"They call Frankie Williamson a jobber." Skeet smiled at Rita. "And right now, he's sure doing his job."

"Ay Dios mio!" Rita pointed at the ring. "The Beast is eating the corner pad. Buzz puts on a wild act, but nothing like this. Uh!" She again covered her eyes. "That green tongue is disgusting. I always tell Rebecca that Wrestling is like the Three Stooges. But Curley and Shemp never did anything that yucky!" Rita pointed to Grant Irons smearing the turnbuckle padding into his chest hair.

"Curley is the funniest." Rebecca laughed.

"Shemp's funny too." Angelica also laughed. "But Mo is my favorite." She opened her arms. "Spread out."

"Give Larry his due." Rita laughed with the girls. "He bridges Mo and Curly. He can also play the violin, and I think he's hilarious."

"Your man has a beautiful body, but without a hair on it." Mary nudged Rita. But this thing's built like an ape, and he's hairy as an ape, but his head's balder than Yul Brynner."

"I keep telling you. Buzz is just a friend. But, Ugh! What an ugly beast!" Rita pointed at Grant Irons. "I'm starting to believe that he was raised in the sewer and ate radioactive rats."

"See Mom!" Rebecca poked her mother's ribs. "I told you wrestling was real."

"But darling, Buzz and Bubby pretend to hate each other. Now you know that they're best friends. They're both our friends. It's just that this beast man is so convincing."

"I know something that's not so convincing." Mary chuckled. "It's you telling me that Buzz is just a friend."

"Stop it, Mary."

"As you wish. It's too early to call him my man. But I'm not here as 'just Bob's friend.' He's wrestling next."

***

The stadium lights dimmed. The sound system played the opening notes to Sergei Prokofiev's *Alexander Nevsky Suite*. The fans booed, hissed, and catcalled as he walked to the ring. A male fan stood and bumped Rita and Rebecca. "Go back to the Soviet Union, you cruddy commie cur!" He flipped his middle finger.

After Yuri entered the ring, the sound system played the choral '*Song for Alexander Nevsky*' from the eponymous suite. He waved the red sickle and hammer Soviet flag.

"Shove that flag up your ass, you pinko fag!" A gray-haired man threw an orange at Yuri. "I'd rather be dead than red!" He extended his middle finger.

The sound system then played one of Borodin's Polovtsian dances. The crowd tried to boo out the music as Yuri performed a traditional Cossack dance.

Al Cohen, Professor Sakamoto, Buzz, and Bart sat together in the dressing room. "I haven't heard so much booing since my Redskin days and playing the Philadelphia Eagles at Shibe Park."

The four of them laughed.

Sakamoto turned to Al. "How long until the state cracks down on Bob's schtick? After all, surely some underage fans are getting some of his beer."

"We've known each other for how long?" Al laughed. "It's near beer." Al grinned. "Alcohol-free. And God bless and keep the government. God bless them and keep them as far away from my operation as possible." Al chuckled. "Especially the IRS. I'm tempted to have a heal play on IRS agent. I can call him the 'Tax Man'." He shook his head. "But they might audit me if I do."

Grant entered wearing only a towel. "I can write an entire dissertation on how beer saved America, and prohibition's biggest beneficiary was Al Capone."

"I'll drink to that." Bart beamed.

"As you mentioned, Al, a worse thief than Al Capone played a major role in ending Prohibition," Grant smirked. "The IRS. As you say," Grant looked at Al, 'You can dream it; they can tax it'."

"We'll all share a few." Al pointed at Bart. "After your match with Buzz. I've got a standing-room-only crowd of over 20,000. They didn't pay to see you drunk and stumbling around the ring."

"We'll need to get Buzz some tequila." Bart guffawed.

Buzz flushed.

"Don't worry, Al." Bart Guffawed and slapped Buzz's back. "Her name is Rita. She cast her spell on him all right. But she's not wicked and evil like Faleena."

"Buzz isn't a cowboy from El Paso either," Al chuckled. "So, I guess I don't have to worry about losing a wrestler."

                                    ***

The sound system next played Chet Adkins's "*Country Gentleman.*" The fans stood and clapped to the music. Rebecca and Angelica danced an elbow swing. The spotlight hit Beer Barrel Bobby. The crowd yelled, "Beer! Beer! Beer!" as he ran to the ring, holding aloft a wooden beer keg with an American flag painted on it.

Bob walked over to the edge of the ring. He made eye contact with Mary. They smiled at each other. Mary crushed her cigarette, walked over to him, and held her cup aloft. Bob filled it with beer.

"Beer! Beer! Beer!" the entire stadium chanted. Several fans at ringside pushed Mary aside and held cups aloft, hoping for free beer.

"Hi there, Uncle Bob!" Angelica yelled and waved.

"Hi there, Bobby!" Rebecca held up her soda cup.

Rita grabbed her arm. "Not until you're twenty-one, honey." She chuckled.

                                    ***

The Rustler brothers stood in the ring with Professor Sakamoto. The sound system played Johnny Cash's "*Folsom Prison Blues.*" Biff swung a lasso; Cletus cracked a stock whip.

The spotlight next shined on the aisle. The Sound system switched to Jerry Lee Lewis's "*Breathless.*"

"Woo! Are they gorgeous!" Mary nudged Rita and pointed to the Samson Brothers as they entered the ring to a rousing ovation. "Professional wrestling is the only place where men can grow long hair like that. It's too bad. I love their hair. Uwe, it makes them look even sexier."

Rita blushed.

"And their bodies. They're not huge or over-muscled." Mary licked her lips. "I don't know about you, but they're just right for this redhead."

"I got news for you Mary." Skeet laughed. "You're not the only lady who feels that way." He sipped his beer. "I assure you that you got some stiff competition."

Mary lit a cigarette.

Ding! Ding! Ding! The ring announcer spoke into his microphone. "Ladies and Gentlemen. Our co-main event of the evening. The American Federation of Wrestling tag team championship. One fall to a finish. In this corner, accompanied by their manager, Professor Sakamoto, they hail from Laramie, Wyoming. Their combined weight is 587 pounds- your challengers, The Rustler Brothers!"

The ring announcer paused so that the audience could boo.

"And in the other corner," the jeers turned to cheers, "the reigning American Federation of Wrestling tag team champions. They hail from Dallas, Texas, at a combined weight of 430 pounds, Shaun and Steve! The Samsom Brothers!"

Rebecca and Angelica stood and cheered. Mary blew them kisses. Rita looked at her daughter and smiled. Skeet sipped his beer.

Ding!

Biff charged Steve. The Samson Brother put him in an arm drag and flung him across the ring. Biff wildly waved his arms over his face in disbelief. He charged him again. Steve again flung him across the ring with an arm drag. Before Biff could rise, Steve put him in a headlock. Cletus ran into the ring to break the hold. Shaun intercepted him with a flying two-legged dropkick. The fans pumped their fists and cheered. The referee turned his back on the Rustler Brothers to usher Shaun back to the corner. Cletus recovered from the dropkick to stomp Steve's head. Biff stood and joined his brother in kicking Steve. Shaun tried to help. The ref, with his back to Biff and Cletus, held Shaun back. Steve staggered to his feet, reached the corner, and tagged his brother. Shaun entered the ring and slapped the ring mat. He looked at the audience with a clenched fist.

"Get them!" An elderly woman shook her handbag. "Kill them!"

"Go Shaun!" Three teenage girls jumped up and down. "Do it for us!"

Shaun hit Biff with a forearm shiver to the chest. He then swung him into the corner. Shaun turned to Cletus. He tried to strike him with an overhead right. Shaun ducked, grabbed his wrist, and flung him into Biff. Shaun charged them, leaped, and drop kicked both at once. He then went to the ring center to receive the crowd's rousing ovation.

***

After twenty-two minutes of action, Steve Samson picked Biff up on his shoulders and spun him around. He then power-slammed him to the mat. After raising his arms in victory, he did a back-over flip and landed on Biff. He lifted Biff's leg from behind his knee for leverage and pinned him. Meanwhile, Cletus had snuck around the outside of the ring. He grinned deviously to the crowd.

"Look out Shaun!" An obese man in a dirty gray shirt pointed. "Look out."

Cletus wrapped his rope around Shaun, binding him to the corner post.

The crowd yelled at the referee. Instead of counting out Biff, the referee chose to confront Cletus. Professor Sakamoto threw salt in the ref's eyes. He rubbed his eyes and stumbled around the ring. Sakamoto ran into the ring and kicked Steve's head, knocking him out. He rolled him from Biff and dragged him on top of Steve. Sakamoto scurried from the ring. The referee's vision cleared.

"Over there ref." Sakamoto pointed to Biff and Steve.

The referee staggered over and slapped the ring mat three times, declaring Biff the winner.

Shaun freed himself from the lasso rope and pummeled Cletus. Biff and Sakamoto ran over and intervened. The three hurled Shaun out to the ring.

Pandemonium erupted. Police and security entered the ring. Oranges and other debris flew into the ring. Rita shielded her daughter with her body.

Ding! Ding! Ding!

"Ladies and gentlemen! For the safety of the wrestlers and others, please refrain from throwing anything into the ring. The time of the match, twenty-four minutes and fourteen seconds. The winner by pin and new American Federation of Wrestling champions, Biff and Cletus Rustler!"

Sakamoto held up his wrestler's arms. The wrestlers raised their championship belts with their other hand.

"Don't you worry about the Samsons." Skeet chuckled at Rita and Mary. "After the show those boys put on, they'll laugh all the way to the bank."

Ding! Ding! Ding!

The ring announcer spoke into the microphone. "Ladies and gentlemen. Security has asked that we have a fifteen-minute intermission until our main event. The American Federation of Wrestling world championship pitting the champion, The Jaguar, against his challenger, Adebe the African Lion."

The Rustler Brothers and Sakamoto ducked their heads and ran to the dressing room amid a shower of debris. Three uniformed police officers and four security guards had to escort the referee to the safety of the dressing room.

The house lights lit.

"Aunt Mary. Look!" Rita pointed to the entrance of the tunnel to the dressing room. Beer Barrel Bobby held up a beer bottle to Mary.

Mary made eye contact, beamed, and tipped her beer cup. They gulped their beers in unison.

***

The house lights dimmed. The crowd murmured. The ring announcer spoke. "Ladies and Gentlemen. The main event of the evening. The best two out of three pin falls or a knockout for the AWF World Championship." They cheered wildly as the sound system played the original 1957 Gallotone label recording of Miriam Makeba's *"Pata Pata."* First, the challenger. He's being led down the aisle by his manager for today, Beer Barrel Bobby. He hails from Kenya, Africa. Weighing in at four-hundred-and-twenty-five pounds, Adebe the African Lion."

"Yay! Yay!" Rebecca and Angelica stood and cheered with the rest of the crowd.

Buzz waited at the entrance portal to the stadium. *'Rita.'* He scanned the ringside seats. His eyes found her. *'So beautiful. I hope you know this is all an act.'* Suddenly, he made eye contact with Rebecca.

"Look, Mom." Rebecca pointed. "It's Buzz!"

"I know Honey." Rita glanced in the direction her daughter pointed.

The sound system played Martin Denny's *"Quiet Village."* Buzz shook the chain wrapped around his waist. "Okay Shigeru, Nigel, let's do this." Buzz nodded to them.

The crowd screamed as The Jaguar resisted his chains. The ring announcer spoke: "He's being led to the ring by his manager, Professor Sakamoto, and his handler, Nigel Earl. He was trapped in the wilds of the Amazon after jungle cats raised him. He has no name. Weighing in at 240 pounds. The American Federation of Wrestling World Champion. The Jaguar!"

Professor Sakamoto held the championship belt aloft before

handing it to Al Cohen.

"Woo! Rita!" Mary gulped some beer. "I adore Steve and Shaun. But your man! Woo! His body can make a statue of a Greek God jealous."

"Mary. Stop it! And not in front of Rebecca." Rita held up her hand. "Buzz is just a friend."

Mary sprayed beer as she laughed.

"He's my friend too, Aunt Mary." Rebecca beamed.

Ding!

The Jaguar circled Abede like a shark sizing up its prey. He suddenly vaulted off the second rope, somersaulted, and kicked Adebe in the chest with both feet. Adebe fell to the mat. The Jaguar leaped and hit a prone Abede with an elbow. He then climbed to the top of the turnbuckle. Abede staggered to his feet. The Jaguar dove skyward, jackknifed, and clotheslined Abede on his descent, knocking him flat on his back. The Jaguar leaped upward and landed with his leg across Abede's throat. Next, he covered him for the three-count. A smattering of cheers was heard above the silenced crowd.

Ding! Ding! Ding!

The ring announcer spoke. "Your winner of the first fall. From the jungles of the Amazon." The ring announcer paused so that the crowd could jeer. "The Jaguar!"

Ding!

The Jaguar charged from his corner and leaped up on Abede's shoulders. Legs wrapped around Abede's neck, The Jaguar shifted his weight to force him into a roll. Abede pried him off his neck, lifted him, and slammed him to the mat. Abede lifted him again and power slammed him to the mat, adding the full force of his weight. The impact caused the ring to quake.

"Huh." Rita put her hands over her chest and gasped.

Abede pulled him to his feet and flung him into the corner. Abede looked and motioned to the crowd for the go-ahead to charge across the ring and slam into him.

"Smash him!" Many in the crowd urged him. "Smash him!"

Before Abede could bolt across the ring, Professor Sakamoto reached across the ring apron and grabbed his ankle, tripping him. Bobby stormed over and prodded. "Oh no, you don't!"

Professor Sakamoto threw salt in his face. Bobby grinned while pointing to his goggles. He then chased Sakamoto back to the dressing room to the crowd's approval.

Abede went into a football three-point stance and blitzed across the ring. He slammed into The Jaguar. The ring post bent backward. The Jaguar staggered to the ring's center. Abede flung him into the ropes. The Jaguar rebounded into the waiting arms of Abede. He put him in a bear hug and smashed him into the corner post. "One!" The crowd yelled. Abede again slammed him into the corner. "Two!" They shouted. Once more, Abede ran him into the corner. "Three!" Abede then lifted the Jaguar overhead and tossed him out of the ring. The Jaguar landed on a ringside table. It gave way as he spilled onto the floor unconscious. The referee counted to ten.

Ding! Ding! Ding!

The crowd erupted. Al Cohen, led by a uniformed policeman and two security guards, entered the ring. "Ladies and Gentlemen! The referee has counted out the Jaguar. Your winner by knockout and the new American Federation of Wrestling champion, Abede! The African Lion!" The referee raised his hand. Al Cohen put the championship belt around his waist.

Rebecca and Angelica stood and cheered for Abede.

Rita looked at Buzz getting rolled onto a stretcher and carried back to the dressing room. She covered her eyes. A tear sifted through her fingers.

"Rita!" Skeet started laughing. "You should know better." He lightly touched her shoulder. "I'll let you in on a kayfabe. Buzz takes the best bumps in the business. He's fine."

Mary smirked at her and nodded. "Ah Hah." She looked away, grinned, and mumbled to herself. "Just a friend." She snickered.

***

Once out of the audience's view, Buzz bounced off the stretcher and walked into the dressing room. "Great job!" Steve Samson shook his hand while clutching his left arm. "Yeah, it sucks giving up a belt. We kind 'a feel the same way. But it's all about the show. A great show means bigger bucks for the rematch."

"It's a win-win for you two." Leslie Van Der Westhuisen chuckled and pointed at the Samsons. "Who else gets the girls because they win but gets even more girls out of sympathy when you lose?"

"Considering that I'm little more than a rookie," Buzz pulled off his mask. "I'm damn grateful to Al for just letting me be the champion, even if I was just table setting for Bubby."

"Here." Shaun handed Buzz a cold bottle of beer. "This Bud's for you." He smiled at Buzz. "You earned it."

"You also earned this." Frankie Williamson handed Buzz a small cup of clear liquid with specks. "Spiced rum." He held up a bottle of Bacardi Spiced Rum. "We celebrate a great match. We drown out giving up the championship."

Buzz took a sip. He spewed it from his mouth. "What the…" He grabbed the bottle of cold beer and chugged it in one gulp.

Steve, Shaun, Leslie, Trevor, and Frankie guffawed.

"I told you it was spiced rum." Frankie grinned at him. "I just no tell you I spice it with habanero powder."

"I ought to." Buzz clenched his fist at Frankie.

"Come on now Buzz," Steve put his hand on Buzz's shoulder and laughed. "You know the saying. 'Fool me once, shame on you. Fool me twice, shame on me'. How many times is he going to fool you before you catch on? You can't kick his ass," Steve pointed at Frankie, "just because he tricked you." He continued laughing. "Get him back by pulling one over on him."

"I ready for you." Frankie pointed to his temple and laughed.

Al, Bart, and Grant entered the dressing room. Al and Grant both wore business attire. Grant's gray pinstriped suit included a matching Fedora hat. Bart wore a tracksuit.

"Excellent match." Al walked over and shook Buzz's hand. "Performances like that advance me, the business, and yourself. The Jaguar is resonating big time. I want to keep the character. Nevertheless, I heard cheers when you leaped from the top rope high enough to do a jackknife and then finished with the flying clothesline. Tonight was one of the last times that you'll play a savage. I am going to adjust your role."

"Are you okay?" Bubby nodded to Buzz.

"I'm fine, except I learned what it's like to survive a trash compacter." Buzz smiled. "I tell people I'm a trashman, not the trash. Thanks a lot."

"You all have guests." Al stepped forward. "Bob cleared them. They're kayfabe. Enjoy your time off. We're at it again in Sarasota on Tuesday. Before the show, I will brief you and Bubby on my plans. Thank you all for your great work. Tonight was a rousing success." Al opened his wallet. "You all earned a bonus." He handed each of his wrestlers fifty-dollar bills.

***

Skeet stood. "Okay, everybody. Let's all go back."

Rebecca beamed. "You mean we all get to go to the dressing room?"

85

"You sure do." Skeet smiled at her. "You're an insider now. Just remember the rules of kayfabe."

"Cross my heart and hope to die." Rebecca tapped a cross on her chest.

Skeet led his daughter by the hand, as did Rita with Rebecca. Mary ran ahead upon spotting Bob. Mary and Bob embraced. They walked away hand in hand.

Buzz stepped out of the dressing room. Rita ran up to him. "Gracias, Dios, you're okay." She hugged him for three seconds before pulling away.

"Oh no, Rita." Buzz chuckled. "I'm hurting. I need another hug."

Rita chuckled and hugged him for three more seconds.

"Buzz! Buzz! Buzz!" Rebecca jumped up and down in front of him, looking up at him with a smile. "Buzz, buzz goes the bumble bee!" She chirped. "Tweedle-dee-dee goes the bird."

Rita lifted her and kissed her cheek.

Al, Grant, and Bart exited the dressing room.

"Hi there Bubby!" Angelica waved at Bart.

"And hi there, little Angel." Bart squatted. "You must be Bob's niece, Angelica. I'll go get your Uncle Bob."

"Rita." Buzz touched her hand. "Let me introduce you to the boss. This is Al Cohen."

"So, you're the one who has my best wrestler under her spell." He shook Rita's hand. "Now I'm under this one's spell." He smiled at Rebecca and waved to her. "You take good care of these two, Buzz."

Rita blushed and looked away. "It's not like that…"

"Uncle Bob!" Angelica threw up her hands.

Rita's mouth and eyes formed a circle on seeing Bob and Mary holding hands.

"Rita, Bob, and I are going out to dinner."

"We'd invite you and Buzz, Rita." Bob squeezed Mary's hand. "But it would break kayfabe if all of us were seen together. Moreover, nobody should get a hint of the Jaguar's identity."

"Bob came here in the wrestler's van, so I'm taking him in my car." Mary smiled. "It looks like you're stuck with Buzz driving you home."

Rita blanched. "But I'm not..."

"Yippie!" Rebecca beamed. "We all get to ride with Buzz."

"Good evening, Ma'am." Grant extended his hand to Rita. "Or dare I say, Estoy encantada de conocerte."

"Gracias." Rita shook his hand. "Hablas Espanol?"

"Si senora. Espanol y Frances."

"I'm afraid we're stuck with him for part of the ride home." Buzz smiled at Rita and Rebecca. "We have to drop him off at his hotel on the way."

"I'm sorry." Grant tipped his hat. "I didn't fully introduce myself. I'm Grant Irons."

"Huh." Rita gasped. "You're..." she pointed, "You're the Beast!"

"He's no more a beast than I'm a savage from the Amazon, and Bubby is from the Savannahs of Kenya." Buzz and Grant laughed.

"Can I see your green tongue?"

"Rebecca!" Rita glowered at her daughter.

"It's perfectly okay, ma'am." Grant smiled. "For a little charmer like her, next time, I'll paint it red, white, and blue."

***

Bob drove his '56 Bel Air. Grant sat in the front seat while Rita and Rebecca sat in the back seat. Grant tuned the radio to a classical music station.

"I'm sorry, Grant," Rita touched her chin, "but I still can't believe that you're the Beast. Why do you do it?"

"It's not my only job. Half of the year, I teach history at Ohio State. I'm not the only one. Shigeru is a professor. He was teaching theater at Temple University in Philadelphia until Al doubled his teaching salary."

Buzz glanced back. "Shigeru wants to break into movie acting. Even though the war ended thirteen years ago, many still see the Japanese as villains. We exploit their bigotry to our advantage. Besides, the best chance for a Japanese man of his size to get a break in Hollywood is to play a villain." Buzz put both hands on the steering wheel. "Wrestling may open that door."

"I understand Professor Sakamoto, but Grant, why are you playing the beast?"

"The same reason that Shigeru is playing a stereotype of his nationality. Al is paying me twice what I make as an associate history professor."

"So, you're demeaning yourself for money?"

"Rita!" Buzz raised his voice.

'It's okay Buzz." Grant held up his hand.

I'm sorry, Grant." Rita lowered her head. "I didn't mean it that way."

"No te preocupe, Signora." Grant chuckled. "It's a natural question, and you're far from the first to ask. Firstly, it's fun. Buzz has a background in Asian martial arts and amateur wrestling. I'm like Bubby. I played football. I made second-team all-Big Ten as a defensive end for Ohio State. I played one year in the NFL for the New York Football Giants. I even got into a game against Bubby. He hit like a Mack Truck." Grant chuckled. "If he didn't hurt his knee, he'd still be playing and making all-pro."

"His knee," Buzz sniggered, "and losing the battle of the knife and fork. His wrestling weight is over a hundred pounds above his football weight."

"Don't I know it," Rita chuckled. "I've seen him tear into Del's pot roast."

Grant laughed. "Rita, we got close to a hundred thousand every Buckeyes home game. The crowds for our games against Michigan, Penn State, and Notre Dame were louder than an artillery range. I missed the cheers and the excitement."

"Rita, may I add that Grant and my images are so bizarre and removed from our real selves, no one connects them to us." He chuckled, "Half the time, we don't even believe it."

"I know that you two are the bestest," Rebbeca chirped. "I also like Tom and Wile E. Coyote even though they're supposed to be bad guys."

Rita squeezed Rebecca's hand and smiled. "Just one more thing Buzz," Rita leaned on the back seat's edge. "I'm starting to understand the show. I now know you need villains that, as we say in Spanish, resonar, with the audience and give reason to root for the heroes, even if you play on the worst of human nature."

"She means 'resonate.'" Grant turned to Buzz.

"Yes. Resonate." Rita laughed. "Thanks Grant. I want to ask you Buzz. All the other wrestlers enter the ring to up-tempo music that 'resonates,'" Rita smiled. "And revs up the crowd. The song that you use, Buzz, could put you to sleep."

"A dreamless sleep?" Buzz glanced back. "Or one that takes you to a dreamland of an exotic, remote village deep in the jungle with clear rivers, spectacular birds, and, of course, ferocious jaguars."

"Buzz's entrance song has its roots in what's playing on the radio," Grant tapped the car radio. "It's Wagner's prelude to Act I of his opera, Tristan and Isolde. Wagner believed that Haydn, Beethoven, and Mozart achieved the peak of genius. Thus, music for the sake of music would always fall short of those grandmasters. Therefore, Wagner believed that music should tell a story. It should reflect a place and mood. Schuman rejected his notion. Tchaikovsky and Braams had mixed feelings. They respected his genius although didn't buy into his theories. Composers such as Gustav Mahler, Anton Bruckner, and Richard Strauss advanced Wagner's premise. The prelude to Act One of Tristan and Isolde featured the chords F-B-D sharp to G sharp. The mysterious Tristan Chord. That progression caused unresolved tension for the listener, thus boosting its emotional intensity. The French composer Claude Debussy sought to distinguish his style from Wagner. Nevertheless, Wagner's influence on Debussy was significant in developing his musical language. It emphasized impression, subtlety, and new harmonic and textural possibilities. The great French impressionistic painters of his time, such as Monet, Renoir, and Degas, also influenced him."

"Wow!" Rebecca chirped. "I wish my teachers were as smart as you."

"I teach college. You're a smart girl. You keep getting good grades, and maybe in the future, you'll be in one of my classes."

"Grant does more than just teach," Buzz added. "He also plays classical and jazz on the piano."

"I always told Rebecca," Rita pecked her daughter's cheek, "that wrestling was like the Three Stooges or a Tom and Jerry cartoon." She laughed. "Never great paintings, symphonies, and operas."

Grant laughed. "Buzz's entrance song, "Quiet Village" by Martin Denny, falls under exotica. Exotica utilizes many of the layered musical textures and non-traditional scales of Debussy's tone poems such as Prelude a l'apresmidi d'un faune, La Mer, and Nocturns, to create an immersive experience into a lush, tropical utopia."

"The bird calls and sound effects add the cherry on top." Buzz glanced back at Rita and Rebecca. "Al chose it for me because he wanted the audience to feel like they are in the Amazon and about to encounter a fierce, deadly jaguar."

Rita chuckled. "Who would'a thunk it?" She turned to Rebecca, "Did you ever imagine that you would be in the car with two professional wrestlers and that wrestling would prove so deep and complex?"

The next sound from the radio was applause. A distinguished voice then spoke, "Ladies and gentlemen. The New York Philharmonic Orchestra is proud to present Kirsten Flagstad." After more applause, Kirsten Flagstad sang *'Isolde's Liebstad'* from Act Three of the opera *Tristan and Isolde.*

Rita closed her eyes. *Buzz lifted and cradled her. She put her hand around the back of his head and pulled him to her.*

"Buzz." Rebecca broke her reverie. "Can we listen to the Alan Freed show?"

***

After dropping Grant off at his hotel, Rita and Rebecca sat in the front seat. Buzz had tuned the radio to the Alan Freed show. "Next is a vocal harmony from a group from New York City. The Heartbeats featuring James Shepard, "Crazy For You."

"You're driving me crazy; oh my darling, where've you been?"

"It seems oh so childish; I always must feel chagrin."

"You don't seem to understand; I'm crazy just for you."

"My nights are so lonely when you're not by my side."

"I think of you, darling, and tears flood my eyes,"

"You don't seem to understand that I am crazy just for you."

Rita inched closer to Buzz. Her floral aroma caused Buzz to lean back in his seat and lower his shoulders.

Alan Freed then spoke, "Ritchie Valens has a big hit with a rock and roll version of a traditional Mexican song, *'La Bamba* .'Here is a vocal harmony group from San Antonio, Texas, and their group harmony interpretation of another traditional Mexican song. Here's Sunny and the Sunglows and *'Le Reloj.'*

As the song played, Rita inched closer to Buzz. He breathed deeply through his nose. *'She's so soft yet so firm. So comfortable.'* He moved his right hand from the steering wheel...

Rebecca sang along with the radio,

"Reloj, no marques las horas

Porque voy a enloquecer

Ella se irá para siempre

Cuando amanezca otra vez

Nomás nos queda esta noche

Para vivir nuestro amor

Y tu tic-tac me recuerda

Mi irremediable dolor

Reloj, detén tu camino

Porque mi vida se apaga

Ella es la estrella que alumbra mi ser

Yo sin su amor no soy nada."

Rita beamed at her.

"She's good." Buzz smiled at Rita. "I mean, she's excellent. Have you considered getting Rebecca professional voice training?" Buzz asked. "Because we may have the next Kirsten Flagstad or Maria Callas."

'We?' Rita thought while pinching her chin.

"I just like to sing with my Mama!" Rebecca arched her eyebrows and smiled.

Rita held Rebecca's hand and grinned.

***

Buzz arrived at 1010 Grimsby Lane. He walked Rita and Rebecca to their front porch. The car was still running. The radio played Bertha Tillman's "*Oh My Angel.*" Rita stood in front of her door and faced him. Buzz gazed into her brown eyes. *'Her eyes. They look bigger. So bright.'*

'He looks even stronger. Tall. Handsome. Blue eyes.' "Tonight was special for me. I never dreamed that I would experience anything like it."

Buzz inched closer to her. He put his arms over her shoulder and placed his palms on her upper back. *'She's not returning my embrace, but she's not moving away either.'* They smiled at each other. *'Those lips are perfect, so full.'* He inched his face closer. She did not move toward him, nor did she back off.

Buzz felt something touch his leg. He looked down and saw Rebecca looking up at him with shiny eyes. "Thank you, Buzz," Rebecca smiled and looked at him wide-eyed. I'm sad you lost, but I still had a wonderful time."

He lifted her with his left arm and cradled her. "Be happy for Bubby. He earned it." He put his right arm around her mother. "Right now, I feel like the greatest victor the World has ever known." He pecked Rebecca's forehead and then Rita's left cheek.

Rita silently kissed the air.

Rita and Rebecca waved to Buzz as he drove away down Grimsby Lane.

Chapter 11

Rita and Rebecca stood in the backroom of Del's diner. Together, they sang the Spanish song, *'Cucurrucucu Paloma.'* Margie watched and listened to them. After they finished, she clapped. "She's good!" Margie beamed. "What a voice!"

Rita smiled and turned to Rebecca, "Thank your Aunt Margie for the compliment."

"Thank you, Aunt Margie," Rebecca chirped.

"Del fought in the big one. Okay, I'll admit, he was a cook. But he was there, and he can tell you that Jo Stafford and Vera Lynn helped the Allies win." Margie turned to Rita. "Mary couldn't make it today, so I'm afraid you will have to wait at her tables too."

Rita walked into the diner. "Where is everybody? Sunday mornings are our big church crowd."

"That's because this Sunday is a major religious holiday around here." Margie chuckled. "There's a big NASCAR race in Daytona Beach. We'll stay open for those who went to a real church and then call it a day."

***

Margie looked at her watch, "Okay Rita, that's it. No use staying open. Del's cooking can compete against just about anything. NASCAR isn't one of them."

"My father can't drive Rebecca and me home until late this evening. Can you give us a lift?"

"I can do you one better. We're invited to a big get-together with Bob and his brother's family. You're invited because they want you and Rebecca's company. I'm invited because they figure I'll bring some of Del's pot roast." Margie shouted to Rebecca. "Rebecca. You're invited to a picnic at Angelica's place. I'm sure she will let you ride her pony." Margie beamed at her. "Would you like to go?"

"Golly gee whiz wow!" Rebecca ran to Margie and jumped up and down. "Yes! I wanna go! I wanna go!" She turned and looked at Rita with bright, wide eyes. "Can we go? Please?"

"Oh, I suppose."

"Cool!" Rebecca hugged her mother. "Thanks, Mom."

***

The Boggs' North Florida farm had a white double-story house, a red barn, and a corral with horses and cattle.

Tammy May greeted Margie, Rita, and Rebecca. Margie held a silver kettle. "I'm sure you wouldn't have invited me if I came empty-handed."

"Nonsense," Tammy May chuckled.

Bart and Bob walked over. "We're sure glad you didn't come empty-handed," Bart beamed.

"I could smell the pot roast before I saw you three." Bob bellowed.

"Why isn't the Pot Roast's creator here?" Tammy May asked.

"Del stayed behind to update the books. He's not the most social person in the world." Margie smiled. "He does the cooking and paperwork. I run the place and hire the personalities. And the personalities don't get any better than Rita and Mary. Mary's one of a kind, and they don't get any friendlier or more likable than this one." Margie put her arm around Rita.

"Or prettier." Tammy May smiled.

"Well, Margie, you sure know how to pick'em." Bob laughed. "Mary is right over there." He pointed to Mary talking with Buzz and a large man wearing denim jeans and a Hawaiian-style shirt.

Rita spotted Buzz; her heart throbbed.

"I'm already dividing my life into before and after." Bob folded his arms and grinned. "Before I met Mary and after."

"Rebecca!" Angelica ran toward them.

"Well, Rebecca, there's someone glad you are here." Tammy May pointed to Angelica. Dressed in blue jeans and a white T-shirt with a picture of Anette Funicello wearing Mickey Mouse ears, Angelica wore her blond hair in pigtails with small pink ribbons on the ends.

Rebecca ran to Angelica. They danced an elbow swing. "Come Rebecca. I want you to meet Sheena. My pony."

"Can I ride her?"

"I only let my best friend ride her."

Rebecca frowned.

"And you're my best friend! Come!" Angelica pointed at the barn. "She's over there."

***

"My husband Del is a good soul and a fine man." Margie turned to Rita. "But he's not much for talking and meeting people. I just told everybody about how friendly and outgoing you are. Only I know you're shy at heart. And now I know matters of the heart make you shy." Margie took Rita by the hand. "Come on. I'll help you. He doesn't bite."

"It's not that…"

"You don't have to tell me what that is. Your Aunt Margie knows. Come."

"Rita!" Buzz beamed and smiled. He gently hugged her. She mildly returned his embrace. "So glad you're here. This is my friend Spence Carter. He's from San Diego."

"Hi. Pleased to meet you." Spence shook Rita's hand. "Buzz has told me so much about you."

Rita blushed. She squinted and looked closer at him.

"Ha! Ha! Ha!" Spence guffawed. "I guess the cat is out of the bag. Spence Carter is my real name. But you can call me Biff Rustler if you prefer.”

“His father is a defense contractor and knows my father.” Buzz beamed at Rita. “It’s a small world, isn’t it?”

“It took a while for us to make the connection.” Spence smiled at Rita. “If you think wrestling’s got its kayfabe secrets, you can imagine how hush-hush a Navy officer and a defense contractor have to keep things.”

“Is your brother here?”

Spence guffawed.

“Cletus Rustler from Laredo, Wyoming?” Biff smiled. “He’s Clayton Farnsworth from Muncie, Indiana.”

“So, you’re not brothers?” Rita shrugged.

“No.” Spence smiled. “It’s often done in professional wrestling. But I can assure you that the Samsons and Van der Westhuisens truly are blood brothers.

“Believe it or not, I remember the Van der Westhuisens from highlight reels of the Melbourne Olympics.” Rita smiled.

"Mama! Buzz! Come here!" Rebecca waved to them. "Look! Angelica is going to let me ride her pony."

"You guys go." Spence tipped his beer to them. "I can hear Bubby and Bobby laughing from here. It looks like that pretty redhead is putting on a kicking good show. I want in on whatever she's saying."

“Be careful Spence.” Buzz laughed. “Once you meet her, you won’t forget her.”

Rita and Buzz walked close enough to rub shoulders but didn’t hold hands.

“About last night.” Rita looked ahead.

Buzz turned and faced Rita. “Are you going to tell me that it was just a big, wonderful dream, and now I must wake up?”

"It's just that..." Rita looked at Buzz with a hint of a tear. "I am worried that Rebecca is growing fond of you. I'm an adult. I can deal with heartbreak and hurt. I accept it as part of life. She's an eight-year-old child. She's already lost a father and has had to adjust to a new country and a new language. Her grandfather helps as best he can. But he's growing old and comes home exhausted after a day working in the field." She looked at Buzz with droopy eyes. "I'm afraid of what may happen if we go beyond just friends." Rita pinched her eyelids shut to hold back a tear. She lowered her forehead and rested it on Buzz's chest; she felt his heartbeat. Buzz put his nose on the crown of her head and stroked her hair. Rita looked up with moist eyes. He braced her shoulders and stared into her eyes before gazing at her lips. *Her breath smelled better than waterfall mist. 'Lub dub; lub dub.'* His heartbeat enhanced his thoughts.

Rita felt comfort in surrender. *'His strength is mine.'* She tingled. "We better join Rebecca." Rita gasped for air. "She's never ridden a horse."

"Look, Momma! I'm riding Angelica's pony. Her name's Sheena."

"You put on a riding helmet," Rita prodded at her. "Right now!"

Angelica handed Rita a riding helmet. "Okay, Momma." Rita donned the helmet.

Angelica walked next to her pony and Rebecca. "Are you ready Rebecca? Squeeze with your legs and hold on to her mane. Trot Sheena."

"Wee!" Rebecca shouted as Sheena trotted around the corral. "Look at me." She beamed at her mother.

Rita gasped and covered her mouth.

"It's okay Rita." Buzz put his arm around her. "That little pony can't go any faster. Besides, it's a small corral. Hey!" He smiled at Rita. "She's a natural."

"Halt, Sheena!" Angelica shouted.

Sheena slowed to a walk.

Rita breathed a sigh of relief.

"Thank you, Angelica." Rebecca chirped. "Thank you so much for letting me ride your pony."

Buzz helped Rebecca down from the pony.

"Oi. Oi." Angelica walked with Rebecca. "Guess what I saw."

Rebecca shrugged.

"I saw my Uncle Bob and your Aunt Mary kissing."

Rebecca and Angelica giggled.

Ding! Ding! Ding!

"That's the dinner bell." Angelica beamed at Rebecca. "My mother made roast pork! Come. I can't wait. I'm starving!"

"It's too bad Bubby and Bob won't be able to enjoy it." Rita linked arms with Buzz. "Not after the way they gorged on Del's pot roast."

"You've only seen them eat at the dinner." Buzz laughed. "I've seen them eat. And I mean eat. There's a reason why they combine for almost eight hundred pounds." He turned and chuckled. "They'll do just fine with Tammy May's roast pork."

***

While the gathering sat at the table, Tammy May excused herself to take a phone call in the kitchen. After answering the phone, she stood in the kitchen doorway. "Margie. It's for you."

Margie took the phone call. Afterward, she knelt beside Rita. "That was Del. He needs to have the books balanced by the start of business tomorrow. I left the payroll in the car. I gotta leave right now." Margie looked at Buzz. "Can you give Rita and Rebecca a ride home?"

"But Margie…"

"I wanna stay Mama!" Rebecca pulled on Rita's sleeve. "I'm having too much fun."

Buzz beamed and nodded at Margie.

"Okay, honey," Rita did not look at Buzz. "We'll go home with Buzz."

"Yippie!" Rebecca chirped.

"And a double Yippie!" Angelica added.

"Can I hear a triple yippie?" Stephanie Johnson sat next to her six-foot-eight husband. She stood five feet two in heels and weighed three hundred pounds less than Bart. "Well, Rebecca, I can see you're wearing the dress I made you."

"It's the prettiest, most wonderful dress ever!"

"Does that mean that you would like another one?"

Rebecca's face lit up like a glow globe.

"And Angelica." Stephanie smiled at her. "What do you think?"

"I think it's the ginchiest! Like coolsville."

"Does that mean you'd like one too?"

Angelica's eyes opened wide as manhole covers.

"I made you both new dresses." Stephanie beamed. "I'll give them to you after dessert."

"Yippie! Yippie! Yippie!" Rebecca and Angelica cheered.

***

Long before Buzz reached 1010 Grimsby Lane, Rebecca had fallen into a deep sleep. Rita carried her inside and tucked her into bed. Buzz waited on the porch.

Rita's vision blurred upon seeing Buzz. Each step closer felt like autopilot. She inhaled once for every two heartbeats.

As Rita came closer, Buzz seemed taller and wider. He raised and spread his arms. Ethereal particles seemed to emit from his hands and onto Rita, drawing her closer and connecting them. He wrapped his arms around her.

Rita rested her forearms on his torso, her hands cupping his pectorals. "Buzz, today was the best day of Rebecca's life."

"How about you?" Their eyes focused on each other.

She felt detached from her body. She shifted her arms around his torso and pressed her breasts into his pectorals; her head moved closer.

'Her heart, it beats like a drum corps; her breath the scent of roses.' The aroma drew Buzz's gaze to her lips. *'So red, so full.'* Buzz kissed her. Their lips pulsated. Mingling tongues stirred a mushroom cloud of ecstasy.

She held him even closer. Each dart of their tongues sparked a scintillating rush throughout her being. "You better go now." Rita pulled her head away and looked down.

"Why Rita? What we're experiencing soars above just a kiss." He gripped her shoulders. "I know it, and you know it."

"Buzz, what do you know about me?" She pulled away. "I have a daughter."

"I know that, and I adore her."

"I am worried that she will soon adore you. Look at you. You're as handsome as a Greko-Roman statue. You're also famous. You can do better than a Mexican waitress with a child." Rita lowered her head. "Someone better will come along. Then what do I tell Rebecca?"

"The Jaguar's famous, not me." He chuckled. "Besides, the Samsons cornered the market on wrestling girls.

"You won't be the Jaguar forever." Rita pursed her lips. "I'm sure Bazz Arlett has no trouble attracting the ladies."

"Rita, I don't care about attracting women. I have an inner drive to pursue excellence. Life is a process. It's more than the destination.

It's what we learn and achieve along the way that counts. Life is a mystery. We don't know what doors will open. I enjoy physical conditioning and athletics. It's not everything, and it's not my end game. The pursuit of excellence is not seeking perfection. Only Jesus Christ is perfect. He gave his life for us, a calling far higher than himself. Through my faith, I can see that you live for something higher than yourself."

"Buzz, love and sacrifice for Rebecca is my greatest reward. Kissing you took me to another world. Before I invite you to my world, I better tell you about Rebecca's father."

"Okay." Buzz raised her hands and kissed them. "Tell me."

Rita lowered their hands but still held them. "I was only fifteen. That's marrying age in my village. I had never even kissed a man, much less known a man. Jose was his name. He was older than me, about your age." She released her grip to tap his chest. "My family was poor. My mother had died of an illness that doctors here could easily treat. My father did the same thing in Mexico as he does here. Farm labor. Jose was rich. I was considered the most beautiful young lady in the region." Rita saw Buzz grin. "Don't say it," she chuckled. "I know what you're thinking. No, Buzz, this is serious. My father wanted me to marry him. Jose promised to help my entire family. His reputation didn't matter to them."

"His reputation?"

He was a mujeriego, and it didn't stop after we married. He also drank and gambled, and nobody knew exactly how he got his money. But he had money, and he was dashing. I went along with what my family wanted. You're a man. You cannot fathom how much the first time hurt, and it never improved. He never made me feel loved. Each time, I felt used. I barely saw him while I was pregnant. At least during this time, he stopped hitting me. I thought things would improve after Rebecca was born. They got worse."

"Why didn't you leave?"

"How? Where would I go? I had no money. No job skills. Girls in my village were raised to be wives and mothers and little else. Besides, our local parish would never approve a divorce."

"Was he at least a decent father?"

"As I said, he was a mujeriego. Often, he came home smelling of another woman. I prayed he only desired grown women. He had Rebecca sleep in our bed. I made sure to sleep between us. He often had friends over. They'd get drunk and say how pretty and sweet they found her. I saw how they looked at her. I hated them. Whenever they visited, I hid a knife under my blouse. If one of those cerdos tried touching her, I was ready to use it. I would gladly face a firing squad in the town square before allowing them to lay one finger on her."

"What happened to Jose?"

"I don't know the details, and I don't care to know. All I know is that he was at the cock fights. They were drinking and betting heavily. A fight broke out. He was stabbed to death. When I heard the news, I felt no sorrow, only relief. I feel guilty about it to this day."

"Don't." Buzz embraced her.

She pushed him away. "The only good to come of it, besides Rebecca, is that he left me enough money to come here for a new start." She pursed her lips. "Without Margie, Del, and Mary's support, I don't know if we could've made it. You're only the second man that I have ever kissed and now the only living man who can make that claim.

"Rita. I, for one, am glad that you made it to America." Buzz took a deep breath and closed his eyes. "Rita." He braced her shoulders and took another deep breath. "I think I love you."

Rita lowered her head and stepped away. "You better go now."

Buzz nodded, turned, and headed for his car. He opened its door and began to climb in.

"Buzz!"

"Yes, Rita." Buzz stood and turned to her.

"I don't want you to leave."

He walked toward her. She ran to him and hugged him with all her strength. She kissed him full and long, turning her head to deepen it.

Buzz kissed her in pulses. He nibbled her ear and kissed her neck before returning to her mouth. He stroked her hair with his left hand and scratched her back with his right hand as their kisses intensified.

Rita closed her eyes. She remembered the gushing waters of the Fuente de la Minerva in the center of Guadalajara. She heard herself moan louder than the fountain's spray. Her knees buckled. She locked her hands behind his neck like a cliff purchase to stave collapse. Freed from conscious thought, her senses magnified. His chest's scent and taste amplified her joy. Buzz lifted her by the buttocks. She wrapped her legs around him. They kissed even deeper and with more passion. Rita reached for the switch and turned off the lights.

Chapter 12

Buzz drove westbound on State Road 64. He turned South onto County Road 675 at the tiny village of Myakka Head. CR 675 ran parallel to the Myakka River, ending at Myakka City and a connection to State Road 70. He spotted a huge flat rock extending into the water, pulled over, and parked his car. Buzz sat on the rock in the lotus position. While living in Asia with his Navy officer father, Buzz learned martial arts meditation. He closed his eyes and tried to clear his head. Late summer rains had swollen the river. The river's mineral scent and the green flora along its banks, combined with the singing of the river cascading through the rocks and fallen branches, evoked memories of the night before. He recalled his words, *'I think I love you,'* and then her melodic voice replete with her exotic and erotic accent, *'I don't want you to leave.'* Euphoria enveloped him. *'Her face, her brown eyes, and her full lips. Touching her, kissing her, feeling her.'* He breathed deeply through his nose. *'Such an aroma; her ambrosial taste,'* He licked his lips. *'Rita. I don't only think I love you. I know I love you.'* The dancing river current had his mind replay Rebecca's singing, transporting him to a place in the heart.

***

Pedro Mendez dropped Rebecca off at school before driving Rita to work. She clocked in and entered the diner. Mary made eye contact with her. They looked at each other for a few seconds. Rita and Mary hugged. They held their embrace for several minutes.

***

About a hundred yards upstream from Buzz, three twelve-year-old boys fished. "Arnie!" One of the boys pointed. "Did you see the size of the fish that just jumped?"

"Yeah, Scott. I didn't see it, but I sure heard it splash." Arnie had short blond hair; he wore white shorts and a white and blue horizontal-striped shirt. "It's gotta be a big one, alright. I'm gonna catch that baby!"

"How, Arnie? You can't cast that far." The chubby boy with black glasses spread his palms.

"I can if I get closer." Arnie started climbing a tree.

"What are you going to do?" Scott stood below the tree.

"Watch me."

Arnie shimmied over a large tree branch. He sat on a bifurcation. "You're mine, big fishy." He cast his line into the current.

***

"I think that, at long last, you've found love, my Rita darling." Mary looked at Rita with moist eyes. "I know I have."

Mary and Rita kissed each other on the lips with closed mouths and again embraced.

"We better get to work," Rita pulled away. "Before Margie thinks we fell in love with each other."

They laughed together.

***

The boys heard a harsh crack. The tree branch broke. The next sound was a splash. Arnie fell into the river.

"Arnie! Arnie!" Scott and Harold yelled.

"Help! Help!" Arnie got caught in the current, swiftly taking him downstream.

The boys' shouts snapped Buzz out of his reverie. He saw a boy struggle with the current. He dove into the river and swam to him. "I got ya kid. I got ya."

Arnie started to struggle.

"Don't be scared. We're going to be fine. We can't fight the

106

current. Just stay with me. It will soon take us to shore."

Scott and Harold ran to the road and flagged down a car. A familiar car, a white '54 Chevy Bel Air four-door, pulled over. "Mr. Wilkins! Arnie fell into the river. It's taking him away!"

Glen Wilkins wore a white collared shirt and round, wire-rim glasses. Bald on top, he slicked down the sides with grease. "Where?"

"He climbed onto a tree branch, it broke, and he fell in! But I saw a man swim out to him."

"Get in. I'll take you to his father." He sped southward on CR 675 to Myakka City.

***

"It looks like we're safe, Arnie. Let this eddy take us to shore." Two minutes later, Buzz helped Arnie onto the bank. "What's your name, kid?"

Arnie cried.

"It all right. You're safe now. Let's climb up the bank and get to the road. We can flag down a car for help."

"I'm Arnie, sir."

"Well, Arnie, you're a brave young man." Buzz chuckled. "But you're not too smart yet. I hope you never crawl out on branches over rain-swollen rivers again."

"My father's the sheriff." Arnie sniffled. "He'll give you a big reward."

***

Mr. Wilkins, Scott, and Harold arrived at the Myakka City police station. Scott ran in first. "Sheriff Martin! It's Arnie! He fell into the river! He got swept away." Scott and Harold's wild eyes and pallid faces underscored the seriousness of the situation.

Sheriff Gerald Martin gasped. His heart skipped a beat.

Glenn Wilkins marched in behind the boys. "It's not as bad as it

107

sounds, Gerry. The boys saw a man swim out to him. Last they saw, he was with him."

Sheriff Martin said nothing. He bolted to his squad car and turned on the overhead lights and siren. He darted out of town, accelerating to over a hundred miles per hour northbound on CR 675. Cars got out of his way. The road looked like a haze to the sheriff; the roadside scenery melted into a long blur.

***

Buzz chuckled, "I don't need a reward, Arnie. I do need a favor however."

"Sure, mister."

"Please don't tell anyone what my face looks like. I can't tell you why. You'll have to trust me and keep our secret."

"Yes, sir, mister." They heard a siren growing in volume. "That's my dad!" Arnie pointed to an oncoming police car.

"You're now officially rescued. I must go. Good luck, Arnie." Buzz disappeared into the woods.

Sheriff Martin felt the weight of Atlas fall from his shoulders upon spotting his son. He pulled over and hugged him.

Chapter 13

Buzz arrived at the Sarasota Municipal Auditorium soaking wet.

"What happened to you?" Steve Samson spread his palms.

"Let's just say I had a little river adventure." Buzz placed his kit bag on a bench. "I can't wait to take a hot shower and wash off this river water."

"Not here. You have to use the locker room down the hall and to the right."

"Sure thing."

After Buzz left, Steve, Shaun, and the Van Der Westhuisen Brothers guffawed.

Frankie Williamson greeted Buzz as he entered the other dressing room. "Hola, amigo. Bienvenida to our locker room."

"What happened to you?" Barry Howard walked over and shook Buzz's hand. "Next time, pack a bathing suit."

"You see, Buzz," Frankie Williamson took Buzz's kitbag. "You no mas champion. Now you one of us. We're amigos. Buenes noticias. I mean, good news, amigo. Tonight, we tag team together."

"You mean I'm wrestling you."

"No amigo. We're tag team partners."

"Yes." Barry Howard smiled. "It's you and Frankie against me and Spider Nel. Spider always has good matches and gives the front liners a run for their money, but, in the end, he has to lose. Tonight, Al wants him to win. So, in the tag team," Barry pointed. "He pins you."

"We wrestle first. But since Al isn't here and you're mi amigo," Frankie slapped Buzz's arm. "Spider can pin me."

Buzz was nonplussed. *'Don't whine about the demotion. These are hard-working, experienced men. Complaining would disrespect them.'*

"I appreciate that, Frankie." Buzz grimaced. "First, I better take a shower. This river water is getting to me."

"What are you doing in here Buzz," Al Cohen entered. "The area is not secured. You can't be seen in this dressing room."

"They said I'm tag teaming with Frankie against Barry and Spider."

Frankie Williamson and Barry Howard tried to stifle their laughter by covering their mouths.

Al sighed and shook his head. "When are you going to learn?"

Steve, Shaun, Leslie, and Trevor barged into the locker room, pointing at Buzz and laughing at him.

"Hilarious, boys," Buzz smirked. "Just hilarious."

"Now that you're all here, I will brief you on what I want for tonight's bill. Leslie, lock the door." Al took a clipboard from his briefcase. "Trevor, tonight it's you against Spider Nel. You've worked together before. He will control most of the match by fighting dirty. Let the crowd think he's going to win. You save the day with clean, scientific wrestling. Remember, he's the 'Predatory' Spider Nel. He's no jobber. You get more credibility if he looks good. Frankie and Barry, you get to lose to Spence and Clay. You two know the routine. I've already briefed them and the Samsons. After you lose, lay on the mat. Spence and Cletus will continue to stomp you."

"Muchas gracias, Al," Frankie chuckled.

Al grinned and smirked. "Steve and Shaun will run into the ring and rescue you. The Samsons and Rustlers will then brawl and hurl insults at each other. I want to build their rivalry. Buzz and Leslie, it's you two tonight. You're the co-main event." Al addressed Leslie. "I want the reverse of your brother's match. You open strong with scientific holds. Buzz, let the crowd think Leslie might pull off an upset. In the end, it's the savage Jaguar. I want you to throw Leslie out of the ring for the finish. The main event will be Yuri and Bubby. Bob, Grant, and Shigeru stayed behind to do a promo and TV spot at Crazy Wally's largest auto dealership." Al grabbed Buzz's arm. "As soon as Bubby arrives, we'll discuss my plans. If none of you have any questions, let's put on a good show."

***

Buzz beelined to a pay phone. He almost fumbled his coin and dialed the wrong number.

"Hola," Rita wedged the phone receiver between her cheek and shoulder.

"Rita! It's me!" Buzz fidgeted with the wire.

"Buzz! I can't stop thinking about you. I'm glad you made it safely."

"Well, I did have a little adventure with the Myakka River on the way, and the boys pulled yet another rib on me. Otherwise, I couldn't be happier."

"There's someone who wants to say hi." Rita handed the receiver to Rebecca.

"I love you, Buzz."

Buzz heard a muffled voice, "Rebecca!"

"I'm sorry, Buzz. Um. You were talking about a river adventure?"

"It's no big deal," Buzz spotted Al and Bubby down the hall looking at him. "I'll tell you later. Bubby and Al are here. They want me in a meeting. I'll call you again after the show."

"I'll be waiting."

"I, I," Buzz felt a lump in his throat, "Goodbye, Rita."

"Adios Buzz," Rebecca shouted.

After hanging up the phone, Rita fixed her gaze and straightened her lips.

"I'm sorry, Mama. Are you mad at me?"

111

"No, Rebecca." Rita lowered her shoulders and beamed. "I couldn't possibly be happier." Rita hugged her daughter and kissed her forehead before kissing her right cheek.

***

The crowd grew restive as Leslie Van der Westhuisen and The Jaguar exchanged collegiate-style wrestling holds. Buzz grumbled in Leslie's ear without moving his lips. "Let's bring it home."

Buzz flung him toward the ropes. Leslie braced his elbow on the top rope, flipped over, and landed on his feet. He stumbled onto a table and flopped onto the floor. The referee counted to ten. The audience did not react. Both wrestlers returned to the dressing room without fanfare.

Al Cohen waited at the dressing room door with his hands on his hips and eyes furrowed. After Buzz entered, Al closed the door behind them. "Care to tell me what the hell that was?"

"I wanted to give Leslie a chance to show his scientific wrestling skills."

"That's bullshit, and you know it." Al prodded. "Leslie was a Collegiate All-American and wrestled in the Melbourne Olympics with his brother. I bill and promote them as Olympic champions. What teams were you named to at West Virginia."

"None." Buzz slumped his shoulders.

"Did you hear any heat from the crowd?"

"Not really."

Al skewed his face. "Not really?" He shook his head. "How about none. They came to see the savage Jaguar, not an ordinary college wrestler. Your match was supposed to tell a story: a clean Olympic champion fighting a bigger and stronger savage brawler. After you beat him, they should love to hate you even more. We discussed our plans. Plans that will make us all big money and boost our promotion to top territory in North America." Al prodded. "Until I tell you otherwise, you're the savage Jaguar." Al placed his hands on his hips. "I like you, Buzz. I have other business connections. I can get you a junior management gig in New York if wrestling is no longer for you. You'll make a fraction of the money you're now earning, and it will take you a few years to climb the ladder. You will have to live in a small apartment, wear a tie every day, and take the subway to work. I can make that happen if that's what you want."

"I'm sorry about tonight's match."

"You're sorry?" Al hinted at smiling. "Go to New York. See Mickey Mantle. You have the potential to be to wrestling what he is to baseball. That will only happen if you do what I say, as I say. Are you with me or not?"

"Yes, Al." Buzz pursed his lips. "I'm in."

"That's good." He shook Buzz's hands. "Let's nip this thing in the bud. Your match with Leslie wasn't televised. By the sound of things, Yuri and Bubby have the crowd in an uproar, and earlier, the Samsons' confrontation with Spence and Clay went as planned. They'll forget your match. Let's move forward with our plans."

"Thank you, Al." Buzz turned to walk away.

Al grabbed his arm. "And give my regards to Rita. She's a lovely lady, and her little girl is adorable." Al held his grip. "I want what's right for you."

Chapter 14

Professor Sakamoto and Grant Irons stood before a 1957 Series 75 Cadillac and a 1956 Buick Roadmaster. Grant ticced his head erratically. Sakamoto grinned mischievously at the camera. "This is Gordan Hanson. I'm here in Tampa at Crazy Wally's largest auto dealership. Professor Sakamoto, what brings you here?"

"My wrestler's parents were American spies in my homeland. They knew America was going to drop the bomb. They hid under the streets of Hiroshima. When they saw what the radiation did to their son, they abandoned him. He survived in the sewers by eating radioactive rats. Now he wants revenge."

"Ah-uh. Ah-uh," Grant flicked his green tongue.

"You always talk about revenge and re-fighting the war." Gordon pulled his face. "But you seem to like it here in America."

"That's because I no like Japanese cars. In Japan cars are very small," Sakamoto held his thumb and forefinger an inch apart, "and slow. American cars are big, powerful, and fast." He smiled broadly. "I like big Cadillac and Buick."

Grant skewed his face at the camera.

"You think he's crazy?" Sakamoto tilted his head at Grant. "Wally is crazier. He's selling this powerful Cadillac and this fast Buick for a crazy low price."

Grant uttered in a loud, primitive, slurred voice, "Low price!"

"Even better." Shigeru smiled at the camera, "Wally is offering crazy easy finance. Come in today, and this Cadillac or Buick can be yours." He moved his arms toward the cars.

Grant blurted, "Easy finance!"

"If you come to crazy Wally's right now," Sakamoto held up a pen, "You'll get a bonus. I will sign for you, in Japanese, a picture of me and The Beast. He will also sign." Sakamoto handed Grant Irons a pen. He put it in his mouth and bit it in two.

"Ah-uh." He kept one half in his mouth and showed the other half to the camera.

***

Gordon Hanson, Beer Barrel Bob, and the television crew stood outside the dealership. "I'm here with Beer Barrel Bob at Crazy Wally's. Bob, what brings you here?"

"Gordon, I'm here because I'm a red-blooded American. What is more American than Chevrolet, Cadillac, Buick, and Ford? Wally also has Chryslers, Studebakers, Nash, and Hudsons waiting for you to drive. Wally knows what America wants and what makes America great. He's crazy about his country. He wants you to see the country in a quality used car for a low price and easy financing."

"How will Wally make this happen?"

"I'm glad you asked Gordon. If you come to Crazy Wally's today, I will personally take you to the boss and get you fifteen percent off his already rock-bottom low sticker price. But you must come and see me right now. Not tomorrow. Now. I know an offer this good sounds crazy. That's because Wally is crazy."

***

After the close of business, Grant, Shigeru, and Bobby met with Wally Garner in his office. "Great job, men." Wally was tall and husky. He wore slick-downed, gray-flecked hair longer than the time's norm. His embroidered western shirt was secured with pearl snaps. A silver bull pendant was set in his turquoise frame bolo tie.

"We sold even more cars than I predicted. In addition to your fees, I want to give you guys a bonus." He held up two sets of keys. "I've got two '55 T-Bird convertibles in my lot. As my show of appreciation, you get to drive them for the next month."

Grant, Shigeru, and Bobby thanked Wally, took the keys, and left the office. Mary Jenkins waited outside the office. She ran up to

115

Bobby, embraced him, and kissed him.

"I've got a surprise for you." Bobby waved the set of keys. Bobby and Mary walked hand in hand through the car lot.

***

Bob and Mary cruised westbound on US Route 92. Their radio blasted "Six Days on the Road" by Dave Dudley. Bob had his left hand on the wheel while his right held Mary's hand. She tilted her head back. The wind blew her red hair like a streamer. "Hey, look!" Mary pointed to a drive-in restaurant replete with garish neon signage. "Let's stop there. I'm hungry."

They pulled in and placed their order with a waitress on roller skates. Their radio played Carl Butler's "Don't Let Me Crossover." Four motorcycles roaring like apocalyptic locusts pulled next to them.

"Uh oh, I know them." Mary's hand trembled as she spoke. "Their leader is named Kenny Schack. He's trouble."

Kenny wore a sleeveless leather vest with a bicycle chain across his shoulder. His black hair was set with excess grease. He braced a muscular, heavily tattooed arm on Mary's side of the car. "Well, if it isn't Mary Double Scoop. I'd order a cherry on top, but I bet you lost that before you were twelve and probably to a family member.

Bob sprung from the car, crossed his eyes at the biker, and punched him.

Kenny didn't budge.

Bob looked at his fist and muttered, "Oh yeah." He punched him again. This time, Kenny stumbled backward and fell. "I know what you're thinking." Bob brandished his fist to the other gang members. "It's three of you and one of me. Fair enough." He tensed his lips and nodded. "Who wants to go first."

"Hey," one of the bikers spread his palms. "He said it." He pointed to Kenny Schack sprawled on the pavement. "Not me. I got

116

no beef with you." He boarded his motorcycle and drove away. The other two did likewise.

"What happened?" Mary asked.

"The first time, I threw a working punch like Beer Barrel Bobby in the ring. The second time was Bob Boggs, for real."

Kenny staggered upward, wiped the blood from his mouth, grimaced at Bob and Mary, climbed onto his motorcycle, and drove away.

"Now that they're out of the way," Bob beamed at her, "I have a little present for you." Bob took Mary's left hand and put a beer can tab over her ring finger.

"What the hell is this?" Mary glared at the beer can tab.

"Oh, I'm sorry." Bob chuckled. "I switched back to Beer Barrel Bobby. Let me do this again as Bob Boggs." He replaced the beer can tab with a diamond ring.

"Are you?"

Bob's eyes glowed. He beamed and nodded his head.

"Yes! Yes! Of course, I'll marry you!" She hugged and kissed him.

***

After the Sarasota matches, Buzz drove through the night, taking a long way as he chose to avoid County Road 675 and the Myakka River. He eventually reached US Route One and took the turn to Autumn, Florida. En route, he stopped at a Mexican takeaway food stand. His heart raced on reaching Grimsby Lane. With each house, 1000, 1002, 1004, 1006,1008, his anticipation felt like a pyrotechnic skyrocket about to burst. In a moment, he would look into her brown eyes, smell her sweet breath, and hold her warm body. 1010 Grimsby Lane. His hand felt detached as he rapped on her door.

"Huh!" Rita gasped on seeing Buzz at the door. "Buzz!" She

beamed. "I thought you just wrestled in Sarasota and tonight you must be in Ft. Myers."

"I don't have to be in Ft. Myers until seven o'clock."

"That means you drove all those extra hours just to see me?" Rita looked back at Rebecca and Pedro, stepped out onto the veranda, and closed the door. She kissed him, their tongues darted. "I see that you brought something for us."

"Yes." Buzz pecked her forehead, "I stopped along the way and picked up some heuvos rancheros."

"They will go perfectly with the molletes that I prepared." Rita opened the door. "Join us for breakfast."

As they walked in, Rebecca grinned mischievously.

'She knows why I closed the door.' Rita blushed.

"Buzz!" Rebecca ran up and hugged him.

"Hola, hombre fuerte." Pedro flexed his right bicep.

"Buzz brought us some heuvos rancheros." Rita held up the takeaway container. "We're all going to eat breakfast together."

"Yippie!" Rebecca jumped up and down. "Swell!"

With each bite, Rita and Buzz stole a look at each other. With each eye contact they smiled; Rebecca smiled broader. She asked, "Are you going to be champion again?"

"That's not my decision." Buzz slid his hand under the table and grasped Rita's hand. She squeezed his hand and grinned at him. "It's up to Mr. Cohen. Bubby's proving a wonderful champion. I'll have to bide my time and do a good job. Mr. Cohen has big plans for me, though."

"Really!" Rebecca beamed. "I wanna know."

"Shh." Buzz put his finger over his lips. "Kayfabe. Think of it as Christmas. You wouldn't want to know what you're getting before Christmas. Wouldn't you rather have a big surprise on Christmas morning?"

"Rebecca wanted to go to wrestling for Christmas, and she got her wish early." Rita beamed at Buzz. "Next, you and Stephanie gave her lovely new clothes."

"That doesn't mean we will shortchange you come Christmas," Buzz chuckled. "What else would you like for Christmas?"

"I want you to marry Mama." Rebecca jumped up and down. Rita gasped and covered her face.

***

Buzz drove Rita and Rebecca to her school. Rita slid over to be closer to Buzz. Rebecca sat on the other side of her. He tuned in his car radio to a rock and roll station. It played Johnny Maestro and the Crests, "Besame Baby." Rita and Rebecca sang along. Rebecca sang in perfect key, tempo, and pitch. Her voice made Buzz smile.

"Rebecca!" Buzz glanced at her and beamed. "You're good. I mean, you sing wonderfully." Buzz held Rita's hand. "Your mother is no slouch either. Now I know where you get your talent."

Rita blushed. "I want her to audition for the school pageant, but she's afraid to sing in front of people."

"Rebecca, performing before an audience is fun. I get a kick out of playing the savage Jaguar, and Bubby has fun playing the African Lion. Even Grant gets a kick out of playing the Beast before a crowd." He turned, glanced at her, and smiled, "Your singing is far different and a much higher calling. It's a gift from God. I'm sure he wants you to share it."

"Buzz is right. Remember, in Sunday school, you learned that Jesus said that one never lights a lamp to hide it under their bed but to light up the house. Jesus wants you to let your gift of singing shine to others."

"Buzz," Rebecca leaned over her mother. "Do you really think I sing good?"

"Rebecca. You're not just good." Buzz imitated the Kellogg's Frosted Flakes mascot, 'Tony the Tiger,' "You're Grrrreat!"

Rebecca laughed. "Mama. Buzz wants me to sing for the school. I think I might"

"Why yes." Rita smiled wider than the mouth of the Amazon River. "That would be fantastic!"

"Okay," Rebecca chirped. "I will."

Rita beamed before kissing her cheek. "Buzz. Turn left. There's her school." She pointed at a one-story brick building.

Rebecca kissed her mother's cheek, "Bye, Mama." She exited the car and closed the door. After running four steps toward the school, she turned and looked back at the car. "I love you, Buzz."

As they drove away, Rita took a clue from the song on the car radio, Paul Anke's *Put Your Head on My Shoulder.* She snuggled up to Buzz, wrapped her arm around his waist, and rested her head on his shoulder. Keeping his eye on the road, Buzz kissed the top of her head.

"I feel guilty, Buzz."

"Why?"

"Because I looked forward to you dropping Rebecca off at school." She lowered her head. "I wanted to be alone with you." She looked up at him with bright eyes. "You're driving. You better pull over." Buzz pulled over to a safe spot along the road. He gazed into her wide and brightening eyes. Rita planted a long, wet kiss on his lips. She caught her breath. "My shift doesn't start for two more hours. Saville Park is just a short way down the road. Let's stop and walk along the lake."

***

Rita and Buzz walked hand in hand along Lake Saville. The morning songbirds were chirping, and the frogs were croaking.

120

"She adores you, Buzz." Rita turned and looked into his eyes. "I don't know if that's a good thing. I've told you my reasons for making sure that doesn't happen. Before you, I never let a man get close to us, never even as a friend." She squeezed his hands. "You're already a good influence. Without you, she never would've risked auditioning for the school pageant. Thank you." Rita kissed Buzz on the lips. "Still, Buzz, I worry. After doing everything possible to save her from hurt and disappointment..." Rita lowered her head.

"Rita." Buzz lifted her chin with his forefinger. "I've also grown attached to her. She's a wonderful child."

"You understand, Buzz. I feel bad for letting this happen. I hope I didn't let her down as a mother."

"You didn't let her down." Buzz put his hands on her shoulders.

"There's a reason I dropped my guard and let this happen." Rita closed her eyes and took a deep breath. "It's because I..." Rita felt her words get trapped in her throat. After inhaling deeply, she smiled. "It sounds like the cicadas are singing your name." She chuckled and touched his nose with her finger. "Buzz, buzz, buzz." They gently kissed.

"It looks like Wally over there also likes looking at you." Buzz winked. "I can't say I blame him."

"Huh," Rita gasped on spotting the large alligator.

"Relax. He has no interest in us. I've lived in Thailand and the Philippines." Buzz chuckled. "There we had saltwater crocodiles twice his size. Those guys you better look out for. Don't worry. I believe in old-fashioned chivalry. I will walk on the lakeside. That way, I'll be Wally's lunch. You can run away before he decides to eat dessert."

"If you say so, Buzz," Rita laughed. "Just don't ask me to go swimming with him." Rita rubbed up against Buzz. A heron then landed on top of the oblivious alligator. "Buzz, I have devoted my last eight years to ensuring that Rebecca has a steady home. But look at you. Everything you own is in your car. Your address is whatever hotel Al books you."

Buzz walked on the lakeside while holding her hand. "I want you to know how much I appreciate you and how you have raised Rebecca. I understand and appreciate every sacrifice you've made for her. You're everything as a parent that I wish I had growing up. As you know, my father was a Naval officer. He was often out at sea. My mother was nice enough to me when I saw her. Unfortunately, she was also often away. At school, I often got teased about the rumors." Buzz closed his eyes and winced. "They were more than rumors. One day, before I could board the school bus, the school's principal took me away. He dropped me off at a group home. I had no idea why. I lived there until my father came back from sea duty. Later, I found out my mother ran off with another man."

"I'm sorry, Buzz." Rita looked at him with moist eyes. She hugged and kissed him.

"My father did his best, but he had a demanding career. I lived with him while he was on shore duty. Unfortunately, when he was called to sea duty," he looked into her eyes, "I got sent back to the group home. My martial arts senseis were my surrogate fathers. They instilled self-discipline but without an ounce of love."

"But you did get to live in exotic places."

"Yes, Rita," Buzz smiled. "I lived in Japan, Korea, Thailand, and the Philippines. My father sent me to a wonderful summer camp for boys in West Virginia. It's called Camp Greenbrier. It's right on the Greenbrier River, nestled between mountains. It's in the idyllic little town of Alderson, West Virginia. I invested in land there. About twenty miles upriver is a girls' camp- Camp Allegheny. It's every bit as nice as Camp Greenbrier. When you think she's ready and you can stand being away from her for a few weeks, I know Rebecca will love it." Buzz smiled at her. "I'm ashamed to say this: I chose to study at West Virginia University because of my summers at Camp Greenbrier and the town of Alderson."

"Do you still see your parents?"

"My father is now a Captain and on the verge of becoming Rear Admiral. The Navy is his life. Keep him Kayfabe. I don't want my jaguar act to hurt his career. I am my father's only child. My mother eventually married the man whom she left him for. I have two half-brothers who I have never met. I am in touch with my mother, but she has a new life and family that doesn't include me."

"I am also an only child. My mother died shortly after my birth."

"I'm sorry," Buzz kissed Rita.

Rita kissed him back. "My mother got sick and never got better. I don't know. Was it because of birthing me weakening her system? My father never talks about it. He never re-married. He had to work long and hard to make ends meet. I respect him for that. He was entitled to relax with beer and tequila when he wasn't working." Rita kissed Buzz. "Our local church helped a lot in raising me. They also protected me from boys and," Rita blushed and lowered her head, "older men."

"I am happy to hear that the church protected you." Buzz smiled. "I wrestle in Naples Friday night. Bubby is more than a former NFL football player, strong man, and wrestler. He is also an ordained Baptist minister. He is the guest preacher this Sunday morning in Daytona Beach. Stephanie will be there. I have plenty of time to drive back to Autumn. If I promise to later go with you to your Catholic church, could I have the honor of taking you and Rebecca to see and hear Bubby's service?"

Rita backed away from Buzz while keeping her hands on his shoulders. "It can't hurt. The damage is already done?"

"Damage?" Buzz dropped his hands to his side.

"Yes," Rita's eyes watered. "Damage. Rebecca's attachment to you has reached the point of no return. I know I talk about it a lot, but I never should have let this happen." She lowered her head. After five seconds, she raised her head. "Earlier, I tried to tell you why I let it happen. I choked on my words." She took a deep breath. "The reason." She stared at him. "The reason I allowed you to get so close to me and Rebecca is, because…" Her vocal cords felt paralyzed. She inhaled deeply and regained her voice. "…I love you, Buzz. I'd be honored to go to Bubby's church with you."

"Rita," Buzz gripped her shoulders. "The other night, I said, 'I think I love you.' Now I know I love you."

Buzz and Rita hugged and kissed. Their hearts beat together in synch with their lips and tongues.

***

"Here we are." Buzz pulled up to Del's Diner. "I wish this morning didn't have to end."

"I feel likewise. But I have my duty to Margie, and you have a long drive to Ft. Myers. You also need to rest up before your show." Rita kissed Buzz. "But I don't want to say goodbye just yet. Come inside with me."

The main jukebox of Del's Diner played Connie Francis's, '*My Happiness*'. Mary held up her hand, showing off her diamond engagement ring. The entire diner cheered. Her smile could make an overcast day bright.

"Mary!" Rita ran up to her. "Did he ask you?"

"Yes!" Mary nodded. Rita and Mary hugged and pecked each other's lips.

Buzz hugged her and kissed her cheek. "Congratulations!" He looked around before talking without moving his lips. "I'm still a rookie and the butt of the other wrestlers' ribs. Now Bob is going to take some of my heat," he snickered.

Rita took Buzz by the hand. "I know we have to say goodbye. I don't want to do it here." She led him outside and around the corner of the diner. They kissed deeply and passionately.

"I love you, Buzz."

"I love you too, Rita."

Margie had watched them leave and walk to a discreet place. She smiled from ear to ear on seeing Buzz and Rita kiss.

***

Buzz felt like he was piloting a hot air balloon rather than a '56 Chevy. The first song the radio played was Billy Eckstine's *"My Foolish Heart."*

He breathed deeply through his nose and dreamed of Rita and Rebecca. The radio now played The Platters' "Remember When."

"Remember when, I first met you,

My lips were so afraid to say, "I love you."

Remember when, to my surprise,

The heaven in my heart leaped into your eyes."

With each smooth and powerful note from Platters lead singer Tony Williams, Buzz could picture, feel, and taste Rita's kisses. He recalled wrapping his arms around her soft yet firm body and imbibing her floral aroma. Fortunately, the road was traffic-free.

***

Rita entered Del's Diner. The main jukebox now played Brook Benton's *'Fools Rush In.'* Her steps felt like walking in lunar gravity. She felt light enough to leap in floating bounds.

Margie smiled at her. "I can see by those dreamy eyes that something special has come over you."

Rita blushed and looked downward. "You can tell?"

"Yes. Darling," Margie beamed, "It shows. I've wanted this for you since I came to love you as a daughter. I know your concerns. I

125

have no worries. Buzz will make a wonderful dad for Rebecca." Margie winked. "And I hope in the distant future Rebecca will have brothers and sisters."

"Stop it, Margie," Rita chuckled. "I'm nowhere near ready for that."

Mary walked over to Rita and embraced her. "I sure know your feeling." Mary smiled. "When you know deep inside that it's more than a feeling and God reassures you, why wait? I believe in showing my faith by grabbing his blessing and being thankful for it." Mary turned to Margie. "Of course, it could be Del's putting something in the water."

The three ladies chuckled.

Mary continued, "I bet you two never dreamed that you would stand in a wrestling ring in front of thousands of people."

Rita raised her eyebrows and spread her palms.

Margie took both of Rita's hands. "I'll fill you in after the lunch rush is over."

Chapter 15

Arnie Martin sat at his father's police station desk.

"Arnie, we've talked about this at length," Sheriff Martin tapped his son's shoulder. "I am extremely grateful to the man who rescued you."

The sheriff smiled, "If not for him, you would've drowned. Regardless of his identity, I will thank him personally. This is Special Agent Conway with the Florida Department of Law Enforcement. We want to help the man who saved you. His muscular physique by itself does not make him a suspect. But keep in mind that convicts have nothing else to do in prison except lift weights. I know," he nodded, "lots of people lift weights. When you add that he wanted you to keep his face secret, and then he fled when he saw my patrol car approach, well, we must put two and two together."

"Your father is a law enforcement officer, and he's a good one. I share his suspicions." Special Agent Conway wore his hair in a flat top. He was dressed in a white shirt and a thin black tie. "Help me find him. I can't promise that he will get amnesty, but I can promise leniency. The sooner we find him, the better for him. Your father took your description to a forensic artist." Conway opened a folder and slid a sketch to Arnie. "Does this look anything like him?"

"Just a little," Arnie nodded.

"I thoroughly examined our files on escaped convicts and fugitives. I also coordinated this with the FBI in Washington. I narrowed our search to White males under forty years old, over six feet tall, and heavy build. Florida has no at large escaped convicts. The FBI found two national escapee profiles that may fit your description." He took two photos from another manilla folder.

Arnie gasped at the mug shots before shaking his head.

"Are you sure?" Special Agent Conway tapped the photos.

"Yes, sir," Arnie nodded. "I'm sure."

"My boy would never lie."

"I know," Conway grinned. "This file has fugitives from the law." He took a stack of photos from the folder. One by one, he showed Arnie a photo collage of a suspect. Arnie shook his head with each one.

"Well, that's all I have." The agent returned the photos to the manila folder and secured it in his briefcase.

"There have been no strong-arm or armed robberies in the vicinity in over a month." Sheriff Martin stood. "None of the fugitives or suspects fit Arnie's description. I guess we must consider that our man was just a good Samaritan who wants to remain private." Sheriff Martin put his hands on Arnie's shoulders. "If we have any new developments here or if you have any new suspects, we give our word that you will have my department and my son's full cooperation."

Sheriff Martin and Special Agent Conway shook hands.

After the FDLE agent left, Arnie looked at his father plaintively, "Did I do okay?"

"You did fine, son. Let's go to the Rexall for an ice cream soda."

Arnie beamed.

Chapter 16

Buzz stopped at a toy store en route to that evening's matches at a National Guard armory on the outskirts of Naples, Florida.

"That should do it." He snickered as he took items from a shelf.

Forty-five minutes later, Buzz entered the Amory dressing room. "I guess you heard the news about lover boy." Buzz guffawed. "I got a gift for him." Buzz had attached toy handcuffs to a toy bowling ball. He cuffed it to Bobby Boggs's ankle. The other wrestlers guffawed.

"I better save it for you." Bobby laughed with them. "My fiancé isn't keeping your secret."

"No," Spence Carter laughed. "It's too light. I saw how you and that hot tamale look at each other. You need an anvil."

"No mas chicos," Frankie Williamson intervened. "I'm his coach. I advise him on romancing Spanish muchachas." Frankie put his hand on Buzz's shoulder. "My advice no good no more. He enamorarse perdidamente. He's too far gone for my help."

The wrestlers laughed at Buzz.

"He needs more of your help, Frankie." Trevor Van der Westhuisen laughed. "He may make her cry when he pulls off his mask."

"At least the mask has some long hair." Shaun Samson held up a lock of his hair. "That's what got her in the first place," he guffawed.

"No, Shaun." Spence donned his black 'Rustler Brothers' western hat. "Mexican beauties go for cowboys."

"Then I guess I don't have to worry about you," Buzz pointed at him. "The only thing you've ever ridden is a surfboard."

The other wrestlers guffawed.

"All you boys need a woman who can take care of you." Shigeru continued laughing. "You all need to meet a nice Japanese girl."

"No. No," Yuri stifled his laughter. "Japanese girls are too delicate. A wrestler needs a sturdy Russian woman."

"You guys argue all you want." Bobby took off the mock ball and chain and held it. "I found the love of my life. She's a good old-fashioned American Country gal." Bobby laughed. "Besides, a beer-drinking gal is my type over a sake, tequila, or vodka drinker."

The wrestlers cheered and congratulated Bobby.

***

After finishing his match with Trevor Van der Westhuisen, Buzz quickly showered and packed his bag.

"Why you leave so early?" Frankie Williamson smiled at Buzz. "Let me guess. You too much enamorarse perdidamente?"

"I know what that means, Frankie." Buzz picked up his bag. "I'm afraid the answer is si, mi amigo."

***

Buzz drove through the night. He checked into a motel just outside of Autumn, Florida. He lay in bed. Images of Rita and Rebecca squashed meaningful sleep. The sun awoke him from a Non-Rapid Eye Movement doze. He hopped out of bed, showered, shaved, and donned his only dress shirt and tie. He drove to 1010 Grimsby Avenue. What awaited exceeded all expectations. Rebecca wore the dress and shoes that he had bought her. Her mother had put two yellow ribbons in her hair. Not even E.B White's Fern Arable from *'Charlotte's Web'* could look more adorable. Rita mesmerized him. She wore a long, elegant red and green skirt topped by a white blouse with an intricately embroidered button placket. Her cheeks were florid and healthy. She wore her hair in a high bouffant. *'She looks elegant and classy. Stunning! Her cheekbones and jawline are striking. Her brown eyes radiate. Dare I kiss her? Her lips look so inviting, so exciting.'*

130

She beamed at him. Her eyes widened. *'A tie? I love that look, so different from the savage Jaguar.'* Rita walked up and braced his shoulders. She gazed into his eyes.

Rebecca ran to them. "Buzz!" She hugged him.

Buzz and Rita dry-pecked each other on the lips.

"I saw that." She wagged her finger.

Buzz and Rita chuckled.

***

Rebecca, Rita, and Buzz, in that order, linked hands as they walked toward the entrance of the Mount Zion Baptist Church in Daytona Beach, Florida. "I can feel by the vibrations and a tad of moisture in your hand that you're nervous. Don't worry. I can see that Rebecca is happy. Aren't you?"

"Yes," Rebecca jumped up. "I'm tickled pink!"

"It's not that." She dropped her head. "I'm ashamed to say this."

"It's alright talk to us." Buzz opened his free hand.

"It's just that, well, I would never work in a segregated restaurant. I think you know that. I made friends with Bubby the first moment he sat down at the diner. I thanked Stephanie abundantly for making Rebecca's dresses. I can tell that she has a heart of gold. It's just that…" Rita inhaled deeply. "We're the only people here who aren't black."

"Bubby will introduce us. Come on, Rita. Everyone is welcome in the house of the Lord. Apostle Paul said in Galatians that we are all united and equal in Christ. The parishioners here agree."

"It's not just that," Rita looked away. "Will they, you know, accept us as a couple."

"A couple of what?"

Rita chuckled and looked at Buzz. "You know… A white man and a brown girl."

131

"Just stay out of the sun and we'll be fine." Buzz chuckled.

"Buzz!" She cuffed his arm and giggled.

"Well," Buzz took both Rita and Rebecca's hands. "Nobody objects to Ricky and Lucy; nobody questioned Tony and Maria's love for each other. How about Marty Robbins?" Buzz sang, "'Out in the West Texas town of El Paso, I fell in love with a Mexican girl.' Or Ricky Nelson," Buzz sang. "I've got a pretty senorita waiting for me, down in old Mexico."

"Well, if you want to put it that way," Rita chuckled. "Look at what happened to Marty Robbins's cowboy and look what happened to Tony."

"You're not wicked and evil like Feleena, and you don't have a brother who leads a street gang."

"If you keep singing, I may have to shoot you myself." Rita laughed. "Buddy Holly married a Chiquita from Puerto Rico, and it hasn't hurt his record sales." Rita again cuffed his arm. "So, leave the singing to Buddy Holly," she chuckled. "Okay?"

"Speaking of singing, this church has an award-winning choir," Buzz nodded toward the entrance. "Let's go in."

"Yeah, Mama," Rebecca pulled Rita by the hand. "I wanna go."

***

Buzz, Rita, and Rebecca found Reverend Bartholemew Johnson even more impressive on the pulpit than in the ring.

"The Lord is our shepherd. We shall not want!" He pointed upwards. "He lays us down in green pastures. He leads us to still waters that refresh our souls. He guides us for his name's sake. But if just one of you should go astray and get lost," he held up his forefinger. "Jesus tells us of the Shepherd who left his flock of ninety-nine! And searched for the one lost lamb. Hear me now, brothers and sisters."

"Yes," the congregation responded.

"In the time of David and Jesus, sheep were not bred just for white wool. Their natural shades of wool were also black, gray, and brown. Some were cream, and some were even the color of a fawn. And you had sheep with mixed colors, even with spots and stripes. Yet they were all still sheep. Likewise, we are all lambs of God and brothers and sisters in Jesus. Glory, Hallelujah!" He threw up his hands.

The congregation shouted, "Amen!"

"Can I get a witness?"

"Yes, Lord!" The congregation replied.

"Now I know you didn't come to see me play football or wrestle."

The congregation laughed.

"And you sure didn't come just to hear me talk. Now for what you've all been waiting for." Reverend Johnson motioned to the choir director. The director waved his arms in a pattern. The congregation stood and clapped as a blue-robed, tall, thin lead singer with a pencil mustache fronted the choir and sang a Black gospel interpretation of Hank Williams's country gospel song, "I Saw the Light."

"I wandered so aimless, life filled with sin.

I wouldn't let my dear savior in.

Then Jesus came like a stranger in the night.

Praise the Lord, I saw the light.

I saw the light; I saw the light.

No more darkness, no more night.

Now I'm so happy no sorrow in sight.

Praise the Lord, I saw the light.

Just like a blind man, I wandered along.

Worries and fears I claimed for my own.

Then, like the blind man that God gave back his sight.

Praise the Lord, I saw the light.

I saw the light; I saw the light.

No more darkness, no more night.

Now I'm so happy, no sorrow in sight.

Praise the Lord, I saw the light.

I was a fool to wander and stray.

For straight is the gate and narrows the way.

Now, I have traded the wrong for the right.

Praise the Lord, I saw the light.

I saw the light; I saw the light.

No more darkness, no more night.

Now I'm so happy no sorrow in sight.

Praise the Lord, I saw the light."

***

Rita, Rebecca, and Buzz waited for Reverend Bart Johnson outside the church. They spotted him leaving with Stephanie.

"Bubby!" Rebecca ran up to him.

"Well, hello, my little angel," Bart picked her up and carried her back to her mother.

"Thank you for inviting us." Buzz and Bart shook hands. "It was a wonderful service."

"I'm Catholic, but I sure felt the presence of the Lord." Rita shook both of Bart's hands. "At first, I was a afraid to go in. Now I am on cloud nine."

"I grew up with Navy chaplains," Buzz added. "Some were inspirational, but nothing like you."

"Thank you again for making those lovely dresses for my daughter." Rita embraced Stephanie.

Stephanie held both of Rebecca's hands. "How did you like the service?"

Rebecca started singing,

"I saw the light, I saw the light.

No more darkness, no more night;

Now I'm so happy, no sorrow in sight.

Praise the Lord, I saw the light."

Bart and Stephanie looked at each other in surprise.

"Wait right here," Bart yelled to his choir director. "Abe!" Bart motioned to himself. "Can you come here for a moment?"

Abe strolled over to them. He was Rita's height and had a round face and round belly.

"Rebecca. This is Abe Collins, our choir director. Will you please sing for him?"

Rita nodded to Rebecca.

Rebecca sang,

"I saw the light, I saw the light.

No more darkness, no more night

Now I'm so happy, no sorrow in sight.

Praise the Lord, I saw the light."

Abe applauded. "Rebecca, will you sing after me?" Choir director Collins sang,

"Go, tell it on the mountain.

Over the hills and everywhere.

Go, tell it on the mountain.

That Jesus Christ is born."

Rebecca sang, "Go, tell it on the mountain.

Over the hills and everywhere

Go, tell it on the mountain.

That Jesus Christ is born."

"Thank you, Rebecca." Abe looked at Buzz and Rita. "Are you her parents?"

Rita shook her head before lowering it.

"I'm sorry," Bart stepped forward. "How rude of me. This is Rita Mendez, Rebecca's mother. He's Buzz Arlett." Bart froze. "Um, he's my trash man."

"I need to get rid of this." Abe patted his belly. "If lifting trash cans can make me look anything like you, Mr. Arlett." He grinned. "Put me to work."

Rita and Buzz shook hands with Abe.

"Rebecca is good. I mean, outstanding. If you can bring her here, I want to work with her. I'd like her to sing lead on a song with my choir."

"We live kind of far away." Rita nodded. "But I thank you for the compliment and the offer."

"Please give it some thought." Abe smiled. "This little girl is a shining light. Please let her gift glow for all to see and hear." Abe bent over and asked Rebecca, "Would you like to sing with my choir?"

"Yes. I love to sing. I often sing with my mommy."

"Maybe you can ask your mommy and daddy to bring you to our rehearsal."

"He's not my daddy yet." She grabbed Buzz's hand. "But I want him to be."

"Rebecca!" Rita spoke without moving her lips.

After the choir director left, Stephanie took her husband's hand.

"You all know he's from Georgia," Stephanie grinned. "I'm from New York City. Two of my favorite street corner harmony groups from New York, The Harptones with Willie Winfield and The Jive

Five with Eugene Pitt, are singing at the Regent Ballroom in Tampa this Thursday. Won't you join us?"

"It's a school night," Rita put her arm around Rebecca.

"You have to be twenty-one to enter." Stephanie chuckled.

"We're not wrestling on Thursday." Bart grinned at them. "I'm sure your father can look after Rebecca."

"I want you to go with Buzz," Rebecca chirped.

"I have the day shift on Thursday." She smiled at Rebecca and took Buzz's hands. "I've never heard of the Harptones or the Jive Five." She winked at him. "But I'd sure like to hear them on Thursday."

Buzz beamed from ear to ear.

***

Rita heard a knocking on her front door. "I'll get it."

A lanky woman wearing a navy-blue dress with a white button placket and wire-framed glasses over her hawk nose stood on the door stoop.

"Good evening. I'm Miss Kathryn Watkins. I'm your daughter's voice teacher."

"Rebecca doesn't have a voice teacher. Who sent you?"

"A Mr. Buzz Arlett. He already paid my fee."

"Oh, really?" Rita scratched her head before breaking into a wide grin. "Come in." Rita led her to Rebecca. "Darling, this is Miss Watkins. She's a music teacher. Would you like for her to teach you to sing better?"

"Yeah! Cool!" Rebecca sprung to her feet. "That would be the utmost!"

Chapter 17

Stephanie, Bart, Rita, and Buzz sat at a prime table near the stage at the Regent Ballroom in Tampa, Florida.

"I loved the Harptones." Rita sipped her drink. "Thank you for inviting me, Stephanie."

"You're welcome, Rita."

"The jukeboxes at the diner have some doo-wop records. Rebecca listens to rock and roll stations, especially Allan Freed. A rock and roll disc jockey named Wolfman Jack has a show on a Mexican station called XERP. We can sometimes pick it up on a clear night. They both mix doo-wop with rock and roll. Yet I've never heard a voice quite like Willie Winfield's."

"His soothing tone and smooth delivery make him tops in my book." Stephanie smiled. "I just wish that he would get a national hit. I can assure you that the Harptones are big in New York."

"Most of rock and roll is from my neck of the woods." Bart sipped his beer. "Little Richard is from my hometown, Macon, Georgia. Most of your rock and roll stars like Elvis, Chuck Berry, Jerry Lee Lewis, Buddy Holly, and Fats Domino are also from the South."

"Doo-wop harmony is mostly from Northern cities like my hometown, New York City, as well as Philadelphia and Detroit. The next act, The Jive Five, are also from New York."

"So, you can see how this Northern gal and this Southern gentleman, a giant man and a dainty lady, complement each other." Bart held Stephanie's hand.

"Growing up as a Navy brat, I never got to attend a church like yours." Buzz grinned. "Our church music was dull or sounded like something from a Dracula movie."

Bart, Stephanie, and Rita chuckled.

"But the music at your church was truly moving." Buzz sipped his beer.

"Just wait until our choir director, Abe Collins, has Rebecca ready to sing some good 'ol gospel." Bart held up his beer bottle. Buzz tapped his bottle to it while Rebecca and Rita tapped it with their margarita glasses.

"I think I know how you two felt going to our church for the first time." Stephanie looked around. "Bubby and I are the only black people here."

"Yeah, and unfortunately, here comes trouble." Buzz pointed to two approaching bouncers.

"Well, if it isn't Johnny Durham." Bart skewed his head.

"Well, Bubby, your Jew promoter may have only booked us in integrated arenas, hotels, and restaurants, but he's not here. This establishment does not admit your kind." He grinned. "We may book black musicians, but they ain't allowed nowhere but the stage and their dressing room. So, unless you want to go on stage and give us a minstrel show, you can…"

Bart jumped up. "Only my friends call me Bubby." He prodded. "It's Mr. Johnson to you."

"Sorry. I don't call your kind, mister." Johnny Durham had platinum blond hair. He stood taller than Buzz, heavier but not as lean. "But you better call him Mr. Kyle." He pointed to the other bouncer.

Kyle held a baseball bat at port arms. He was tall and muscular. Prison tattoos covered his arms. He used copious grease to style his black hair in a faux hawk.

Bart scowled at them both. Kyle tapped the end of his baseball bat in the palm of his free hand.

"Johnny Durham," Buzz took a sideways glance, tilted his head, and nodded. "Al booked you as 'The All-American Boy.' You had the fans convinced. You had me believing it, too." Buzz folded his hands behind his head and smirked at him. "Only I couldn't figure out which America."

"The only America that matters is my America." He prodded at Bart and Stephanie. "Now, you two get out and take the cute little wetback with you."

Buzz leaped to his feet and shoved his chair aside. He glowered at Johnny. Suddenly, quick as a lizard snatching a flying insect with its tongue, Buzz snatched the baseball bat from Kyle. Buzz perused the label. "Hmm…Hank Aaron. I thought you didn't allow black people off-stage."

Kyle backed off.

Buzz handed Bart the bat. "That's only for safekeeping." He focused on Johnny. "What do you say you and me in a shoot? Right here and now. If you win, the four of us leave. I win; we not only stay, but you leave." He pointed at him.

Johnny hesitated. Suddenly, he threw a punch. Buzz evaded it, grabbed his wrist, twisted it, and exploited his momentum to fling him to the floor. Buzz went into a fighting stance. Johnny jumped up and charged him like a raging bull. Buzz dropped on his back. He put his foot on Johnny's abdominals and flipped him skyward. The other patrons screamed as he flew into a table. Buzz ran over and put him in a sankaku-jime choke hold. "Tap the floor, and I will let you go. Otherwise, I kill right here and now."

Johnny tapped out. He scrambled to his feet. Bart then approached with the baseball bat. "You made a deal. You lost. Now get your candy ass out of here."

Johnny glowered at them before walking out of the club with his shoulders slumped and head down.

"Go home, loser!" a patron heckled him. Other patrons added derisive remarks. Kyle had returned to his post.

The patrons cheered as Buzz and Bart sat down.

Rita gasped, covered her face with her hands, and wept. Stephanie put her arm around her.

A man in a blue pinstriped, double-breasted suit approached their table. "I'm Luca DeMarco. I own the joint. I know you. You're Adebe. The World Champion professional wrestler." Luca extended his hand.

Bart pursed his lips, looked at Luca's hand, and glanced back at Stephanie. She nodded. He shook his hand.

"You're welcome to stay. Waiter!" He snapped his fingers. "Bring them a bottle of Dom Perignon." He looked back at Bart. "Don't worry. It's on me."

"So, what am I? Your token black or honorary white?"

"Neither. Times are changing, and I want to change with them." He snickered. "Besides, my favorite color is green, like on currency notes, and I don't care who spends it on my operations. I want to introduce you to my club."

"Only if this is the first day the Regent Ballroom is officially integrated."

Luca pinched his chin. "I voted for Ike. Yes. I will. The Regent Ballroom is now officially open to all." He looked to Buzz. "Oh, and your friend… It looks like I tag-teamed with your promoter, Al Cohen. I just fired Durham as well. I'm giving Mr. Kyle one last chance, but only after a man-to-man talk." Luca put his hands on his hips and tilted his head. "You're one hell of a fighter. You also a wrestler?"

"No. I'm Abede's trashman."

"I bring him when I think there might be trouble with more than one foe." Bart slapped his back.

"So, how does a trashman get such a gorgeous lady?" He smiled at Rita and then turned to Buzz. "Please give me some tips after the show."

Rita, eyes still moist, turned tomato red.

Luca walked onto the stage and took the microphone. Greetings, ladies and gentlemen. You got a bonus tonight. You got a little rasslin' in addition to the music. Our special guest tonight needs no introduction. Presenting the World Champion Rassler. Adebe: The African Lion."

The spotlight shined on Bart. The audience cheered.

"And now, they come all the way from Brooklyn, New York. The Regent Ballroom proudly presents… The Jive Five!"

Eugene Pitt fronted two of his brothers and two other singers. They sang their opening number, *The Girl With The Wind In Her Hair.*"

Buzz looked at Rita. He imbibed her floral aroma and the salt of her margarita drink. His mind drifted. He imagined Rita on a tropical beach with her ankles in the ocean. Behind her, the surf formed a tubular curl. Its trough a deep cobalt, its face turquoise, and the white spray from its peak reflecting a prism of colors. Palm trees swayed in the mountainous backdrop. She wore a two-piece bathing suit. The sun gave her smooth body a burnished bronze sheen. She beckoned him as the wind fluttered her long brown hair.

Chapter 18

Over 5,000 people packed the Silver Spurs Arena in Kissimmee, Florida. Maid of honor Margie Anderson stood in the center of the ring. She wore a flowing pink gown with white ruffles along the seams. Bridesmaids Stephanie Johnson, Rita Mendez, and Tammy May Boggs stood beside her. They wore shorter, baby blue gowns. Bobby Boggs and his brother Skeet wore tuxedos. They stood next to Margie. Bart Johnson wore his dark blue minister robes and held a Bible.

Three musicians: a guitar player, a banjo player, and a fiddler, stood behind them. Reverend Johnson nodded to the musicians. They played a country interpretation of the Bridal Chorus from Act III of Wagner's opera *Lohengrin*. Mary held Al Cohen's arm. He led her down the aisle toward the ring. She wore a white wedding gown with a long train. Al lifted her gown's train as she climbed into the ring. He then stood between her and Margie. *'Ding Ding Ding'* the timekeeper rang the ring bell.

"Ladies and Gentlemen," Reverend Johnson spoke into the microphone. "Over five thousand of you have gathered here to witness the wedding of Beer Barrel Bobby Boggs and Mary Jenkins. Who gives this woman to be married to this man?"

"I do." Al stepped aside. Maid of honor Margie Anderson then moved next to Mary.

"Mary Jenkins." Bart moved in front of Mary and Bobby. "Do you commit yourself before God and these witnesses to be the loving wife of Beer Barrel Bobby Boggs, in sickness and in health, for richer and for poorer, and to forsake all others." He put the microphone before Mary.

"I do."

"Do you, Beer Barrel Bobby Boggs, commit yourself before God and this audience to be the loving wife of Mary Jenkins, in sickness, and in health, for richer and for poorer, and to forsake all others." He put the microphone before Bobby.

"I do." His brother and best man handed him their wedding ring. Bobby put it on Mary's finger.

"If anyone here knows any reason why these two should not be joined in holy matrimony, speak now or forever hold your peace."

Professor Sakamoto had snuck into the ring and confronted them. He pulled his salt pouch from under his jacket and smirked. He then sprinkled dry rice on them.

"I declare you husband and wife. You may kiss the bride."

Bobby lifted Mary's veil and kissed her. The five-thousand-strong audience gave them a rousing standing ovation. The three musicians played a country interpretation of Mendelssohn's Bridal March from 'A Midsummer Night's Dream overture.

Mary threw her bouquet over her shoulder. It landed flush in Rita's arms. Rebecca, sitting next to her grandfather, stood and cheered.

***

'Ding Ding Ding.' The timekeeper rang the bell. The wedding party, save the groom, departed the ring. A referee and the ring announcer entered the ring. Beer Barrel Bobby took the microphone. "We have made a change in tonight's bill. I am sure you will understand. After all, I just got married." The crowd cheered. "My new wife and I want to start our honeymoon. We have tickets to the Grand Ole Opry in Nashville, Tennessee. I am sure you won't mind if we change the order of the bill and I wrestle right now."

The crowd cheered and yelled, "Beer! Beer! Beer!"

Frankie Williamson entered the ring. Beer Barrel Bobby handed the microphone to the ring announcer.

"Fighting out of this corner, from Columbus, Ohio, weighing in

144

at 238 pounds, Frankie Williamson." Faint applause. "And, in this corner, he weighed in at 345 pounds. He hails from Tallahassee, Florida, Beer Barrel Bobby!"

The fans stood and cheered. "Beer! Beer! Beer!" They chanted. "Beer! Beer! Beer!"

'*Ding!*'

Still wearing his tuxedo, Bobby threw Frankie into the ropes. He rebounded into his arms. Bobby put him in a bear hug and power-slammed him into a pin. The referee slapped the ring three times.

'*Ding ding ding.*'

The ring announcer spoke, "Your winner, after 26 seconds, Beer Barrel Bobby."

Frankie Williamson and Beer Barrel Bobby shook hands. The crowd yelled, '*Beer! Beer! Beer!*'

Bobby took the ring microphone. "In celebration of my wedding, for the next hour, draft beer is on sale at the concession stands for a dime a cup."

The crowd stood and applauded. Some ran toward the exit portals en route to the concession stands.

Chapter 19

Buzz's mind felt helium-filled, but his accelerator foot felt cast in concrete as he drove through Autumn, Florida. As he turned onto Grimsby Lane, the radio disc jockey spoke, "Good afternoon, Florida. This next singer needs no introduction. He's a native Floridian from Jacksonville. Now he's a national star. Johnny Tillotson and 'Dreamy Eyes.'"

Buzz turned into the final stretch. He pictured Rita greeting him with a smile. An imaginary gaze into her large brown eyes made him sing aloud with the radio, "Dreamy eyes, you've got such dreamy eyes; when I'm away from you, I'm so alone and blue. When I take you home, I feel so alone, and then I realize I love you, Dreamy Eyes. Your eyes hold a dream of a love for two. A love so warm and rare. I hope to see that dream come true. A dream we both can share."

'Too bad she hates my singing. Maybe the voice coach I hired for Rebecca can help me sing that song for her?'

Upon pulling into the driveway of 1010 Grimsby Lane, he noticed another car, a yellow '52 Hudson Hornet, parked in the driveway. He rapped on the door. Rita answered. *'Oh, those dreamy eyes. That smile is making my dream come true.'* Buzz smiled back at her.

Rita said nothing. She gently closed the door behind her. She put her arms around his neck and kissed him.

"Shh," she next placed her forefinger over her lips before taking Buzz by the hand and leading him into her house. They sat together on a couch and held hands.

Katheryn Watkins tapped a note on her portable keyboard. Rebecca sang the matching note.

"Excellent, Rebecca. You're the most gifted young student that I have ever taught. When is the audition for your school's talent pageant?"

"Two weeks from tomorrow." Rebecca smiled.

"Can you choose your song?"

"Yes, Miss Watkins. We can."

"Children's songs have their place. But I think you've progressed enough to sing a more grown-up song. Would you like me to teach you the song I have in mind?"

"Yes! Please!"

"It's not too grown-up." Katheryn chuckled. "Rosie Hamlin wrote the words when she was only fourteen. You'll like her. She's half Mexican, and her mother even has your same last name, Mendez. The song is called '*Angel Baby.*' The record is in English, but I want you to sing it in Spanish. Would you like to try it?"

"Yes!"

Kathryn took the sheet music from her portfolio and placed it on her keyboard.

"Can you read the words?"

"Yes. Miss Watkins."

"We'll start by singing together." She played the introduction on the keyboard. Katheryn and Rebecca sang together.

"Es como el paraíso

Estar aquí contigo

Eres como un ángel

Demasiado bueno para ser cierto

Pero después de todo

Te amo, lo hago

Mi bebé angelical

Mi bebé angel

Cuando estás cerca de mí

Mi corazón da un vuelco."

Buzz gazed into Rita's eyes, "You're my Angel Baby, and I love you, I do." They stole a kiss.

Kathryn and Rebecca continued to sing,

"Apenas puedo estar de pie

Sobre mis propios pies

Porque yo te amo"

Rita put her finger on Buzz's nose, "When you are near me, my heart skips a beat. I can hardly stand on my two feet." They again kissed.

Kathryn and Rebecca continued to sing,

"Te amo, lo hago

Mi bebé angelical

Mi bebé angel

Woo-hoo, te amo

Woo-hoo, lo hago

Nadie podrá amarte."

Rita and Buzz walked over and applauded.

"Wonderful, Rebecca! Maravillosa! Your daughter's got it!" Kathryn beamed. "She has true talent!"

Buzz and Rita squeezed each other's hands. Rebecca opened her eyes wide and beamed at them.

Chapter 20

Al Cohen had summoned Buzz, Bart, Shigeru, Nigel, Frankie, TV announcer Gordon Hanson, and an actor dressed as a policeman into an office at Crazy Wally's Tampa, Florida, dealership for a closed-door meeting.

"This is phase one of our plan. Wally Garner had his main showroom cleared for tonight's telecast. I made a deal with Wally to use his showroom as he also uses it for TV commercials." Al folded his hands.

"I'm sure Wally doesn't mind the free advertising," Buzz smirked.

"You majored in business, didn't you?" Al narrowed his gaze.

"Yes, sir."

"So, you understand how partnerships work?" Al put his hands on his hips. "And how deals are made?"

"Of course, Al." Buzz smiled, "And you have never failed to cut us our fair share."

"Keep that in mind for your performance tonight. That goes for all of you. Pull this off, and you'll all get the biggest paydays of your careers. As I mentioned, I chose to stage our show here because the telecast infrastructure is already in place. Tonight, we perform the first episode. We have one more episode until the final event at the Orange Bowl in Miami. If all goes well tonight and in the next three acts, our Miami show may go national and attract over 60,000 in live attendance. Again, you all know what that means for you. I have already syndicated tonight's show to several out-of-market TV stations. Think of this as a TV show. It requires a controlled environment and a pre-selected live audience. A fake cop with a prop gun would never pass legal muster in a public setting. Besides, my TV people can make it look like we have a bigger attendance."

"Gordon," Al motioned to his TV broadcaster, "Tonight you

must shine."

"I've rehearsed this. I am ready, even if it goes off script."

"That's good, Gordon." Al pointed, "And Shigeru, tonight you act your worst." Al laughed. "Hollywood scouts may watch, so don't hold back. And that goes for you, too, Buzz. Tonight, take your act to the next level. This is it. Your last act as the savage Jaguar. Make it memorable. Nigel, thus far, I have only used you as a stand-in extra. Now, you get your chance to perform. Frankie, I chose you for tonight. You're as professional as any wrestler in the business. I have total faith in you." Al pointed to the outside actor. "You have the script. You're a professional. Do your job." Sam steepled his hands. "Last but not least, Bubby, you're the star of the show. You know what to do." Al smiled. "You've never let me down before. That's just one," he led up his forefinger, "reason why I made you the champion." Sam stood. "Okay. We're all on the same page. The first match is in two hours. Let's do this."

***

Rebecca sat in front of the TV. "Hey, look, Bobby is on!"

Rita washed dishes in the kitchen. "That's good, darling. Call me when Buzz is on."

"Okay, Mom." Rebecca pointed at the TV. "Bobby is fighting Spider Nel. He's mean and fights dirty, but I know Bobby will win."

***

Ding! Ding! Ding! "In this corner, from Colombus, Ohio, weighing in at 236 pounds, Frankie Williamson!"

The audience clapped politely.

The house lights went out. Strobe lights flashed on an open door at the showroom's rear. The sound system played Martin Denny's *'Quiet Village.'* Nigel Earl, dressed in a safari suit and wearing a pith helmet, led Buzz, wearing his spotted mask with head and facial hair protruding from its edges, by a chain. Professor Sakamoto walked in

150

front of them. "And now, being led to the ring by his handler, Nigel Earl, and his manager, Professor Sakamoto, he was trapped in the deepest and darkest reaches of the Amazon jungle, The Savage Jaguar!"

***

"Mama! Buzz is on!" Rebecca pointed at the TV.

Rita ran into the living room and stood in front of the TV.

***

Frankie Williamson faced the ring corner. He held the ropes and stretched. The Jaguar ran across the ring. *'Ding! Ding! Ding!'* Before the bell's final echo, the Jaguar pounced on Frankie Williamson. The Jaguar dropped Frankie to his knees with three straight forearm strikes to his back. He then lifted him and flung him into the ropes. The Jaguar vaulted from the second rope and launched himself skyward. He pivoted in mid-flight and struck him with a two-handed chop across the chest, knocking Frankie onto his back. The Jaguar picked him up and body-slammed him. He then went to the corner and climbed up on the third rope. After pausing to let Frankie Williamson stagger to his feet, The Jaguar sprung high in the air, jackknifed, and came down in a close line across Frankie's upper chest. Frankie clutched his throat as he went down. The Jaguar pinned him.

The referee slapped the mat. "One, two." The Jaguar lifted Frankie and tossed him out of the ring. The referee counted Frankie out. Suddenly, the Jaguar attacked the referee with a forearm strike, staggering him backward. The Jaguar pounced over and threw him out of the ring. *'Ding! Ding! Ding!'* The Jaguar ignored the bell and paced about the ring like a caged animal.

***

'It's just a show.' Rita winced. *'It's just a show'*

151

***

Professor Sakamoto and Nigel Earl, carrying his chain, came into the ring. The Jaguar ignored Nigel's commands and continued stalking about the ring. Suddenly, Professor Sakamoto threw salt into the Jaguar's eyes and kicked him twice in the gut with side karate kicks. The Jaguar put his hands over his eyes and fell into the ring's corner. Nigel beat him with a chain four times before wrapping the chain around his throat and binding him in the corner.

***

"What's going on, mama!" Rebecca pointed at the TV. "Why are they doing that to him?"

Rita stood stiffly. She frowned before pinching her chin.

***

The Rustler Brothers then ran into the ring. They pummeled the bound and chained Jaguar with kicks and punches. The four then fled the ring. Gordon Hanson grabbed Professor Sakamoto. "What is going on here? Turning on your own man like that was worse than Pearl Harbor."

"Pearl Harbor? Te he he." Professor Sakamoto cackled. "It was a smart move."

Sakamoto pointed to his temple. "We destroy four American battleships. The Jaguar? He's a savage with no brain." Sakamoto twirled his finger by his temple. "He no more champion? He no more use to me. I get rid of losers like yesterday's garbage." He grabbed Gordon Hanson's necktie and wiped the sweat from his brow with it. Gordon Hanson pulled his face in disgust.

The Jaguar tore apart the turnbuckle pad. He leaped from the ring and chased away ringside officials before throwing chairs into the ring. He flipped over a table and threw it into the ring. He re-entered the ring and smashed the chairs and tables.

Rita stood stiffly. She put her hands on her hips.

Gordon Hanson broadcasted, "What is going on here? The Jaguar has lost it! He's out of control! He's a crazed, rabid animal! This is a dangerous situation! He may attack someone in the audience."

She jutted her head and glowered at the TV.

The preliminary wrestlers ran into the ring. The Jaguar knocked the first out of the ring with a drop kick. He dispatched the second with a punch. He hurled the third over the top rope.

Gordon Hanson shouted into his microphone, "No one can stop him. No one!" The TV camera panned to Gordon. Someone handed him a slip of paper. Gordon read it aloud, "Oh no! Nigel Earl has the only tranquilizer dart, but he has fled the arena!"

The Jaguar continued his rampage.

"No! No!" Gordon stood with the microphone. "What's this!"

The actor playing the policeman stood on the ring apron with a prop gun.

"They may have to shoot him with a live round! You may hate the Jaguar, but no one wants this! I'm going to have to cut for a commercial break. We can't broadcast what is about to happen."

Rita lurched over and turned off the TV.

"Mama!"

"Got to your room, Rebecca."

"But…"

"No buts!" Rita prodded. "Now!"

Rebecca ran to her room crying. She slammed the door.

Rita collapsed in a chair, lowered her head, and cried.

***

"Wait just a minute!" Gordon shouted. "What's this? Abede is running to the ring. The champion is the only wrestler to have beaten the Jaguar!"

Bart entered the ring. He oscillated his head and made hand gestures that resembled sign language.

"He's not fighting the Jaguar." Gordon paused for effect. "I get it! Abede once joined a lion pride in Africa. He knows big cat language. It looks like he's getting through to the Jaguar!"

The Jaguar returned Abede's gestures before nodding. Both walked out of the ring in separate directions.

"Abede has diffused a deadly situation! Make sure you never miss an episode of '*Big Time Wrestling.*' You never know what you might see. After a word from our sponsor, Crazy Wally's Used Cars, we will be back with more."

***

Al Cohen greeted Buzz by clasping his right hand with both his hands. "Excellent, Buzz! Excellent! You set the foundation for your transition to a face wonderfully!"

"Thanks, Al." Buzz beamed.

Bart entered the room smiling from ear to ear. "What did you think, Al?"

"You're my champion, and you performed like a champion. You're a star, and tonight you were a shining star."

After Al and Bart left the room, Buzz walked over to a pay phone, put a dime in the slot, and dialed Rita's number. She answered after seven rings. "Rita! Quite a show tonight! I'm about to leave. I should reach your place in about ninety minutes."

Rita took a deep breath and wiped away a tear. "I don't want you

154

to come over."

"What?" Buzz felt his heart drop into his gut. "I don't understand."

"I don't want you to come over." She sniffled. "Not now or evermore. Understand this. I am a mother. You are always telling me that The Savage Jaguar is just an act. Tonight, I saw something dangerous in you. What if you lose it with me, or worse, Rebecca?"

"Rita. Please. Tonight was the last…"

"You already know how much Rebecca is attached to you. I need to cut this off now before it gets worse. She wants you to hear her sing at the school pageant. Her schoolmates will see we're together."

"I wear a mask in the ring and on TV. How will they know?"

"Your physique unmasks you. Will you tell Rebecca's classmates you're a trashman?" Rita fought back a tear. "Nobody is buying. Your presence would embarrass Rebecca and set her up for bullying."

Buzz breathed in gasps. His tenor plunged to hadalpelagic depths. His head spun. Speech got trapped in his throat.

"You already got in a bar fight while with me."

"I was defending your honor." Buzz rasped. "He also insulted Bubby and Stephanie."

"Defending my honor by fighting in a bar? You're forgetting that I'm a widow. I was married to a man who put machismo before common sense. He made my life a living Hell, and he was a terrible father." Tears flowed from Rita's eyes. "Rebecca and I were doing fine before you came along. I love you, and Rebecca adores you. But the hurt will fade with time. I'm sorry, I think it best that we no longer see each other." Rita hung up the phone. Five seconds later, she bawled.

"Rita? Rita?" Buzz dropped the receiver, leaving it dangling. He pinched his eyes closed, picked up his kitbag, and left Crazy Wally's silently and quickly.

Chapter 21

A large banner in red letters spelling "Goodbye Mary" was strewn across the Del's Diner ceiling from wall to wall. Red, white, and blue streamers hung from the ceiling. The main jukebox played Patsy Cline's *"Walkin' After Midnight."* The guests cheered the bittersweet moment as Mary cut a chocolate cake. After the guests got a slice, Mary clanged a spoon against a glass.

"I know that you didn't come to hear a speech." Mary wiped a tear from her eye. "I want to tell you all that I love you." The gathering cheered. "Del's Diner is my first real home and all of you are my family. Many of you know that my parents abandoned me as a child. Margie, you are a mother to me, and Del, you're the father I never had. And Rita, my sister. Last but not least, you customers. I can't thank you all enough for your love and support. Tallahassee is not too far away. This is not the last you will see of Mary," she paused for effect, "Boggs."

The gathering cheered and milled around Mary. Rita sat in a corner booth, staring blankly at the festivities. Mary looked over the crowd and spotted her.

"Excuse me." Mary worked her way through the party. "Excuse me." She made it to Rita, sat beside her, and put her arm around her. "What's wrong, darling? I've never seen you like this. I know that you're not crying over me. Is it Buzz?"

Rita failed to hold back tears. "You don't have a daughter. I do. You wouldn't understand."

"Try me." Mary clutched Rita's arms.

"Rebecca's classmates will tease her and bully her if they know that I am with the Savage Jaguar" Rita held up her hands with two fingers in imitation of quotation marks, "And what if he goes savage on me or worse, Rebecca?"

"I just married a wrestler. Never in my life did I think I would find such joy."

The main jukebox played Elvis's *Teddy Bear.*

"Everybody loves Bob both inside and outside the ring. Everybody hates Buzz."

"Certainly not Buzz Artlett, the man. Bob will be the first to tell you that Buzz is well-liked among the other wrestlers. They often play practical jokes on him. Bob says he never loses his temper but laughs and takes it in stride. As for the wrestling fans, I don't know about everybody." Mary braced Rita's shoulders. "More than a few fans admire his athleticism and physique."

"You also forget that I was married to a violent and abusive man. I never," Rita shook her fists, "never want to go through that again."

"You already know, Rita." Mary stroked Rita's hair. "That I have had a string of abusive boyfriends."

"Yes, Mary, I know. You wear your heart on your sleeve; I'm a private person. I don't talk about my late husband. My experience with him was so awful I never dated a man until Buzz."

"We've worked together long enough to know that, Rita." Mary smiled. "Trust the woman's intuition of two ladies that love and care about you. Margie and I have done everything possible to grease the skids in bringing you and Buzz together."

Rita gazed into Mary's green eyes. "You don't know this, but Buzz got into a fight while we were together."

"I heard. Seeing that it was Johnny Durham, he got what he deserved. Buzz, along with Shigeru, Grant, Spence, Clay, and Yuri, play bad guys in the ring but are good guys outside of wrestling. Johnny Durham was a good guy in the ring but an asshole and a bigot in real life. Come on, darling," Mary kissed Rita's forehead. "It's all an act. He loves you and Rebecca."

"You know what I mean." Rita lowered her head. "That barfight was no act, and he did it right in front of me."

"Well, Bob beat up a motorcycle gang leader while we were together. A real man does what a real man must do. He will defend his woman's honor while being gentle with her. Buzz has only been kind to you, right?"

"Yes."

"Grant Irons looks and acts like a Neanderthal in the ring, but he's a gentleman outside the ring." Mary nodded. "He's smarter and better educated than anyone I know, and he even teaches a college class."

"Buzz is no college professor. Wrestling and fighting is all he knows."

"It's not all he will ever do. He's a smart man with a college degree. Moreover, Grant Irons is happily married with three kids." Mary beamed. "I can only imagine what gorgeous kids you and Buzz will have."

"Stop it, Mary!" Rita furrowed her brow and tensed her lips. "I'm sorry, Mary." Rita took a deep breath. "I know you mean well. I was married to a handsome man, that's the only good thing I can say about him, and he made me miserable. I already have a beautiful daughter." Rita put her hand on Mary's arm. "I am thrilled you found what you're looking for. Let me be. I'll get over this. God will comfort me." Rita half smiled. "Don't let me be a party pooper. Go have fun."

Mary dropped her head.

"Before you go," Rita raised Mary's head with her forefinger. "I second what you said in your toast. You are a sister to me, and I love you."

Mary beamed, "I love you too, sis."

Mary and Rita hugged.

Mary went back to the party. Margie came over to Rita. Margie clasped her hands and kissed her forehead. She then rejoined the party. Rita continued to sit in the corner booth. Its private jukebox played Jo Stafford's *"Haunted Heart."*

***

Buzz silently packed his kitbag and walked toward the dressing room exit.

"Not so fast, buddy." Steve Samson blocked his way. His brother Shaun stood next to him. "We can't let you sulk and brood. You're coming with us. There's someone who wants to meet you. You're his favorite wrestler."

"Come on, guys." Buzz pushed past them. "How is meeting a mark going to cheer me up?"

"He's more than a mark, buddy." Shaun grabbed Buzz's arm. "Trust me."

"Trust me?" Buzz opened his hands. "I can trust you to put a rattlesnake in my kitbag as a rib. But that's as far as it goes with you two." Buzz laughed.

"Come Buzz," Steve laughed and touched his shoulder. "You can't just go to your hotel room and brood. You gotta get out and meet people."

"The girls flock to you two like they do movie stars and rock and roll stars. Those aren't the girls I'm looking for." Buzz started walking. "Leave me alone. I'll be fine."

"Hey!" Shaun grabbed Buzz's kitbag. "We're not hooking you up with no arena rats." Shaun grinned. "You're coming with us."

Buzz grabbed his kit bag. He focused on Steve and Shaun. They looked relaxed. They smiled gently at him. Buzz released his grip on his kitbag. "If you guys say so." Buzz chuckled. "Just don't expect a tip for carrying my bag."

***

159

Steve Samson drove his '56 Cadillac Coupe Deville southbound on US Route 41. Buzz rode beside him while Shaun sat in the back. Steve soon reached Tampa's Central Avenue district. "I hope it's kayfabe to be seen with you," Buzz alighted the car, "especially without a mask. You guys are famous enough as it is, and everybody else knows that only professional wrestlers wear long hair like yours."

"Let me do a switcheroo on the words to a song." Steve sang, 'Wrestlers rush in where white men fear to go, but white men never hear great music, so how are they to know?"

"As far as great music goes," Buzz chuckled. "Your singing doesn't qualify. Not that I'm any better, Rita won't even let me sing to her." Buzz dropped his head.

***

"Here we are," Steve pointed. "The Cotton Club."

"Look at the line," Buzz stopped walking, "How are we going to get in? Moreover, it looks like we're going to be the only white people."

"What are you afraid of? They don't bite. Besides, they're dressed to the nines. We'll get in." Shaun grinned. "Solomon Burke is the headliner. You expected less than a full house? He's only nineteen. You gotta hear him. Some still consider him up and coming. When you see and hear him, you will agree that he's great now and will only get better."

"You're wrong about something else, too." Steve smiled conspiratorially. "We won't be the only white guys. A big-time white guy is waiting to meet you." Steve slapped Buzz's shoulder. "You so happen to be his favorite wrestler." Steve raised his palms. "Don't worry about not wearing your mask. He's kayfabe."

As Steve, Shaun, and Buzz walked to the front of the line, several girls screamed, broke the queue, and ran over to touch Steve and Shaun. A large black man with a knife scar greeted them. Steve said,

"We're a guest of 'you know who.'"

"I know he's expecting you two." The doorman pointed at Buzz. "But who is he?"

"He's our trashman." Shaun smiled. "Trust me. Our man wants to see him."

"When a white guy says, 'trust me,' to a black man, it often means, 'screw you.'" The bouncer laughed. "My man said you might be bringing a guest." He stepped aside and head motioned for them to enter.

The dimly lit club had a large stage and a dance floor surrounded by tables. Two long bars manned by four busy bartenders were on each side of the club. On stage, a local harmony group sang their interpretation of the *Ink Spots, "If I Didn't Care."* Several couples slow-danced.

Steve, Shaun, and Buzz weaved through the crowded nightclub. A man with a pencil mustache and a white jacket with a black bow tie led them to a private lounge. A stout young Black man with a wide crown, sharp jawline, and pointed chin sat in a padded armchair. A young white man sat beside him. He stood, "Steve, Shaun, you brought him. I never saw him without his mask. He's not what I expected, but I can see by his body that he is The Jaguar."

He looked to Buzz as around six feet tall with a trim, athletic build. He wore his hair in a slicked-back pompadour with a pronounced quiff, longer on top, styled upwards and back. His confident smile was asymmetric enough to be both attractive and unique. "You're my favorite wrestler." He extended his hand.

Buzz's eyes opened wide; his mouth formed a circle, "You're, You're…"

"Elvis Presley," he extended his hand. "I'm thrilled to meet you, sir."

Buzz and Elvis shook hands.

Steve Samson cuffed Buzz's shoulder. "I told you I wasn't introducing you to just another mark."

"Mark?" Elvis chuckled. "I know you guys only fake fight," Elvis smirked. "But you put on a great show. It's worth every dime. I've been a fan my entire life. And you," Elvis placed his hand on Buzz's shoulder, "are my all-time favorite."

"You're the best singer in the world." Buzz beamed.

"Thank you very much for saying that. But I'm not even the best singer in the room." Elvis chuckled. "I want you to meet Mr. Solomon Burke." Elvis nodded to the young black man who sat beside him.

Solomon Burke stood and shook hands with Buzz.

"Steve and Shaun tell me that your father is a Navy officer, and you lived in Asia. They also told me that you learned their martial arts." Elvis smiled. "It looks fun and useful. Can you teach me some techniques? I'm thinking of mixing it into my stage routine."

"Sure. Anytime."

"How about now?"

"Okay. Start with this." Buzz stood sideways. He put the edge of his right hand against his abdomen and held his left arm outward at a thirty-five-degree angle with his hand open. "Turn your hips, retract your left hand, and strike, keeping your elbow in, with your right."

Elvis mirrored Buzz's move.

"You're a natural, Elvis!"

"When I include it in my next show, you can tell everyone you taught me."

"Are you going to perform tonight?"

"I wish I could, but I can't." Elvis nodded to Solomon. "He's better than me, so I don't want to look bad."

Solomon Burke chuckled.

"Well," Elvis put his hand on Solomon Burke's shoulder, "I'm not as good as him, but, well, right now, I am more famous. If I go out first, I may take some of his electricity. If I go on after him, people may talk about me instead. As much as I'd like to sing for the Cotton Club, tonight is Solomon's night."

The pencil-mustached man in the white jacket and black tie peered through the door. "You're on in five minutes, Mr. Burke."

"Break a leg, Solomon. Okay, Steve, Shaun, and Buzz let's go up to a private balcony and watch a true master perform. I leave for Memphis after tonight." Elvis beamed. "I had the Colonel check the TV Guide. Your next show will be on Memphis TV. I'll be watching."

***

Kathryn Watkins set up her portable keyboard in the Mendez living room.

Rita went to Rebecca's bedroom, "Miss Watkins is here. It's time for your singing lesson."

"No!" Rebecca stood and folded her arms over her chest. "I'm not coming out, and I'm not going to sing. Not now, never!"

"You come out right now!" Rita marched into Rebecca's room. "Miss Watkins is here, and you're going to sing!"

"No, I'm not!" Rebecca jutted her jaw. "And you can't make me."

Kathryn clasped Rita's arm. "It's okay. We can't force her to sing. Singing must be joyous. It must come from the heart. If you force her now, she won't enjoy singing in the future and may stop as soon as you let up on her." Kathryn faced Rita. "Give her time to get over whatever is bothering her. I am sure she will want to sing again. She's wonderfully talented, and I can tell she enjoys singing. Let's not do anything to risk it."

After Kathryn left, Rita sat on her couch and wept.

163

Chapter 22

Al Cohen met with Bart, Shigeru, Spence, and Clay in the Ft. Lauderdale, Florida, War Memorial Auditorium dressing room. "This is act two." Al steepled his fingers and placed his hands on a table. "We performed act one in an ad hoc TV studio with a controlled audience. Tonight, we go live. We're expecting over two thousand people. After we pull this off, the crowd will be livid. Gordon," Al pointed at Gordon Hanson. "I signed a deal with ABC to broadcast tonight's bill throughout the Southeast, Memphis, as well as New York City and Philadelphia. I think you know what that means for your career."

"How many more people will see me get my pants pulled down?" Bart pursed his lips.

"You're an ordained minister, right?

"Yes."

"I may be Jewish, but I know and respect the New Testament." Al spread his arms. "Did not Jesus say, 'He who humbles himself will be exalted?' Everyone is talking about act I from Wally Garner's showroom. Do this for me tonight, and the stage is set for you to be on national TV and in front of a 60,000-strong live audience as a World Champion winning yet another belt." Al opened a folder. "Shigeru, Spence, Clay, tonight you will act as nasty and dirty as it gets. Playing the heal is fun. Have fun with this, and it will go over better. And, of course, a touch of sadism will rile the marks up even more."

***

Rita stood by her front door. "Rebecca, I'm leaving for work now. Papi will take care of you. You can play outside, play with your toys, or watch children's shows on TV." Rita prodded. "You are forbidden to watch wrestling."

Rebecca slid a toy horse on wheels across the room. "Okay, mama."

"I'll miss you, honey." Rita kissed her forehead. "I love you."

"I love you too, Mama."

***

The house lights were turned off. The electric anticipation of the crowd sparkled. It surged as a spotlight hit the dressing room exit portal. The sound system played Johhny Cash's *"Folsom Prison Blues."* The crowd booed and hissed as Professor Sakamoto led Biff Rustler to the ring. Biff climbed into the ring and cracked his whip at the audience. Professor Sakamoto worked the crowd on the other side of the ring. The music stopped, and the houselights went off.

The crowd stood and cheered in the darkness. Suddenly, the spotlight hit the exit portal. The sound system played the original Gallotone label recording of Miriam Makeba's *"Pata Pata."* Strobe lights flashed on Adebe as he approached the ring and climbed into it.

Ding! Ding! Ding! The ring announcer spoke into a microphone, "Ladies and Gentlemen. The moment you've all been waiting for, our main event of the evening…"

***

Rebecca heard snoring reverberate off the walls. Her grandfather had passed out in his easy chair. A tequila bottle sat on the floor. *'You are forbidden to watch wrestling,'* Rebecca's mind heard her mother's voice and pictured her mother's image. Rebecca glanced at the TV. A *Lone Ranger* rerun was on. She turned the dial, hoping to find a Bugs Bunny, Tom and Jerry, or Mighty Mouse cartoon. She briefly stopped dialing, "…The American Federation of Wrestling World Championship. This contest is one fall to a finish. In this corner, your challenger, accompanied by his manager, Professor Sakamoto. He hails from Laramie, Wyoming, weighing in at 265 pounds, Biff

165

Rustler." Biff cracked his whip. "And in this corner," the ring announcer paused so that the crowd could cheer. "He comes all the way from Kenya, Africa, weighing in at 435 pounds, Adebe the African Lion." The fans cheered uproariously. Everyone except Biff, Adebe, and the referee left the ring.

'Ding.'

Rebecca's nerves jittered as she stepped back. She looked both ways, checked to ensure her grandfather slept, and returned her gaze to the TV. Biff Rustler charged across the ring. Adebe planted his feet and extended his torso. Biff bounced off him and fell on his buttocks. He slammed the mat with his fists as the crowd laughed at him. He stood and propelled himself off the ropes. He again hit Adebe as if crashing into an immovable barricade. He again fell on his buttocks to the derision of the crowd. Professor Sakamoto called him over to the corner. He made certain the crowd saw him smirk and look in each direction. Sakamoto then slipped Biff a foreign object resembling a white tape-covered bottle opener. Biff struck Abede in the throat with it. Abede fell to his knees while clutching his throat. Biff hid the object in his tights. The referee confronted him. Biff held up his open hands. The fans screamed and pointed to the hidden object. The referee examined Biff's hands and ordered the match to continue. Biff again struck Adebe in the throat with the object. Adebe again clutched his throat."

Biff backed away and tossed the foreign object to Sakamoto.

"No fair! No fair!" Rebecca yelled at the TV.

This time the referee pat searched Biff and signaled that he found nothing.

Biff then flung Adebe into the ropes and clotheslined him on the rebound. Abede fell on his butt. Biff put him in a headlock and raked his knuckles over his eyes. Abede flopped around the ring while massaging his eyes. Biff beamed at the audience and slapped his palms together three times in an up-and-down motion. He lifted

Adebe by the hair, kneed him in the gut, and started punching him. Rather than hurt him, each punch seemed to energize Adebe. After taking four punches, Adebe smirked and brandished his right fist.

Biff begged for mercy.

"Punch him!" Rebecca yelled at the TV. "Punch him!"

Adebe reared back and hit Biff with a forearm. Biff staggered back into the ring corner. Adebe struck him twice with forearms to the chest. He grabbed Biff's arm and flung him into the ropes. Biff rebounded into Adebe's arms. He power-slammed him and covered him for the pin. The referee slapped the mat twice. He lifted his arm for the final count.

Gordon Hanson broadcasted, "Oh no! What's going on here? Cletus and Sakamoto have entered the ring."

"Stop them!" Rebecca pointed at the TV. "They're cheating!"

"No!" the broadcaster shouted. "Cletus stomped Adebe's head. Sakamoto is striking him with karate kicks! The referee has just signaled for a disqualification."

'*Ding! Ding! Ding!*'

"The referee is standing in front of Cletus. Can the referee stop further mayhem? Oh no! Cletus just tossed him from the ring. Cletus and Sakamoto are mercilessly kicking Abede. Abede is climbing to his feet! Oh, will they pay!"

"Yeah, Bubby! Get them!" Rebecca yelled at the TV. "Give it to 'em."

"Oh no!" Gordon broadcasted. "Biff just lassoed Abede. He's pulling him to the ropes. What's this? Sakamoto and Cletus locked Adebe's arms between the second and third ropes! They're taking turns punching him in the gut! The crowd is in a frenzy. How much lower will the Rustlers and Sakamoto stoop?"

"Free yourself, Bubby!" Rebecca jumped up and down. "Free yourself!"

"Oh no! What's this? Biff Rustler has Adebe's traditional lion headdress! No! No! It can't be! Biff is tearing it to shreds! No! He's rubbing it in Adebe's face! This is disgusting! This is despicable! Oh, will you get a load of Sakamoto's laughter? This is the most evil and depraved act I have ever witnessed in over ten years as a wrestling announcer!"

"No!" Rebecca burst into tears. She turned off the TV and ran to her room. She buried her face in her pillow and bawled.

Adebe freed himself from the ropes. Biff threw his tattered headdress in his face. Biff, Cletus, and Sakamoto fled to the safety of their dressing room.

Adebe picked up the remains of his headdress, leaned back, and screamed. As he left the ring, Gordon Hanson stopped him, "Abede, I know you're too angry to talk, but can you say something?"

"Those sons of (a loud bleep covered his word). This was my traditional headdress." Adebe shoved the remains into the camera. "Now look at it. The Rustlers and Sakamoto have dishonored me, my ancestors, and my people! There's gonna be payback! Big-time payback! I am not only going to punish them physically, but I'm going to take what they value most. Their championship belts!"

"You're a mighty warrior, Abede. But you can't do it by yourself."

"That's right, Gordon. I have been training a tag team partner. We are going to make them pay! Next week at the Miami Beach Auditorium, I will introduce him. Vengeance will be ours!"

"The matches and Adebe's announcement will be telecast live!" Gordon held his microphone. "You can tune in and find out. Better yet, come to Miami Beach and see it live. Hurry. Tickets will go fast. Stay tuned. First, a word from our sponsor. Crazy Wally's Used Cars."

Chapter 23

Pedro Mendez sat in his armchair holding a tambourine. Rebecca sat on the couch with her mother. Rebecca held red, white, and green maracas in each hand. Rita rested a guitar on her knee.

"Mama, let's sing Guantanamera."

"Sure, Rebecca. It's a Cuban folk song written in the guajira style. But we sing it in Mexico." Rita smiled and strummed the opening chords on her guitar. Pedro rapped his tambourine on his leg while Rebecca shook her maracas. They sang,

"Guantanamera

Guajira guantanamera

Guantanamera

Guajira guantanamera

Guantanamera

Guajira guantanamera

Guantanamera

Guajira guantanamera

Con los pobres de la tierra

Quiero yo mi suerte echar

Con los pobres de la tierra

Quiero yo mi suerte echar

El arroyo de la sierra

Me complace más que el mar

Guantanamera Guajira guantanamera Guantanamera Guajira guantanamera."

Rita closed her eyes and pictured Buzz. She then spoke the lyrics in English while imagining Buzz speaking. As she spoke, Pedro and Rebecca sang the chorus in Spanish.

"I am a sincere man

From the land of the palm trees.

And before dying I want to

share my poems from my soul.

My poems are soft green;

My poems are also flaming crimson.

My poems are like a wounded fawn seeking refuge in the forest.

With the poor people of the Earth, I want to share my faith.

The streams of the mountains please me more than the sea."

Rita fought back tears. A lump formed in her throat. She dropped her head and cried.

"It's okay, Mama." Rebecca put her arm around her mother. "It's okay." Rebecca cried with her.Pedro placed his tambourine on his lap and stared straight ahead.

***

Buzz paced back and forth in the Hollywood, Florida, Sportatorium's dressing room, sometimes stopping to stare at the phone.

Frankie Williamson walked up to him. "Your actions speak for itself. You're antonado. Besotted. Enamorarse perdidamente! That's okay. It's macho to love a woman with a manly passion. We're more than amigos. We're Hermanos. Brothers. Hable conmigo."

Buzz looked around and pursed his lips. "Okay. I'll tell you. My savage jaguar act embarrasses her, and now she's afraid of me. She doesn't want any of her daughter's acquaintances to know their mother is dating a wrestler in general and the Savage Jaguar in particular. She also worries I might flip the switch and act like the Jaguar in real life."

"We protect the business with kayfabe. But most people have figured us out. Look at me. If wrestling were real, I would be dead a hundred times over." Frankie chuckled. "But I play my role as a jobber; you play yours as a headliner."

"I've explained it to her. Bubby's explained it. And Bobby's explained it. I guess my last performance was too much for her. It's not just Rita that I've lost. Her little daughter is adorable. I miss her. I'm worried that I may never see her again."

"I'm sure that they both miss you." Frankie grinned. "I may be a lousy wrestler, and I may be no guapo like you. But I do know my muchachas. Don't call her just yet. You say she's afraid you might be the uncontrollable savage Jaguar? Show her self-control by not calling. Let her miss you." Frankie pointed upward. "But don't wait too long."

"First of all, Frankie, the marks may think you're a lousy wrestler because they always see you lose. You may think you're a lousy wrestler. But the people that count know that you're a professional. You do your job, and you do it well. Therefore, I trust you as a hombre who can advise me with the muchachas. I'm all ears." Buzz cupped his right ear. "When do I call her."

"Seeing that you're my brother, I got a plan." Frankie beamed. "Wait until after the Miami show. It's going to be big. Even if she doesn't watch it on TV, word will get back to her. Here's what we're going to do. Call Margie at the diner. Find out what time Rita gets off work. Margie believes in you, so I'm sure she'll tell you. Rita will be riding home. I'm amigos con Ricardo Sugar, the lead disc jockey for America's strongest Spanish radio station."

"Yes, Frankie." Buzz smiled and raised his arms. "I know that she listens to his show."

"Tell me what time she'll be riding home. I will call Ricardo and have him dedicate a romantic song to Rita in your name. Wait an hour or two. Then show up at her front door with a bouquet of roses."

"You think that will work?" Buzz shrugged.

"Well, if I steer you wrong." Frankie pursed his lips. "Maybe you beat the merde out of me for real."

"If I ever intended to beat the shit out of you." Buzz slapped Frankie's shoulder. "I would have done it long ago, after one of the many ribs you've played on me. Besides, I don't have a plan, so what choice do I have? Thanks, brother."

"No es nada."

Chapter 24

Two beefy men sat at a booth in Del's diner. They had placed their white Western hats on the table. "We'll have the chile con carne. Is it as hot as you?"

Rita wrote down their order without changing her expression. "I'll have Del add extra spice."

Before he could respond with, *'You're everything nice.'* Rita walked away and hooked their order on the carousel by Delbert's station. Margie winced. *'Professional as always. Yet she's lost her flair.'*

Rita brought Rebecca to work as today was Saturday and Pedro had to work. She sat in the Del's Diner backroom. She turned the TV dial past a game show and a rerun of *'Sky King,'* stopping on hearing Gordon Hanson's voice. "Welcome to Big Time Wrestling. Last week, Professor Sakamoto and the Rustler Brothers committed the most atrocious, disgusting, and despicable act in wrestling history. At the end of this broadcast, Adebe the African Lion will introduce his new tag team partner. Adebe has sworn revenge on Sakamoto and the Rustlers. His new tag team partner will be his battle ally."

The Miami Beach Auditorium matches were spirited. Beer Barrel Bobby treated the audience to near-beer before his contest with Spider Nel. Grant "The Beast" Irons created his usual bedlam during his match with Shaun Samson. The crowd's anger at the Rustler Brothers was palpable as they wrestled the Van der Westhuizen Brothers. The main event pitting Steve Samson against Yuri the Red invigorated the crowd. Nevertheless, the buzz was for the big announcement.

Rita used her break from waitressing to check on her daughter. "Are you watching wrestling again?"

"Mama, look!" Rebecca pointed to the TV. "It's Bubby! He's

going to tell us his tag team partner to get back at those terrible Rustler Brothers."

"You met Spence Carter, and you know he's a nice guy. You also know I don't want you to watch wrestling." Rita put her hand on Rebecca's shoulder. "Turn it off."

***

The arena silenced as Al Cohen and Bart Johnson stood in the ring. Gordon Hanson held the microphone up to Bart in character and accent as Adebe from Kenya. "Last week, Professor Sakamoto and the Rustler Brothers dishonored me, my ancestors, and my people."

Al Cohen held up a sheet of paper and spoke into the microphone. "Right here is an open contract signed by Professor Sakamoto and the Rustler Brothers. They are obligated to put their tag team title on the line. Three weeks from today, the fight will take place in Miami. Only this one is so big that we have booked Burke Stadium, home of the Orange Bowl football game."

The crowd roared.

"I want to fight Professor Sakamoto, Biff Rustler, and Cletus Rustler one by one and punish them for what they did to me. But I want to inflict more than just physical pain. I want to take from them what they cherish most." Adebe paused for effect. "Their tag team title!"

The crowd yelled, "Adebe! Adebe! Adebe!"

***

"If you won't turn it off," Rita reached for the dial, "I will."

"No, Mama!" Rebecca raised her hands. "Please let me see who's gonna be Bubby's new tag team partner."

Rita sighed. "Oh, okay." She watched with her hands on her hips. "But afterward, you're watching something else."

174

Gordon Hanson handed the microphone to Al Cohen. "Adebe. The wrestling world doesn't want to want any longer. Who is your new tag team partner?"

"In Africa, we measure intelligence by jungle savvy, not diplomas. No one in the wrestling world has more jungle savvy than my new partner. Together, we will make Sakamoto and the Rustlers pay. Introducing my new tag team partner and future co-holder of the American Federation of Wrestling World Tag Team Championship…"

The house lights extinguished. A spotlight shined on the dressing room exit portal.

The crowd erupted.

The Jaguar sprinted toward the ring. He vaulted over the top rope. His mask no longer had the straggly hair and beard. Al Cohen raised the Jaguar and Abede's arms. He then spoke, "In just ten days, The Jaguar has learned to speak English." He held the microphone to the Jaguar.

"Professor Sakamoto withheld me from civilization, then he turned on me like a viper. Adebe's fight is my fight, too." He paused for the fan's ovation. "I learned about the big war. I also learned that America and Japan are now friends. But Sakamoto still wants war. Well, Sakamoto, you should be careful of what you wish for, because, three weeks from tonight, in the ring at Burke Stadium, you and the Rustlers are getting it!" The Jaguar brandished his right fist. "War!"

Gordon Hanson spoke. "There you have it! Three weeks from tonight! The Big Cats against the Rustler Brothers. If you can't drive to Miami, Crazy Wally has chartered buses from his Orlando, Tampa, and Palm Beach dealerships to Burke Stadium. All qualified buyers who test drive a used car with Wally can ride to Miami for free. Anyone who buys their wrestling ticket from Crazy Wally gets, now this is going to sound insane, two dollars off face value. Why is

Wally doing this? Because he's crazy. You'd be crazy too to pass on his offer."

***

Rita smiled wide enough for the overhead light to shine on her teeth.

***

"Mom! Dad!" Arnie Martin pointed at the TV. "Come quickly!"

"What is it, Arnie?" Gerald Martin and his wife Susan rushed into their living room. "That's him!" Arnie pointed to wrestling on TV. "The Jaguar! He's the one who saved me from the river!"

"Are you sure?" Sheriff Martin asked.

"I'm sure, I'm sure! That's his muscles, and that's his voice! I'll never forget!"

Sheriff Martin glanced at his wife and his son. "You know something, Arnie?" He pinched his chin. "It's starting to make sense. Now I understand why he didn't want you to describe his face. I want to meet this man. When is the next wrestling?"

"They're wrestling in Ocala next Friday."

"Would you like to go?"

"Yeah! That would be coolsville!"

Chapter 25

Pedro Mendez waited by Del's Diner's rear entrance in his '46 Ford 59c pickup truck. Rita smiled and waved to him on exiting the diner. He leaned across the truck's bench seat and opened the passenger side door.

"Hola Papi." Rita boarded the truck.

Although grit and sweat clung to Pedro's weatherworn face, seeing Rita made him smile.

"Hola, Mija." Pedro pulled out of the parking lot and onto the main road en route to Rebecca's school. He had the radio tuned to Ricardo Sugar's Latin music program.

"Buenes dia America. Ricardo Sugar transmitiendo desde Miami. Mi gringo amigo, Buzz, pide esta canción para su amor Rita. Álvaro Carrillo y *Saber A Mi*.

Pedro felt energized, "Tu hombre tiene grandes musculos y un gran corazon." He beamed.

Rita pressed her hand over her heart. The tingling spread throughout her, amplifying each romantic note and lyric. For the rest of the ride to Rebecca's school, Rita stared out the window, half expecting the car to take off like a jet.

***

Buzz and Frankie Williamson sat at a table in Horrible Hank's Tavern on a lonely stretch of State Road 27 between Ocala and Autumn, Florida. The tavern boasted a roller derby motif. Two picture-framed Florida Bombers roller derby jerseys, one front and the other back, hung on the wall behind the bar. A pair of white, high-ankle roller skates sat in a glass case at the tavern's near corner; and three roller derby "jammer" helmets were displayed on a hat rack. A large, framed photograph of the tavern owner in roller derby action adorned the wall by the entrance. A pitcher of Schlitz Beer

177

and a Sony TR-69 transistor radio sat on Buzz and Frankies' table.

"Suguru wasn't kidding about this radio." Buzz sipped his beer. "It blasts."

"Listen!" Frankie pointed to the radio. They heard Ricardo Sugar dedicate Alvaro Carrillo's "Saber a mi" to Rita in Buzz's name. "See! I told you I take care of mi amigos." Frankie tapped his beer mug to Buzz's mug. "You know what to do next."

***

Rita sprung from her father's truck. "Rebecca!" She ran up and hugged her daughter, picked her up, and carried her back to the truck. Rebecca laughed. The three sat together on the pick-up truck's bench seat. "Are you still sad, Rebecca?"

"A little bit," Rebecca lowered her head.

Rita clasped her daughter's hand. "I hope that will change."

***

Buzz pulled over to a roadside kiosk. He found what he was looking for. He glanced at his watch. Perfect timing. He would reach Autumn, Florida, in little more than an hour.

***

After tucking Rebecca into her bed, Rita sat on her couch and sipped a glass of Casa Madero wine by candlelight. She placed her glass on a side table, steepled her hands, closed her eyes, and prayed. After fidgeting with her watch, she looked upward, inhaled deeply, and sipped more wine. She stood, paced to her record player, looked at the telephone, and walked over to gaze out the window. Sitting back down, she stared at the flickering candlelight and got lost in thought.

***

Buzz turned onto Grimsby Lane. His radio played the Five Satins 'To The Aisle.' '1006, 1008, 1010,' He pulled into the Mendez

178

driveway. Bracing the steering wheel, he said aloud. "This is it, Buzz. It's now or never." He walked up to the front door, waited five seconds, and gently rapped on the door.

Rita sprung to her feet and answered the door. Her heart skipped a beat before shifting into overdrive. Buzz waited with a dozen roses. Rita cracked a smile. She took the roses and buried her nose in them. "Come in. Wait a minute." She strolled to the kitchen and returned with the roses in a water-filled vase. After placing them on a table, she turned on her record player. A stack of 45 RPM discs waited on the spindle. "Buzz." Rita put her arms around his neck. She waited for the sound of the disc dropping onto the platter. "Will you dance with me?" Her phonograph played Alvaro Carrillo's "Saber A Mi."

Buzz pulled her closer to him and held her tight. She rested her chin on his shoulder and pressed her cheek to his cheek as they swayed. After the record finished, they stared into each other's eyes. Another disc dropped onto the platter. The Belmont's rendition of Roger's and Hart's "Where or When" played.

"It seems we stood and talked like this before,

We looked at each other in the same way then,

But I can't remember where or when.

The clothes you're wearing are the clothes you wore.

The smile you are smiling, you were smiling then.

But I can't remember where or when."

A force beyond the laws of gravity pressed Buzz and Rita's bodies even closer together. They looked at each other and smiled as never before. They kissed. Their tongues mingled in synch with the music. They didn't stop kissing until the record finished.

"Buzz?"

"Yes, my love."

"Can you do one little thing for me?"

"I would move a mountain for you."

"Just a little thing." Rita chuckled. "Tomorrow morning..."

"Yes," Buzz moved his hands to her lower back and pulled her closer.

"I'm not ready for Rebecca to walk in on us." Rita winked. "So, can you sneak out before she wakes up, get some takeaway breakfast for us, and then come back and dine with us?"

Buzz picked up Rita and cradled her. She put her hand behind his head and pulled him closer. They kissed in gushing pulses as Buzz carried her to her bedroom.

The phonograph now played "El Reloz" by Sunny Ozuna and the Sunliners.

***

Rebbeca and Rita sat at the breakfast table. Pedro had already left for another hot day of agricultural work. They heard knocking on the door. "Will you see who it is?" Rita grinned.

Rebecca got up and opened the door. "Buzz!" She jumped up and down. "Mama! It's Buzz!" She ran over to her mother. "Look! He brought breakfast!"

"Don't be rude, honey." Rita beamed. "Invite him in."

Rebecca ran over to Buzz, took him by the hand, and pulled him toward their kitchen table.

Buzz placed the takeaway containers on the table. "I got some huevos rancheros and fresh cantaloup. And look at what I bought just for you." He held up a box of *Rice Krispies* and shook it. "Snap, crackle, pop. It comes with a prize." He handed her the box. "Why don't you see what it is?"

Rebecca rifled through the cereal box. "Wow! Look at this prize! It looks expensive!" Rebecca held up a gold ring with a two-carat diamond.

"Oops." Buzz took the ring from Rebecca. "That prize is for your mother."

Rita gasped. "Is that?" She tried to smile, but her face froze.

Buzz slipped the ring onto her finger.

Rita held the diamond up to her eyes. The rising sun sparkled from its fifty-eight-facet, round cut. She smiled brighter than the sun and diamond combined. "Yes! Yes! Yes!"

"Mama! Mama!" Rebecca ran over and clutched her mother's arm. 'Did Buzz just?"

"Yes! Rebecca! Yes"

"Daddy!" Rebecca ran to Buzz and embraced him.

Chapter 26

Rita and Rebecca waited outside the Ocala, Florida, Marion Theatre dressing room. The Jaguar had finished his first match as a face. His opponent, Spider Nel, performed professionally as a villain. His ability and willingness to sell Buzz's acrobatics enhanced his transition to a crowd favorite. Buzz left the dressing room wearing a navy-blue sports shirt and matching slacks. A plain white mask hid his identity.

"Daddy!" Rebbeca ran up to Buzz. He picked her up and held her with his left arm. He held Rita's hand with his free hand.

A uniformed police officer appeared. He pointed at Buzz. "Were you in Manatee County on September 9th?"

Rita blanched. Rebecca had to fight her bladder.

A twelve-year-old boy and his mother followed the policeman.

"Arnie?" Buzz smiled. "Is that you? I see you're high and dry. I hope you stopped climbing tree branches over flooded rivers."

"I told you he wasn't a convict." Arnie grabbed his father's arm and pointed at Buzz. "I told you it was him!"

"I'm Sheriff Gerry Martin. Arnie's father." He shook Buzz's hand. "You will never know the lengths I went to find you. I'm thrilled to finally thank you in person for saving my boy's life."

"I'm Suzanne Martin." She shook Buzz's hand. "Arnie's mother. I thank you from the bottom of my heart."

"I'm not the one to thank. It was divine providence. I just happened to be in the right place at the right time." Buzz nodded to them. "This is my fiancé Rita and my soon-to-be-adaptive daughter, Rebecca."

"Buzz? What's going on here?"

"You may remember when I called you from Sarasota. I

mentioned that I had a little adventure in the Myakka River?" Buzz grinned at Rita. "I told you it was a long story."

"I am pleased to meet you," Suzanne shook Rita's hand. "If not for your fiancé, I would have lost my son." She knelt to Rebecca. "Your soon-to-be daddy is a hero."

"It is a long story." Sheriff Martin put his hand on Arnie's shoulder. "So, let me give you a chance to tell it to your fiancé and soon-to-be daughter under the best possible circumstances. Come to our place outside of Myakka City for lunch tomorrow. Suzzane is going to roast a turkey with all the trimmings. Consider it Thanksgiving in October. Our way of thanking you. Please join us."

Buzz looked at Rita. She nodded.

"I'm not wrestling tomorrow, and Rebecca doesn't have school." Buzz smiled. "Roast turkey with all the trimmings is too much for us to turn down." Buzz laughed. "Well, Arnie here knows what I look like without this thing." Buzz pinched his mask. "But I'll give the rest of you something to look forward to."

***

The Martin property sat on three acres. Three oak trees with intertwining branches and hanging Spanish moss shaded the eighty-five-degree Florida Fall heat. Buzz, Rita, Suzzane, and Gerry sat under the trees, sipping Budweiser from the bottle. Rebecca, Arnie, his ten-year-old brother Dave, and eight-year-old sister Debbie played a noisy game of hide and go-seek tag.

"I love the sound of children playing." Suzzane was slightly underweight. She had short brown hair and wore a yellow sun dress. She smiled at Rita. "And if not for your fiancé, it would be much quieter."

Rita wore a traditional Mexican dress. She blushed. "I'm sure your husband saves many lives in his line of work."

"We perform some dangerous stunts in the wrestling ring." Buzz sipped his beer. "But, unlike you, Sheriff Martin, we never face anyone with guns or knives."

"Call me Sheriff Martin again, and I'll lock you up." He guffawed. "It's Gerry."

Rebecca ran up to the adults. "Mama! I'm having so much fun! You're it, Dave!" Rebecca ran back to the game. "Close your eyes and count to ten. You can't find me."

Rita chuckled. "Thank you for inviting us. Rebecca is an only child. It's been tough for her since her biological father was killed. She doesn't always have playmates."

"It's my pleasure to have you here." Suzzane flicked her hair. "I know I shouldn't say this, but I must." She sipped her beer. "Buzz, you hardly have a face that anyone should cover with a mask."

"Thank you." Buzz smiled. "I'll take that as a compliment.

"It is a compliment. She doesn't say that to just anyone." Gerry laughed. "At least not in front of me."

Suzzane blushed before holding her husband's hand."

"Reasons exist for starting with a mask." Buzz folded his hands. "Professional wrestling is an art. I am still a rookie. I have much to learn about the business, and I have a long way to go before perfecting the art, although no one has ever truly perfected it. The business is always changing, presenting new challenges. We must change with it. Moreover, wrestling fans have long memories. My promoter doesn't want to over-expose me at my present skill level. He wants to wait until I'm more advanced and experienced before reintroducing me without a mask and a different character."

"But Arnie tells me you were a champion as the Savage Jaguar." Suzzane crossed her legs.

"Briefly," Buzz laughed. "All I had to do was gymnastic flips and act wild."

"You seem like a fine young man." Sherrif Martin looked directly at Buzz. "Acting like a savage is beneath you."

"I second that." Rita pursed her lips and nodded.

Buzz laughed and held Rita's hand. "We almost lost each other over it."

"Wrestling in general." The sheriff leaned toward Buzz. "Shouldn't a young man like you aspire to better things?" Gerry steepled his fingers. "And wrestling is like any other sport. It doesn't last forever. Have you made plans for after wrestling?"

"Better? Right now, it's my niche in life. Not everything is the end game. Sometimes, we should stop and enjoy the journey along the way. Wrestling does open other doors. If a door to a better opportunity opens, I am prepared to enter. I am investing part of my earnings for the future." Buzz squeezed Rita's hand and gazed softly into her eyes, "especially now."

Suzanne smiled at Buzz and Rita. "I second that." She chuckled. "Look at you two. I can see that you're both enjoying the journey. Keep that feeling when you reach your destination."

Rita blushed and lowered her head. She then looked into Buzz's eyes. They pecked each other on the lips.

"Gerald." Buzz folded his hands. "What is the highest-ranking law enforcement officer in the United States?"

"The Attorney General."

"A door may open for you, too. Yet right now, are you not doing more for your community and family as a local sheriff?"

Gerald looked at his wife. They smiled at each other.

"You know something?" Gerald laughed. "For a wild savage raised by wild cats and trapped in the deepest reaches of the Amazon jungle, you make a lot of sense."

Buzz, Rita, Suzzane, and Gerry all tapped beer bottles.

Chapter 27

Gordon Hanson stood before a wrestling ring in an empty arena. "Gordon Hanson here at the West Palm Beach Auditorium, just ten days before the biggest event in wrestling history. The Big Cats will challenge the Rustler Brothers for the American Federation of Wrestling World Tag Team Title at Burke Stadium, home of the Orange Bowl football game, in Miami, Florida. Professor Sakamoto and the Rustlers, in costume, joined Gordon on camera. "Professor Sakamoto. The Rustlers have never faced such stiff competition. They're up against a former world champion and the current world champion. Do you have a strategy to keep their belts?"

"You Americans have a saying, 'There's more than one way to skin a cat.' In Japan, we don't eat cats. You want to eat cat? Go to a Chinese Restaurant. I hear it tastes like chicken." Sakamoto guffawed. "In Japan, we eat Beef Tataki, Kobe Beef, and Beef Teppanyaki. My wrestlers rustle up the world's best beef cattle. After we're finished with the Big Cats a week from Saturday, the Chinese can round up what's left of 'em for chicken chow mein."

Biff Rustler grabbed the microphone. "You think we can't beat a phony lion and a fake jaguar?" Biff twirled his lasso, "Last week, my brother and I lassoed a thousand-pound grizzly bear, ate him for lunch, and, afterward, made a rug out of him."

Cletus cracked his whip. "After next Saturday night, while you people eat chicken chow mein, we'll be enjoying our new lion and jaguar rugs."

Sakamoto and the Rustlers departed. Adebe and The Jaguar took their place. Adebe wore his new lion regalia and spoke in his faux Kenyan accent. "A week from Saturday will be more than a wrestling match. It will be more than a war. It will be personal. I am going to avenge my people and my heritage. Sakamoto, you and the Rustlers will pay like no one has ever paid." Adebe looked sternly at the camera and prodded.

"Each day, I learn more about civilization." The Jaguar wore his mask sans long hair and beard. "I had encountered missionaries while living deep in the jungle. Professor Sakamoto is what they taught us about Judas. Judas hanged himself. If you and the Rustlers knew what Adebe and I have in store for you, you three would do likewise."

Gordon spoke, "Stay tuned for a word from our sponsor."

Al Cohen approached them. "Excellent!" He applauded.

"You're not kidding, Al." Spence cuffed Bart on the arm. "This one had me worrying." He laughed.

"Yes, Spence. Not only that, but I will have our promo go national. That leads to my big news. The live feed or film of our big event will be broadcast throughout most of the nation. We have already sold over 30,000 tickets and counting."

Sakamoto and the wrestlers shook hands with Al before departing for the dressing room. Al grabbed Buzz by the arm, "Great news, Buzz, my contacts are expediting your adoption of Rebecca. When you and Rita are legally married, it will happen."

***

The TV feed cut to a pre-recorded commercial taped at Crazy Wally's Used Car showroom in Tampa, Florida. Frankie Williamson and Barry Howard flanked Wally Garner. "Crazy Wally here to tell you about my crazy new offer. I am already crazy enough to charter buses to take any qualified buyer test-driving one of my certified pre-owned vehicles for a free ride to Burke Stadium in Miami. I am already crazy enough to chip in two dollars for every wrestling ticket you purchase at one of my dealerships. If you come to my Tampa showroom on the morning of the matches, wrestler Frankie Williamson will ride the bus with you! Come to the Orlando showroom and ride with Barry Howard. Why am I doing this?

Because I'm crazy and you would be too if you pass on this one owner, low mileage, '55 Pontiac Chieftain Coupe.

***

Buzz pulled off his mask as he entered the dressing room.

"Here comes Loverboy," Steve greeted him first.

"I saved this just for you." Bobby Boggs handed Buzz the toy bowling ball, plastic chain, and toy handcuffs."

"We don't have any champagne." Trevor Van der Westhuisen moved beside Buzz.

"But we do have The Champagne of Beers." Leslie Van der Westhuisen stood on Buzz's other side. The brothers poured Miller High Life beer over him.

"All right." Buzz laughed and covered his head. "Enough out of you guys." He walked over to a vacant locker next to Frankie Williamson.

"Hola Mi Amigo." Frankie smiled. "Si, I told you I know my Spanish muchachas." He put his hand on Buzz's shoulder. "When is the big day?"

"This Sunday," Buzz beamed.

"So soon?"

"Yes, Frankie." Buzz smiled. "Al is helping with the adoption papers for Rebecca. He says it can't happen until Rita and I legally marry."

"Where are you getting married?"

"At Rita's Catholic Church in Autumn. Yet Bubby is going to conduct the ceremony, and a Baptist gospel choir is going to sing."

"Who's gonna be best man?" Frankie asked.

"Well, Bubby is my best friend here, but he's conducting the ceremony. My father is flying in from the West Coast. This will be his first time meeting Rita, and it's the first time I've seen him in

188

person since graduating from college. There's no bad blood between us, and I'm glad to see him again, but all things considered, I can't see making him my best man."

"How about Al?"

"I thought about him. The problem is that he is the same age as my father. I am already snubbing dear 'ol dad, so rather I don't pile on by picking someone his age." Buzz took his gear from his kitbag and placed it in the locker.

"All of you guys are great. If I pick Steve, then I'm snubbing Shaun. If I pick Leslie, then I'm snubbing Trevor. Grant flew home for his daughter's birthday. Bobby's wife, Mary, and his sister-in-law, Tammy May, are already in the wedding as bridesmaids, so, Bobby would be one Boggs too many. I can't pick Spence, Clay, or Shigeru as that would violate kayfabe. Spider and Barry are coolsville, but I don't know them well enough. That leaves the wrestler whose advice got Rita back."

"Me?"

Buzz nodded.

"But I'm only a lowly jobber."

"You're also a professional and an excellent man. Are you in?"

"Si! Si! Mi amigo. Si!"

Buzz and Frankie shook hands.

Chapter 28

Teachers, students, and the custodial staff had cleared tables from Autumn Elementary School's cafeteria. Rows of chairs were added for the Fall pageant. The teachers and pupils decorated the cafeteria in a Northern Fall motif. Orange and black crape paper streamers spanned the ceiling, and a pumpkin and gourde display sat on a long table. Turned heads and murmurs accompanied Buzz and Rita as they entered hand in hand. They continued to hold hands while watching individual or small groups of youngsters perform talent acts such as piano playing, singing, poetry recital, and dancing. They squeezed hands and beamed at each other when they saw Kathryn Watkins getting up and moving behind a piano. Rita rested her forearm on Buzz's leg and leaned forward. Miss Watkins played the opening notes. Rebecca stood on stage with her right foot slightly forward and her shoulders squared. She smiled for the audience and sang Rosie Mendez-Hamlin's "Angel Baby" in Spanish.

She bowed to the audience upon finishing. The guests applauded enthusiastically. Buzz and Rita embraced.

***

A paunchy man in his early fifties, school principal Dick Warnick, wore a blue pin-striped suit with a red striped tie. "I thank every one of you for attending our pageant. I am proud of each and every one of our students. You all will agree that Autumn Elementary School is rich with talent." The audience clapped. "I wish I had a trophy for every student who participated. Nevertheless, we can only award trophies to our top three. Our third-place trophy goes to Betty Lou Thompson for playing '*Twinkle, Twinkle, Little Star*' on the piano."

The audience *applauded* as a pony-tailed girl in a blue dress accepted her trophy and stood on stage. "Second prize goes to Benjamin Jordon for singing, '*America the Beautiful*'." A blond-haired third-grade boy accepted his trophy to applause.

"And now the moment that you have all been waiting for. The winner of Autumn Elementary's 1958 Fall pageant, she sang the popular song '*Angel Baby*' in Spanish…"

Buzz and Rita clasped both hands, looked into each other's eyes, and beamed.

"…Rebecca Mendez."

The audience applauded. Rebecca walked up to the principal. He handed her the first-place trophy. They posed together for flash photographs. Afterward, Rebecca joined Betty Lou and Benjami for pictures with the principal.

***

As Buzz, Rita, and Rebecca walked out of the cafeteria, six students gathered around them. One stepped up with a piece of paper and pen. "Rebecca's father. Who do you think will win the tag team championship?"

Buzz raised his palms. "I don't know. If your parents won't take you to Miami for the matches, make sure you watch on TV."

The boy thrust his pen and paper at Buzz. "I heard you were The Jaguar. Can I have your autograph?"

"I'm just the wrestler's trashman." Buzz looked at the boy staring at him like a puppy dog for a treat. He took the piece of paper. "But The Jaguar does have me sign on his behalf." Buzz signed autographs for all the kids.

Afterward, Rita clasped Buzz's hand and snuggled up to him. "I can't wait until you're no longer a trashman."

"I can't wait until you're my daddy." Rebecca handed him her trophy.

"I'm already prouder of you than any father was ever proud of a daughter."

Chapter 29

The organist played the wedding chorus from Act III of Wagner's opera Lohengrin. Pedro Mendez led his daughter up Autumn, Florida's Holy Family Catholic Church aisle. Rita wore an elegant White gown. The sun gleaming through the stained-glass windows radiated on her smile. A gossamer veil alluded to her flowing tress. Buzz wore a form-fitting Tux. Best man Frankie Williamson's tux looked three sizes too large. The Reverend Bart Johnson wore dark blue minister's robes and held a Bible in front of him.

Rita faced Buzz. She raised her head. The sparkle in her eyes, the florid glow of her cheeks, and the fullness of her lips shone through her gossamer veil. *'Is it possible to be so blessed?'* He focused on the texture and angles of her face like an aficionado appraising a priceless painting. *'Her perfumed skin has the texture of rose petals; her warm breath has its aroma. I hear our heartbeats strumming like harps'.* Buzz fell into a trance.

'Both of my feet are on the ground, but I fear I'm about to float away. His eyes, blue like the deepest sea. All my life, I have searched, and at last, I have found. The security and peace of everlasting love.'

They faced each other while holding both hands. Buzz spoke first, "Rita, I take you as my wife, I promise to be faithful in good times and bad, sickness and health. I will love you and honor you all the days of my life."

"I, Rita, take you, Buzz, to be my husband. I, too, promise to be faithful to you in good times and bad, sickness and health. I will love you all the days of my life."

Reverend Bartholomew Johnson held his Bible in his right hand and raised his left hand. "Before I pronounce you man and wife, someone dear to you both wants to sing for you."

Abe Collins stood before ten members of his choir. He raised his left hand and motioned with his right hand. Rebecca sang,

"Go, tell it on the mountain

Over the hills and everywhere

Go, tell it on the mountain

That Jesus Christ is born

While shepherds kept their watching

O'er silent flocks by night

Behold throughout the heavens

There shone a Holy light

Go, tell it on the mountain

Over the hills and everywhere

Go, tell it on the mountain

That Jesus Christ is born."

Father Jose Vargas Sprinkled Buzz and Rita with Holy Water, "May the Father, the Son, and the Holy Ghost bless this couple in Holy Matrimony."

Frankie Williamson handed Buzz the wedding ring. Buzz held it up to Father Vargas. He nodded. Buzz slipped it on Rita's finger. Reverend Johnson raised his Bible. "I now pronounce you man and wife. You may share your first kiss as husband and wife."

Buzz lifted Rita's veil and kissed her to the applause of the church. The organist played Mendelssohn's Wedding March Op.61 from '*A Midsummer Night's Dream.*' Buzz and Rita held hands and hurried down the aisle.

At the church steps, Rebecca ran up to them. Buzz picked her up. Al Cohen joined them. "I want to be the first to give you a wedding gift." He handed Buzz a document.

Buzz beamed.

"What is it, Buzz?

He showed it to Rita. Her face lit up. "Rebecca, it is final. Buzz is your legal father."

"Daddy!" Rebecca pecked Buzz's cheek.

Chapter 30

Vehicles jammed Southern Florida's Dixie Highway, Tamiami Trail, and State Road A1A. Cacophonous horn honking failed to speed traffic. The Parking lots around Burke Stadium were filled two hours before the big show. Al Cohen had all the wrestlers on the bill gather in a dressing room under the stands. He stood next to Shigeru Sakamoto. "I'm relieved to see you all here and here on time. We have a lot at stake tonight. Thanks to you all, I have one less thing to worry about. First, Shigeru would like to say a few words."

"This is a bittersweet moment for me." Shigeru stepped forward. "I have achieved a long-term goal. I have landed a co-starring role as the chief villain in a major Hollywood secret agent movie."

The wrestlers applauded.

"I must be on set Tuesday morning. That means tonight is my last gig with you guys. I want to thank Al and each one of you. Your performances enhanced my performances and my notoriety. Hollywood scouts never would have noticed me without you. Moreover, I will remember my time with you all as the happiest days of my life."

Each of the wrestlers shook Shigeru's hand and congratulated him.

***

Grant Iron's wife Michele accompanied Rita to Burke Stadium's press box. Rita was surprised. Michele was a dainty, well-groomed woman. She wore an olive-green skirt, a black belt with a gold buckle, and a white blouse. "Does it bother you watching your husband's act? I almost lost Buzz over his savage jaguar act."

"No," Michelle chuckled. "I'm quite used to it. Besides, he teaches a college class in the off-season. Wearing custom business suits and Fedora hats outside the ring serves as much a disguise as

Buzz wearing a mask inside the ring."

Rita blushed and lowered her head. "I didn't mean it that way."

"It's okay," Michele laughed. "Besides, Grant's act makes him more an attraction than a figure of hatred. Moreover, it would have been far worse had you asked about sleeping with such a large man and especially his copious body hair."

Rita laughed with her.

"Is tonight your first time watching Buzz as a face?"

Rita nodded.

Michelle pointed at the stands. "Will you look at how quickly those seats are filling? I know they came to see our husbands, but give Al Cohen credit for promoting it."

"I couldn't be more grateful to Al. He gave us the best wedding gift imaginable. He used his connections to speed up the adoption. Buzz is not only my husband; now he is Rebecca's father."

"Grant flew to Ohio for our daughter Ronnie's birthday party. Please invite me to Rebecca's ninth birthday party."

"You know I will." Rita clutched Michele's hand.

***

Al Cohen waited for the wrestlers to depart the dressing room. He asked Buzz, Bart, Biff, Cletus, and Shigeru to remain. He locked the dressing room door. "You men have performed admirably in every promotion leading to tonight's event. This can boost your career and professional wrestling in general. The carryover effect will impact everyone in the business. We are expecting an even bigger crowd than the Orange Bowl football game. You guys know what to do. Make it a good match. Make it a memorable match."

***

Grant "The Beast" Irons and Steve Samson revved up the crowd. The polar contrast between their physical appearance, Steve's athleticism, and Grant's brawling was stark.

***

"Your husband is putting on quite a show." Rita smiled at Michele.

"Maybe too good. Your husband's match is the one that can make professional wrestling a major attraction. Grant and Steve are sparking too much electricity. Let's hope it doesn't blow a fuse before the main event."

***

Steve flung Grant out of the ring. Al Cohen sat at ringside. He covered his mouth and whispered to him, "Throw a table into the ring and run back to the dressing room."

Grant threw a table in the ring. Steve leaped to avoid it. He ran over and reached through the ropes to grab Grant.

"Ah-uh! Ah-uh!" Grant ducked backward, slapped his bald head in circular motions, and wagged his green tongue before retreating to the dressing room."

The ring announcer entered the ring. "Your winner. From Dallas, Texas. Steve Samson!" The referee raised Steve's hand in victory to the thunderous approval of the audience. Many young female fans screamed and swarmed to touch Steve as he walked back to the dressing room portal.

"Ladies and gentlemen. Our next match will be the one you've been waiting for. The American Federation of Wrestling tag team title. First, a fifteen-minute intermission."

Few people left their seats during the intermission. Their anticipation was palpable. Murmurs escalated to shouts as the stadium lights dimmed and the ring lights brightened. *Ding! Ding! Ding!* All 61,836 people in attendance stood. The boos started with the first beat of the sound system playing Johnny Cash's "Folsom Prison Blues." Professor Sakamoto led the Rustler Brothers to the ring. After entering the ring, Biff twirled his lasso, and Cetus cracked his whip. Professor Sakamoto grinned mischievously.

The sound system next played Link Wray's "Rumble." The fans erupted as Adebe and The Jaguar marched to the ring with purpose. They climbed into the ring and glowered at their opponents.

"Ladies and gentlemen. Our main event of the evening and the biggest match in wrestling history. This match is the best two out of three falls for the American Federation of Wrestling World Tag Team championship!"

The crowd cheered.

"First, the challengers. The big cats. Your first big cat hails from the Amazon jungle. Weighing in at two hundred and forty pounds, The Jaguar. And his tag team partner, the American Federation of Wrestling champion of the WORRRLD! Weighing in at four hundred and twenty-five pounds, Adebe. The African Lion!"

The ring announcer waited for the cheering to subside. "In this corner, first their manager, from Tokyo, Japan, Professor Sakamoto." The ring announcer paused so that the audience could jeer. "And now, the reigning American Federation of Wrestling world tag team champions, from Laramie, Wyoming, at a combined weight of five hundred and eighty-seven pounds, Biff and Cletus, The Rustler Brothers!" Boos, hisses, and catcalls greeted them. Crumpled programs and popcorn boxes rained into the ring. "Ladies and gentlemen, please. Limit expressing your feelings for the wrestlers to words. Do not throw any objects into the ring. Our special guest referee for the match is Stanley Christodoulou." The ring announcer departed.

"*Ding! Ding! Ding!*"

***

"Go Daddy! Go!" Rebecca shouted at the TV.

Pedro Mendez beamed and laughed.

***

The Jaguar opened the match by leaping across the ring, twisting, and chopping Biff in the chest. Biff went down. The Jaguar pulled him to his feet and flung him into the ropes. He clotheslined him on the rebound. The Jaguar put him in a headlock and pulled him back to his feet. Buff waved his arms as he struggled to move toward his corner. After six steps, he extended his arm far enough to tag Cletus. He entered the ring and twice kneed the Jaguar in the gut. Biff and Cletus then double-whipped him into the ropes and double-clotheslined on his return, knocking the Jaguar to the canvas. Cletus leaped and dropped his leg over his throat. Cletus pinned him. The ref slapped the ring canvas and counted, "One, two…" The Jaguar kicked out, staggered to the corner, and tagged Abede. He pounded his chest and dashed across the ring. He slammed into Cletus, sending him flying into the corner. Abede stepped back, shuffled his feet like a bull, and charged at him. He turned and squashed Cletus into the corner. The ring post bent backward. Biff snuck behind them, wrapped his lasso around Abede's neck, and choked him. The Jaguar ran across the ring. The referee turned his back to the action and ushered him back to his corner. Sakamoto threw Cletus a chair. He slammed Abede over the head with it and tossed it back to his manager. Abede collapsed on the mat. Cletus leaped in the air and body-splashed him. He lifted Abede's leg for leverage and pinned him. The referee slapped the mat three times.

'*Ding! Ding! Ding!*' The ring announcer walked into the ring and spoke into his microphone. "Your winner of the first fall. The American Federation of Wrestling Tag Team champions, The Rustler Brothers." An orange struck his chest. The fans cheered. "For the safety of everyone involved, please refrain from throwing objects into the ring."

'*Ding! Ding! Ding!*' Abede staggered from his corner. Cletus struck him twice with overhead forearm strikes to the chest. He then flung Abede into the Rustler's corner. As Abede bounced off the turnbuckle, Buff tripped him with his whip. Abede fell to his stomach. Cletus stomped on him, grabbed his ankle, and pulled him toward his corner. The fans clapped in unison as Abede resisted by crawling to his corner. He reached out and tagged the Jaguar. He somersaulted over the top rope and thumped Cletus with a flying dropkick. Cletus staggered off the ropes. The Jaguar leaped, wrapped his legs around Cletus's neck, and rolled him over. He held him in a leg lock. Cletus kicked out and tagged his partner. Biff charged the Jaguar. The Jaguar leaped and used his right hand on Biff's shoulder to vault over him. He then hit him with a flying mule kick to the back, sending him to the far corner. The Jaguar corralled him in the corner, struck him twice across the chest with forearm shivers, body-slammed him, and knee-dropped him. The Jaguar climbed to the top rope and waited for Biff to stagger to his feet. The Jaguar leaped high off the top rope, jackknifed, and clotheslined him. He then covered him for the pin. The referee slapped the ring for the three count. The audience stood and cheered, soon chanting, "Jaguar! Jaguar! Jaguar!"

***

Rebecca smiled and pointed at the TV. "That's my daddy they're cheering!"

***

Michele Irons tapped Rita's hand. "Did you ever imagine hearing such adulation for Buzz?"

Rita stood and beamed.

***

The ring announcer entered the ring. "Your winner of the second fall. The Big Cats! It all boils down to this. The final fall to a finish for the world tag team championship. Are you ready?"

The crowd stood, shook their fists, and cheered.

'*Ding. Ding. Ding.*'

The Jaguar circled Biff Rustler like a shark; after closing the gap, he leaped up and attempted to lock his legs around his neck. Biff caught him and dropped him, ribs across his knee. Biff then stomped him, pulled him to his feet, and flung him into the ropes. The Jaguar bounced back; Biff put him in an arm drag, and threw him across the ring. The Jaguar bounced up and tagged Abede. He charged Biff and knocked him down with his chest. Biff retreated to his corner and tagged Cletus. He stayed in the corner. Abede charged. Cletus eluded. Adebe crashed into the corner. Buff lassoed Abede from outside the ring and tied him up by wrapping his rope around the corner post. The Jaguar ran in to help. The referee intercepted him. Turning his back to the action, he forced the Jaguar back to his corner. Meanwhile, Cletus worked Abede over with forearm strikes before raking his knuckles across his eyes. Sakamoto snuck into the ring with Abede's lion regalia. He grinned with a slight curl while baring his teeth.

The fans stood in shocked silence.

***

Rebecca stood and pointed at the TV. "No! No! Not again! Somebody stop him!"

***

The Jaguar ran around the outside of the ring. He attacked Biff with right and left punches. Biff released his grip on the lasso. The Jaguar slammed Biff's head into the ring apron. Abede knocked Cletus to the canvas with a forearm shiver. Sakamoto dropped his lion regalia and fled. The Jaguar reached under the bottom rope and grabbed the lion garb. He ran around the outside of the ring, back to his corner. Adebe joined him. The Jaguar handed him his regalia. Abede donned it. He faced the Rustler's corner, shook his fists, and roared. Biff dropped to one knee, steepled his hands, and begged for

201

mercy. Abede stalked in, lifted him, and power slammed him. Next, he body splashed him and stayed on top for the pin. Cletus ran into the ring to stomp him. The Jaguar intercepted him, picked him up, and slammed him on top of Biff. Abede sat on them both. The referee slapped the mat. "One, Two." Sakamoto ran in with his pouch of salt. The Jaguar leaped off the top rope, flew clear across the ring, and thumped him with both feet. As Sakamoto fell, he threw the salt in the air. It landed in his own eyes. He staggered around the ring, rubbing his eyes. The crowd went into a frenzy. The referee slapped the ring and shouted, "Three!"

Burke Stadium erupted into bedlam. Al Cohen entered the ring and handed The Jaguar and Abede their championship belts. The referee raised their hands; the wrestlers raised the championship belts with their other hands.

***

Rita stood and applauded.

"Even though we know this was Al's plan, it's still exciting," Michele laughed. "Buzz, Bart, Spence, Clay, and Shigeru all did a great job."

***

Rebecca jumped up and down and cheered. Pedro smiled and laughed.

***

Buzz, Bart, Spence, Clay, and Shigeru shook hands in the dressing room after the match and congratulated each other for a successful show. Al Cohen entered. "Excellent! Each one of you was a superstar. In my mind, every one of you is a champion. You will all get cash bonuses."

Frankie Williamson walked over to Buzz. "Mi amigo. We have a fourteen-hour drive to our next show in Tallahassee. Mi amigo in Miami wants to fly us in his airplane. It's three hours instead of fourteen."

"Thanks anyway, Frankie." Buzz put his hand on his shoulder. "But Rita and I have planned our honeymoon on South Beach. Besides, Rebecca is waiting for us back in Autumn."

"Comprendida. How about you, Bubby?"

"Are you kidding me?" Bart beamed. "Three hours in a plane rather than fourteen hours with my knees against the dashboard of the wrestler's van?" Bart slapped Frankie's shoulder. "You got it, my man."

"Did I hear that you got a plane going to Tallahassee?" Bobby Boggs walked over to them. "I sure would appreciate more time with Mary. I can pay you."

"No es necesario." Frankie held up his hands. "The pilot and plane owner is a huge wrestling fan. El es encantado."

"Okay." Bobby shook Frankie's hand. "I'm in."

Chapter 31

Frankie Williamson, Bob Boggs, and Bart Johnson took a cab to the Tamiami Airport. "There's my friend, Juan Cordova," Frankie waved to a thin man in his early thirties wearing gray slacks and an untucked white collared shirt. He stood with his hands on his hips.

"We're going to fly to Tallahassee in that thing?" Bob pointed to the fifteen-year-old single-engine aircraft.

Juan's brownish skin tone turned ashen. Frankie shook hands with him. Juan listlessly returned his handshake. "My friends need no introduction, Beer Barrel Bobby Boggs and the reigning individual World Champion and now Tag team champion Bart Johnson."

Juan limply shook their hands. He next grabbed Frankie by the arm and pulled him around the airplane. "You told me I was taking Buzz the Jaguar and his hundred-and-twenty-pound wife. Those two combine for over eight hundred pounds. I don't know if it's safe to ask this old bird," Juan slapped the plane's fuselage, "to fly that much weight."

"Come on amigo. Your plane will be fine. After all, you're flying a World champion and one of the most popular wrestlers in the game. Someday, you can tell your grandkids about it."

"Okay." Juan scratched his chin. "I'm a huge wrestling fan and thrilled to fly such big names. Still, I'm unsure about stressing my plane with such weight."

"You'll be fine, amigo." Frankie grasped Juan's arm. "Trust me."

"This thing has less legroom than the van." Bart sat in the front seat. His knees were pressed against the dashboard. "But, hey, I ain't complaining. Three hours beats fourteen."

Bob's shoulders scrunched against Frankie's shoulders. His knees dug into the rear of the front seat. "Only when traveling with you,

Bubby, do I have to squeeze into a back seat.”

The airplane taxied to the runway’s edge before ascending at a twenty-degree angle. They looked out the window. The buildings and vehicles below seemed larger than they should be. After fifteen minutes, the airplane flew parallel to US Route 41. The plane flew only a bit faster than the cars and trucks below. Juan then banked to the north. The Everglade’s vastness sat below.

“Hey!” Bart pointed at the control panel. “What’s that red light all about.”

“Oh, it’s nothing.” Juan glanced at it. “It’s only the engine’s running a little hot. No te preoccupe.”

“Speak English,” Bob leaned forward. “What’s with the plane.”

“I said,” Juan glanced back, “not to worry.”

After five minutes, Bart pointed out the front window. “Nothing to worry about? That damn light is still on, and I see smoke coming from the engine.”

“Este nada.”

“Nothing?” Bob grabbed the front seat. “Your engine is sputtering like my damn lawnmower!”

“If it will make you feel better, the Seminal Indians have a landing strip about five miles ahead. I’ll land and check it out.”

“Hey, Juan,” Frankie leaned forward. “I promised my amigos we would get to Tallahassee in three hours. How long do we got to stay at the Indian reservation.”

“It’s nothing to worry about. I’m only going to check the fluids and let the engine cool off a bit, and we’ll be on our way.”

The engine’s cylinders started misfiring. Black smoke billowed and cloaked their vision.

“There it is.” Juan pointed to the packed dirt landing strip. “Hold on! This may be rough.”

Bart tucked his head between his knees and prayed. Bobby closed his eyes and thought of his new wife, Mary. Frankie remailed stolid.

Juan pulled back on the control stick. The plane's nose struck the landing strip first. The engine burst from the cowling; the propeller blade crashed through the windshield, decapitating Juan and impaling Frankie, killing him instantly. The plane spun sideways. The right-wing hit the runway first; the impact ripped it from the fuselage. A second later, the tail section bashed into the runway, severing the horizontal and vertical stabilizers and the rudder. It bounced into a swamp. After dribbling like a basketball, the airplane halted beside the runway.

***

Buzz and Rita sat together on their couch, holding hands. Rebecca sang the popular Mexican children's song, "Los Pollitos Dicen." The shrill ringing of the telephone interrupted her. Buzz chose to ignore it. "You better answer it." Rita nudged Buzz in the ribs.

Buzz took the call in the other room. He emerged chalk white. Four tears dripped from his left eye and two from his right eye.

"What is it?" Rita felt her heart skip a beat. "What is it?"

Buzz gestured for her to join him in their bedroom. He closed the door.

Rebecca heard her mother scream. She ran to the bedroom. Both of her parents were crying. "Better sit down, honey." Rita sniffled. "I can't sugarcoat this. Nobody wanted this to happen." Rita put her arm around her daughter. "There's been a plane crash…"

Rebecca's screaming awoke Pedro.

Chapter 32

The dishwater gray clouds granted the mourners a small favor by holding its rain. An estimated four hundred cars took every available parking space. Many had to park over a mile away. Police directed the hearse to a designated opening. A rope barricade marked a path to the gravesite. Rope barriers around the gravesite sequestered the two thousand public attendees from the invited mourners. People outside the ropes chanted, "Beer! Beer! Beer!" while Buzz, Yuri, Spence, Clay, Leslie and Trevor Van der Westhuisen, and Steve and Shaun Samsom carried the oversized casket along the path to the gravesite.

Grant Irons wore a black suit, Fedora hat, tie, and white shirt. He stood with his wife Michele, wearing a dark navy blue dress. Shigeru Sakamoto and Al Cohen, both dressed in black, stood with them. Tammy May and Skeet Boggs stayed with Rebecca and Angelica. Rita and Margie stood with Mary, wearing a black dress with a black shroud covering her face. Both Rita and Margie had their arms around Mary's shoulder. Mary lowered her head and bawled.

The wrestlers placed the coffin by the gravesite. The minister sported a thick, handlebar mustache. He wore his black, tailed coat open. He wore a white shirt topped by a clerical collar. A large ornamental belt buckle of a steam locomotive and a white Western hat completed his attire. He held a Bible in his right hand. "We stand here at the door to eternity. As Bob Boggs passes through that door to the glories of Heaven, we are to grieve not as those without hope. While our parting with Bob brings sadness, God the Father has sent his Holy Spirit to us as our comforter. Let us rejoice that our grief is only temporary. For one day, we shall pass through that door and reunite with Bob. Our Lord Jesus has prepared for us golden mansions in the new Jerusalem. If you call upon the name of the

Lord Jesus, your name shall join Bob's in the Book of Life. We will live with Bob and our Lord and Savior, Jesus Christ, in Heaven for eternity. Today, we celebrate Bob's transition from mortal to immortal, from the corruptible to the incorruptible. We now lay Bob's remains into the Earth while his spirit ascends to Heaven." The casket was lowered six feet into the ground.

Yuri stood by the gravesite, lit a candle, and recited the "Memory Eternal" in Russian.

Mary fell to her knees and wailed, "Bobby! Bobby! No! Bobby! Please!" Rita and Margie dropped to one knee to comfort her. Angelica bawled. Rebecca cried and hugged her. Tammy May embraced them both. Skeet stood stoically still. A single tear ran down his face.

The clouds now rained tears on the gathering.

"Please, come with us," Margie and Rita helped Mary to stand. Her knees buckled. Margie and Rita caught her and helped her regain her footing. She now wept in mummers. "Bobby…Bobby…Bobby." Margie put her arm around her and Rita held her hand as they led her from the gravesite. Rebecca held Angelica's hand while departing with Tammy May and Skeet.

"Steve, Shaun, give me your autograph." A wrestling fan held a paper scrap and pen over the rope barrier. "Me too." Another fan with paper and pen pleaded.

Steve and Shaun ignored them. Al Cohen scowled at the autograph seekers.

After the gathering had dispersed and security had departed, four mourners snuck up to Bobby's grave. They opened a barrel tap and poured beer on his casket.

Chapter 33

Bart Johnson lay in his hospital bed at Jackson Memorial Hospital in Miami, Florida. Stephanie sat next to him and held his hand. The doctors had secured his head and neck with a halo brace. His right leg was in traction. Dr. James Benson entered his room carrying a manilla folder. A much younger and smaller doctor accompanied him. Dr. Benson compared a chart attached to Bart's bed with some papers in his folder. "How are you feeling today, Mr. Johnson?"

"I'm feeling, and that's what counts." Bart beamed. "How about calling me Bubby rather than Mr. Johnson."

"Force of habit." Dr. Benson closed his folder. "It is a miracle that you're alive and an even bigger miracle that you can feel and move your limbs." The younger doctor handed Dr. Benson an X-ray photo. "As you know, you suffered a fracture of the third cervical vertebrae." He pointed to the X-Ray photo of Bart's neck. "A millimeter more, and you're a quadriplegic. Another millimeter, and you're dead. After watching the film coverage of the wreckage on TV, I can't believe you're alive and in one piece."

Stephanie smiled at the doctor. "God was with my husband."

"Faith or no faith is not a job requirement for my profession. Therefore, I won't confirm or deny that."

"How long until I can shake this stuff off and get out of bed."

"Be patient. You're going to fully recover. Your fractured fibula will require two more months in that cast. I hope to have that halo brace off you in about three months. Let's err on the side of caution. I am also going to have a psychiatrist take your case."

"A shrink?" Bart laughed. "Why do I need a head shrink?"

"The head shrink is only a back-up." Dr. Benson tightened his lips and narrowed his eyes. "I will have the head shrink commit you to an institution to prevent you from even thinking about playing football or wrestling again."

***

Bart and Stephanie beamed as Buzz and Rita entered the room. "Well, if it isn't the newlyweds." Bart raised his right thumb.

"Dr. Benson gave us the great news that you're going to get up and walk out of that bed." Buzz returned his thumbs up.

"I feel guilty each time I smile." Bart pursed his lips. "After all, Bobby, Frankie, and the pilot weren't so blessed. I couldn't even pay them my last respects."

"On Monday, Buzz, Rebecca, and I are flying to Puerto Rico to pay our respects to Frankie's family." Rita rested her hand on Bart's bed frame. "We will send them your condolences. Unfortunately, Mary has taken this extra hard. Al and the other wrestlers have been great with her and Bobby's family."

"Yes." Buzz held Rita's hand. "And Al paid to have Frankie's remains shipped to Puerto Rico and also gave his family a generous donation."

"The doctors decided for me on God's behalf. I'm through wrestling. I knwq all along he had a higher purpose for me. All Midwestern Athletic Association college football player, NFL with the Washington Redskins, and individual and tag team World wrestling champion is a fine legacy. Yet I always knew that my ultimate calling in life is to preach the word. I made some phone calls from here. Stephanie," he nodded at his wife, "finalized the deal in person. I've got my own church in New York's Upper Westside waiting for me. As soon as I'm up and about from this, I'll be in charge and preaching the word."

"I accepted an offer from Elizabeth Arden to work for them as a designer. They are not only on the cutting edge of the fashion industry, but they work closely with the movers and shakers in the recording, stage, and screen fields. I told them about Rebecca's

210

singing. One of my new colleagues knows Abe Collins. He raved to her about Rebecca's singing. My agency made some phone calls. They got Rebecca an audition for the Julliard School of Performing Arts."

"That's wonderful." Rita touched Stephanie's hand. "But we live a thousand miles away."

"Rebecca is welcome to live with Bubby and me." Stephanie squeezed Rita's hand.

"God gives everyone a talent." Bart added, "Some are given more than others, and some are given much more. Our obligation to our creator is to use our talent fully and to his glory. Jesus teaches us not to hide a lamp under the bed but to let it shine so others can see the light."

"No better way exists to let others experience Rebecca's wonderful gift of song than to develop her talent at Julliard." Stephanie spread her palms.

Buzz and Rita looked into each other's eyes and nodded. "You have given Rita and me much to think about and pray about."

"Rebecca has a say in this as well." Rita nodded. "But it is our duty as parents to point her in the right direction."

"I think we should all pray together," Bart blinked his eyes rapidly. "Let's join hands."

The four linked hands.

Bart continued, "Heavenly Father, in the name of Jesus, we first ask you to send the Holy Spirit to comfort the Boggs and Pumarillo families. I thank you for preserving my life my health, and your amazing, everlasting mercy. I thank you for Stephanie's offer from Elizabeth Arden and for trusting me with a church. We all pray for guidance to best utilize the unique and precious talent that you gave young Rebecca. We ask this in the name of the Father, the Son, and the Holy Spirit. Amen.

Buzz, Rita, and Stephanie replied with, "Amen."

Chapter 34

Buzz sat across from Al at his desk. Al stood. "This setting is too formal. Let's talk over a beer." Buzz and Al moved to a teak bar set at his office's far wall. Al reached up and grabbed two mugs. He leaned over and filled both with beer from a tap. "As you already know, I have shut down the American Federation of Wrestling for three months out of respect for Bobby and Frankie. I can't speak for the dead. Nevertheless, I am sure they would not want us to fold up altogether. I am now restructuring the operation. Thanks to you, Bubby, Shigeru, Spence, and Clay, the Miami show has made us the number one territory in the nation. Many wrestlers from other territories want to join us."

"It's not just because of us. Your generosity and benevolence to your wrestlers is well known within the business."

"Buzz," Al sipped his beer, "I would love for you to stay, but I'm afraid that you won't reach your full potential here. There's no turning back to the Savage Jaguar. Moreover, Grant is staying with us. I explained, before transitioning you to a face, that we only need one wild man, especially seeing that your roles preclude forming a tag team." Al placed his beer mug next to Buzz's. "The champion represents our organization. I would rather not have a masked wrestler hold the belt."

"I was champion before."

"Yes." Al nodded. "You were. And you did an outstanding job. But we both know that you served as a placeholder for Bubby."

"It was a courageous move to have a black champion."

"Bubby was no token promotion. His charisma transcended racial bigotries. He was also among the world's strongest men, a true athlete, and an outstanding actor. My next champion has huge shoes to fill."

"How about we scrap the Jaguar mask."

"The problem is it would take too much time to establish your new identity. I considered keeping you as the masked Jaguar, wrestling as a face. You and Rita could help bridge the Spanish and English-speaking markets. But Hercules Cortez is returning. He is already a huge favorite with Mexican fans and popular all around. As for tag teams, Spence is leaving for the West Coast Territory. He is trimming his physique and dying his hair blonde. He is going to portray himself as a friendly beach boy and wrestle as a face. Clay is staying and will continue as Cletus Rustler. Both Van der Westhuisens are staying. They are outstanding wrestlers and, as you know, exemplary people outside the ring. I plan on using them more as individuals than as a tag team. Spider Nel is staying. I want to elevate his status. He's too good a wrestler and too professional in attitude to lose every night. Yuri has chosen to wrestle in Europe. I am going to replace him with a German wrestler. I'm trading the Cold War angle for World War II. It worked brilliantly with Shigeru. No reason exists to not do it again."

"I would be happy to pay my dues and work my way up."

"I know you would, Buzz, and I appreciate that." Al sipped his beer. "My plan is for a face to be my long-term champion. You would have to wait too long. That would not be in your best interest. I am going to make Steve Samson our champion. His brother is just as worthy, but Steve is bigger and older. The fans see him as the big brother. Steve has that combination of the ladies wanting him and the men wanting to be him. He's got an athletic physique without looking like a musclehead. He has a handsome face with the Biblical Samson hair that only a professional wrestler can wear. Moreover, he is an outstanding wrestler. He knows the business, and his image is well established. He's also nothing like Johnny Durham. Steve's a decent man outside of the ring."

"That's another thing I appreciate about you. You only keep decent people in your territory. You got rid of Johnny Durham even though he made you money." Buzz sipped his beer. "What about a tag team? I'm still your tag team champion."

"Yes. You are." Sam chuckled and slapped his arm. "But I am totally restructuring the American Federation of Wrestling after the tragedy. Shaun has Steve's qualities. I am blessed to have them both. Therefore, I am going to make Shaun a tag team champion."

"Shaun and I are friends. I would be honored to share the tag team title with him."

"A masked wrestler would not make a good pairing with him. You're plenty handsome without the mask, but you have a different look from Shaun. He can also boast the Biblical Samson's hair. You have a crewcut and were raised in the military. You have an admirable look. I am looking for that adorable pop star look. I think I've found the perfect tag team match for Shaun. One of my scouts met him on a golf course. His name is Kelvin Vonn. He's somewhat like you. He has a great physique and a handsome face. He can grow his hair out, but I will leave the Biblical Samson hair to Steve and Shaun. I am going to change his first name to Lance, after the All-American quarterback from Pennsylvania. I like the last name, but I am going to change it a bit. I will spell it V-a-u-g-h-n, after my favorite singer, Vaughn Monroe. Combining the names of a dashing All-American quarterback and a singer with a powerful, masculine voice should resonate with the wrestling fans. I thought of calling my new wrestler "Fabulous Lance," but the woman's champion, Mary Lillian Ellison, already calls herself The Fabulous Moolah. Rather I call my tag team of Lance and Shaun the "Fabulons.""

"Where do I fit in?" Buzz shrugged.

"This is often done in wrestling, Buzz." Al opened a manilla folder and slid it to Buzz, "just like with baseball and football players."

Buzz perused the paper. "You've sold my contract to Vince McMadden in New York for ten thousand dollars." Buzz opened his mouth in a circle.

"I heard your daughter sing at your wedding." Al grinned. "I'm not a music talent scout. Nevertheless, she sounded magnificent. Bubby's wife told me she got her an audition for The Julliard School. That's the finest school for music in the United States and perhaps the World. You can't pass on that opportunity."

"But New York City? That's a hell-of-a-change for us."

"I see that you and Rita are selling the house in Autumn."

"Yes. And her father, Pedro has decided to retire in Mexico. I plan on helping him financially."

"Think in the best interests of your career and your daughter's future. Besides, you will already have friends there in Stephanie and Bubby."

"I don't know, Al."

"Buzz, that ten thousand dollars is contingent on your reporting."

"I feel like I'm being sold like chattel."

"Go to New York and make me look as bad as the Boston Red Sox for selling Babe Ruth."

Buzz pursed his lips and closed his eyes.

"There's something else I need to tell you. Can you keep a secret?"

"Sure, Al."

"Go to New York, and I will give you and Rita McMadden's ten thousand dollars. Keep that between you and me. Otherwise, every wrestler will expect it."

Buzz beamed. "You can't do that."

"Sure, I can." Sam shook Buzz's hand. "I just did."

"As always, Al, you've parted the sea for me." Buzz returned Al's handshake. "Now it's up to me to follow the path."

Epilogue

New York City, October 1969

Buzz, Rita, nine-year-old Bobby Arlett and seven-year-old Frankie Arlett waited under their Upper Manhattan apartment's porte-cochere. A long black limousine pulled up. A uniformed doorman opened the rear door, smiled, and made an exaggerated entrance gesture. Rita lifted her red evening gown's hem while Buzz held her other hand as she entered. After Buzz joined her, the boys piled in. The driver grasped the steering wheel and looked back at them.

Frankie Arlett blurted, "Do ya know how to get to Carnegie Hall?"

"Yes." The driver answered. "Practice."

Rita and Buzz laughed. Bobby lightly elbowed his younger brother in the ribs, "Butthead."

"Stop it, boys." Rita smiled. "This is your sister's big night."

"Hey," the driver beamed. "Now I know who you are. You're the world champion professional wrestler."

"Nah, I'm just their trashman."

"Yeah, a trashman who owns thirty percent of the company and can afford to hire a stretch limo. You must be proud of your daughter. It's in every newspaper in town, and I don't miss a beat. Here, I thought the Mets winning the World Series was a miracle. A nineteen-year-old girl singing at Carnegie Hall for Sir George Solti is miracle enough, but to sing Brünnhilde's Immolation from Gotterdammerung after he just finished working with Brigit Nilsson is a bigger miracle than Jets beating the Colts in the Super Bowl and the Mets combined. Wagner took twenty-five years to compose the Ring. If he were alive, I wonder what he would think of a nineteen-year-old singing the Ring's climax?"

"How do you know all of that?" Bobby Arlett asked.

"I'm a New York cab driver. It's my job description to know it all." The driver turned to Rita. "You sure must be proud of her."

Rita smiled from ear to ear. "All of us are."

***

Stephanie, Bart, and their twenty-year-old son, George, joined the Arletts in a private balcony box at Carnegie Hall. Rita marveled at the gold lighting ambiance and the double circular chandeliers. "I've never been so excited in my life."

"I can feel it Rita," Stephanie clutched Rita's arm. "Your glow says it all."

"We haven't heard her sing since Sir George Solti chose her." Rita beamed.

"Sir George Solti is a genius. The word on the street is that he's a mad genius for choosing a nineteen-year-old girl to sing the Immolation scene. That's what they said about you and Grant." Bart bellowed, "But look at you now."

"They said we were mad but never geniuses." Buzz laughed, "We posed as illiterate savages. Mr. Solti learned from musical masters. And unlike Grant and I, he is a true genius."

"Grant is still at it as 'The Beast.'" Bart raised his hands. "It seems his act never gets old. Can't say I blame him. He's making more money than all of us."

"See, Dad!" George beamed. "You just said it. There's big money in professional wrestling."

"We'll talk about it later, son."

"Why not now? I'm on the Rutger's wrestling team and I'm getting good grades like you asked. Why don't you want me to be a wrestler."

"We talked about this before."

217

"I'll tell you what, George." Buzz looked at him. "Stay on the wrestling team, get your degree from Rutgers, and I will have a meeting with you and your father about professional wrestling."

"But I'll be over twenty-one." George crossed his arms. "I can do what I want."

"If wrestling is what you want," Buzz tilted his head, "You will go a lot further and a lot faster if your father and I help you."

"I bet you're glad that your daughter chose music over trying to beat The Fabulous Moolah." Stephanie laughed.

Rita chuckled. "Rebecca, when she's not exhausted, tells me about the length and intensity of Mr. Solti's rehearsals."

"It's necessary," Buzz added. "She's going to have to sing over a hundred-piece orchestra. Experts are in near agreement that the roles of Isolde and Brunnhilde have the highest degrees of difficulty in all of music. Usually, only a singer in at least her thirties with a mature voice can sing them."

"I'm sure Rebecca growing up bilingual helped her master the German libretto." Stephanie nudged Rita.

"First, the orchestra is going to play Siegfried's Funeral March." Buzz held up the program. "The Immolation scene closes the eighteen-hour Ring cycle." He read from the program. "It says here that Wagner's *Ring* ranks among the greatest achievements in music history. After over a century and with traditional instruments, it's still the music of the future."

"Yes." Rita smiled and squeezed Buzz's hand, "Rebecca told me Julliard taught her that Wagner changed the direction of music with *Tristan and Isolde,* and he took music into the future with the Ring.

Bobby pushed Frankie. Frankie shoved him back. "Shh, stop it." Rita put her finger over her lips. "They're about to start."

The orchestra tuning their instruments created a cacophony. The house lights dimmed. The first violist stood. The orchestra silenced.

The audience applauded. The orchestra then stood. Sir George Solti walked across the stage to a standing ovation. The first violinist nodded to the orchestra. They sat. The first violinist next sat. The conductor stood on his podium and faced the orchestra. He waved the opening notes. The orchestra played *Siegfried's Funeral March*.

***

The audience applauded the piece's conclusion. The conductor signaled silence.

She sauntered across the stage poised and confident. Her lavender gown was modest, albeit elegant. Rebecca stood an inch taller than her mother while commanding every micro-millimeter of her beauty. Her brown hair was styled in an aristocratic bouffant. Carnegie Hall went silent as a subterranean cavern as she faced the audience. Rebecca glanced at the conductor and sang.

***

After Rebecca sang the final note, she walked off-stage. The orchestra played the final seven minutes of frenzied, powerful, and lush instrumental music, bringing the epic Ring saga to a sweeping resolution. The audience stood and cheered. Shouts of "Bravo! Bravo!" could be heard over the clapping and cheering. Sir George Solti nodded. Rebecca re-entered the stage. The audience erupted. A black-tied patron handed her a huge bouquet of flowers; a female in a formal dress walked across the stage from the other direction and handed Rebecca a second bouquet. Three more bouquets were tossed onto the stage.

Rita stood and applauded. Her tears flowed like a fountain. Buzz smiled from ear to ear. He felt several inches taller. Bobby and Frankie jumped up and down. Buzz and Rita gazed into each other's eyes. They warmly embraced. Their hearts beat in synch with the long, thunderous ovation.

219